*The prostitute clutched the priest's face and put a gun to his mouth . . .*

"I . . . will . . . kill you." She cocked the gun. "I told you, don't go thinking I'm here for sunshine and salvation. You want to save me? Hide me! And don't *preach!*"

The priest could breathe finally. He nodded, gasping.

In the depths of the hallway toward the darkened chapel, they heard the thudding and thumping noise at the same time.

She whispered frantically, "What the hell was that?"

He managed to get up, limped to her. "Someone is in the chapel. Go. In the attic there's a huge wooden Christ. Get behind him. And Caressa, be very quiet. You'll be right over the altar below."

The priest limped toward the chapel. The whore tiptoed into the last safe place in her woebegotten world, counting on a stranger of the Lord to save her from a horrible death at the hands of a powerful killer.

The priest put his hand tightly around the silver crucifix at his chest. He listened. Through the door the footsteps echoed. Slow. Deliberate. Uninvited. He crossed himself, kissed the crucifix and gently opened the door to the chapel . . .

# Holy Terror

**Books by Jane Holleman**

Killer Gorgeous
Hell's Belle
Holy Terror

Published by POCKET BOOKS

# Holy Terror

# Jane Holleman

**POCKET STAR BOOKS**

New York   London   Toronto   Sydney   Tokyo   Singapore

This book is a work of fiction. Names, characters, places and inci-
dents are products of the author's imagination or are used ficti-
tiously. Any resemblance to actual events or locales or persons,
living or dead, is entirely coincidental.

An *Original* Publication of POCKET BOOKS

 A Pocket Star Book published by
POCKET BOOKS, a division of Simon & Schuster Inc.
1230 Avenue of the Americas, New York, NY 10020

Copyright © 1999 by Jane Holleman

ISBN: 1-4165-0176-2

This Pocket Books paperback printing May 2004

10   9   8   7   6   5   4   3   2   1

POCKET STAR BOOKS and colophon are registered
trademarks of Simon & Schuster Inc.

Cover photo by Mitsuru Yamaguchi/Photonica

Printed in the U.S.A.

# Holy Terror

# 1

Forget the old saying about whores being nervous in church.

This whore—the one with the pearl-handled pistol pressed deep against the priest's moistening forehead—was as calm as a cat on a porch in the summer sun.

The lanky priest with the marble smooth voice said, never meaning to hide his glibness, "Let me guess. You're our new mail carrier."

She cocked the gun, gritted her teeth at him. He sized her up from the sweaty inches between them, covered in part by her steady pistol. She had a quality, something like a feral clown. A thunderstorm of dirty blond hair that spiked up like loose ocean-bottom flora in all directions. Her face needed a fresh wet rag to swab away the goo, which looked as if she had set her face into a paint palette and wallowed. Bosoms like Fat Boy bombs bulging ruthlessly from the tightest sweater he had ever seen outside the girlie magazines the nuns found in the schoolboys' bathrooms. Oh, and the gun of course, her most salient quality at the moment. He licked a pearl of sweat off his top lip.

She snarled at him. "Don't be a wiseass. You're my hostage." Outside thunder rolled. Her tiger eyes had a hopped-up quality, a hurricane on a radar screen.

The priest smiled very dimly. "If it's money, they won't pay for me." He looked at her over his wire rims. His insouciance—if she had known such a big word—was pissing her off. "What I mean, Miss, is that nobody negotiates for a penniless priest who is half-crocked half the time on cheap gin. For a hostage, you need a celebrity or a sheikh."

She had reason then to give him a renewed once-over. "You got gin?"

He hated his own wartorn hipness. "Do we have gin," he said. "This is a Catholic rectory, isn't it?"

"You know, you're messing with me, old man. And I could shoot you, just shoot you dead right here." It wasn't defiance that leaked through her Texas drawl. It was desperation he recognized. "I might, too, just shoot you until you're dead."

He flicked the brow that propped up the gun point. "Yes, but then you'd never find the gin I've hidden."

She smirked. He saw the youth in the gesture, and he knew that what he thought was a fifty-year-old crackled complexion belonged to a much younger girl. "You're a sorry hostage," she griped. Her gun hand fell to her side and she sat dejectedly in one of the rows of small, shiny pews in the candlelit chapel.

He kneeled beside her. Wanted to, but did not, touch. "What is your name?"

She stared at him harshly, an optical dare. "Caressa Dicks."

He threw himself backward in laughter that hardly ever came from the craters of his bleak and profound depths.

She fought her own repugnant grin, disarmed the gun's hammer, and jammed it into a giant carpetbag that loped at her side. "You're not very polite for a man of the cloth."

He eyed her grimly. "My cloth, these days, young lady, consists mostly of cocktail napkins and my own wet laundry."

She sighed greatly. "Shoot fire. Leave it to me to pick a sad-sack martyr for a hostage. I swear, without even trying I could fuck up a two-car funeral."

The storm suddenly knocked out the rims of small lights mounted along the walls, beneath the high stained-glass windows. The stations of the cross—those vignettes of Christ's last walk with the Cross crushing him—blinked into darkness. The priest and the whore were lost in shadows from the candles. The typically forlorn Christ dangling over the altar looked down at them through a pale wash of candlelight.

"How old are you, Caressa?"

"Yeah, sure, like there's still pretty little parties and cute Hallmark cards in the mail to remind me." She shrugged, feeling sad that saying her age reminded her that she was way too young to have lived down so many twisted miles. Her sigh was cold air. "I guess I'd be, maybe, I don't know, about thirty, maybe." She looked up at him, woeful as a wet puppy. "When you're nothing to anybody, you're age-old trash, anyhow." There was no self-pity, only venom.

He wanted to hug her, to fall onto her with his head in her lap and sob until his tears were blood. But he stayed calm.

"And why do you need a hostage?"

She turned her face toward the wintry white light of the candles over the Christ. Her words, so intoned, didn't fit the profile of the monstrous, garish girl at his hands. She said, "Bless me, Father, for I have sinned and offended God." She cut her tiger eyes at him so suddenly it chilled the candles into a mass flicker. "Now this is a Confession, so you can't tell anyone what I say, you understand? You're my hostage, but right now you're my priest, and what I say to you is private, right, jack-off?"

He nodded. She bent to him. He smelled liquor and male body fluids on her tongue. The candles and the Christ leaned closer to hear over the rain tickling the dark stained glass. "Just now, out there, I saw a man kill somebody. We were in his car. He was driving. I was—" She swallowed, stuck a grotesquely long fingernail in her mouth for a second, then took a breath. "I was facedown in his lap, if you get it. He ran over her, a bag lady, and he kept going. I heard it, the hit, and he cursed real loud. I heard the front wheels and then the back wheels, and I heard her shopping cart go over the car like somebody scratching a blackboard real hard. The car stopped. I was blindfolded—somebody in the backseat had blindfolded me when I got into the car—so I ripped it off, after the hit and run, and now nobody's in the car. The door's open and the rain sounds like it's burning the ground from falling so hard, and the bag lady is twisted like a pretzel, blood gushing everywhere. So I ran. I walked at first, slowly, through some of the skyscrapers down here, just tried walking along the sidewalks. This end of downtown is deserted by midnight, so there was nobody around."

She put a hand on the priest's long black sleeve, and the gross fingernails dented his skin. "He shot at me from somewhere. Like from between the buildings. A bullet chipped brick over my head, and down where I live that's a sound I don't mistake, so I ran. He shot twice more, and he was screaming my street name. When I got in, I told him my name!"

He listened, rapt, and realized he had been holding his breath. Her gory story had mesmerized him for a few moments. This creature before him, so slight and almost frail, yet so vile and violent, was pelting him with meteors of emotions. Holding people's hands through their fears and sadnesses was his lifestyle, but this wild child was, he believed, the most fractured little soul he had known. And in holding his breath beside her panic, he had held in a thought as well, a thought too morbid and at once marvelous, in fact a whole world of thoughts about a plan he had for her if she ever came to him. How he would take her to himself and cure her, fix her, how he'd open her up and end her pain.

Now, with her fingernails digging his black sleeve, when he let out the air caught in his chest, it was not a sigh of relief that the story had crescendoed. It was instead a sob of air. He had not

dreamed that when the girl came to him she would
be so destroyed. And seeing such a wash of self-
destruction inside her crushed the air from his
lungs when he realized it was she, she was it. The
plan wouldn't go so smoothly now. Now there was a
murder, and now there was a murderer out there
somewhere shooting at her, and now there would
be police. But most importantly his keen and clean
plan to remove her demons was complicated by
her, herself, because he had planned that she'd be
needy, controllable, maybe even grateful. His plan
had not allowed that she would be lost to the world,
lost to him, and so supremely damaged.

She thrust out her other hand, clamped the
priest's other arm, crushing his flesh, her eyes afire.
"I ran and ran. He shot at me a couple more times.
I tried some doors on the warehouses around here.
Then I jumped your little fence and yanked on the
chapel door and it was open. My god." She didn't
cry, just went steely and more coarse. "You came a
few weeks ago, remember, to the whore district,
and you gave us those fliers about the food bank
here, so I knew as I was running that I was going
north on the sidewalks, toward this church. Toward
you."

The chill fluttered down his long, lean frame and
eddied as a thick thud in his belly. He resisted the
urge to double over in agony or ecstasy. He spoke
softly, looking away from her because his suspicion
was at hand, and the truth was too prophetic and
horrendous.

"You've made reconciliation before. So, as a girl
you went to Catholic school."

She said acerbicly. "I just told you I saw a man kill a woman." She shoved him hard, from nowhere, and bent her fiery face into his. "You forget who I am, you jack-off, because it's what I am that counts. I'm dead if I don't get someplace to hide until I can get the hell out of town. Knock off the warm-fuzzy crap. You're going to hide me in this rectory until I can get money and get out of here, and I'm going to hold this gun next to your sappy, saint-sucking heart every minute so you won't call the cops."

Sounds were droning in his ears, the bereft memory of a little girl's screams decades ago, echoes like a terrified blind kid alone in the horror house at an amusement park. Now his palms were soaked in sweat. He said to her lamely, "We could go to the police."

Open handed, she slapped him so hard it reeled him backward off his knees. He stayed there, feeling himself panting.

"Right, sure, great idea, Father Dumbshit. Me, with a police record about as long as your leg. And this rich guy, with his big Jeep Wagoneer and his diamond and gold Rolex and his fucking cell phone, and the police are going to believe me over him?" She yanked him up by the clerical collar of his black robes and seethed into his swelling cheek. "He's somebody. I'm nobody. Now screw all your divinely inspired do-gooder nonsense, pal. This is real grit and danger and pain. I need help. And since I'm the one with the gun, you're going to help me."

She fished in the filthy, worn bag as she ranted, stopping only long enough to light a cigarette right there in the chapel and toss the match into the quiet air. "When the trouble dies down on the streets—just a couple of days—I'll board a bus, maybe L.A., who knows." She blew a long, acrid plume of smoke and said to the priest like a wizened gypsy soothsayer, "They'll look for me everywhere. He's got a lot to lose, this powerful guy with the pricey wristwatch. They won't want me to tell what I saw, so they'll look for me in every building within a mile of here. And they'll kill me."

To look in her eyes, he could hear flames crackling. She jerked him beside her on the pew. He straightened himself, his hair and collar. He was quiet by nature, so only the thunder punctuated her panting.

She said quickly, putting a fingernail as long as a purple pencil into his sunken chest where the silver cross lay, "Don't you go thinking, Father, that I'm the whore with a heart. I'm not. You betray me, you call the cops or try to run away until I'm out of here, I'll cut your nuts off and leave you the doctor bill. Got it?"

He said, "Who is 'they'?"

She sniggered cruelly, stomped the cigarette out on the shiny wooden floor. "He has people, whoever he is. He has money, power, probably a respectable family, a good job. And he wouldn't want anyone to know that he first picked up a hooker and then ran down an old lady pushing all of her busted-up world in a shopping cart and then kept going." She went distant on him, maybe contemplating how painful her death would be if they found her. "They'll protect him, his people will.

And to do it they'll murder me—and you if you're in the way when they find me."

He stood. She realized that he was not old. He had boyishly blond, short hair and oasis-blue eyes set on high cheekbones and a slender, Nordic nose. The wire-rim specs were disarming in their simplicity. He was cowboy tall, but noticeably thin in his black robes, like a refugee. The rosary that dangled on a small chain should have been at his waist, but his gauntness made it wear like a holster at his hips. It clicked when he stood. He put out a hand. She felt an odd shiver when she saw it, and she started to speak, but a sliver of lightning shot through the stained glass, and she felt speechless a moment and shut her usually rattling trap.

His hand was there in her vision, an opened lily, and she stared at his wrists. Slash scars. Thick, heavy ropes of regret, signs of a doomed night when he had fallen to his knees on the altar and slashed a fresh blade repeatedly across the blue veins under his fair skin. Lightning ticked again through the glass and splintered into hot rainbows that sliced the dark.

"Jesus. What'd you do?" She was indelicate, crass. "Run your wrists through a meat grinder? Man, for a priest you sure are a lousy mess."

He said dully, "Lucky guess. Please carry that cigarette into the rectory so we can throw it away."

She yanked up the gun again, pointed it at him across an alley of shadowy candlelight. There was no fear in his eyes, and she felt empty, somehow undressed in a new, shameful way, as he glared at her. "No cops, Father. Just you and me. Before you go to sleep I'm going to tie you to the bed."

He smiled for a split second, grinned at the gun's opening as if it were a flashbulb and he had just said cheese. "No need, Caressa. I'll help you."

She squinted at him. "Yeah? Why? Nobody ever helped me do anything except get my panties down faster. And I didn't just get to be a worthless piece of human junk tonight, ya know. I've been a pile of smelly dung since I can remember. Why should you help?"

"I can get to the resources. It's called charity."

Her squint became a narrow-eyed sneer. "Well, it's not a piece of ass you want, is it? No. I'm not a little altar boy. Charity? From strangers? It won't work, because you can't tell anyone I'm here, or I shoot you, remember?"

He became so serious when he spoke that it put dark shadows over his sunken cheeks. "I do not intend to tell anyone that you came to me."

She heard herself swallow. "Hey, why aren't you scared?"

He was in the dark. He had to ask now, even though the words tangled in his labored breaths, even though he knew that if the answer was yes she'd have shot him through the head by now. But if the answer was no, then maybe just the sordid, secretive question itself would jar her, and then they could start the ... extraction of pain. If she remembered when he asked, they could begin the ending of it all.

She could see only the candles glowing in his eyes, tips of light penetrating his words when he asked precisely and softly, "Don't you know me?"

She swallowed hard. He and the storm and the candles and Christ looking all . . . executed, up there were spooking her. She answered him. "So. Okay. You came to the whore district once, and so maybe I blew you or spanked you or whatever. I don't ask questions. I don't see faces. I don't care about much."

He walked. At the altar he genuflected without missing a gracious beat of his stride and crossed himself. She heard him. His whisper pinged through the silence and up to Christ as clear as a bird's wings.

He whispered, "Thank you, Lord. Please guide my words and deeds so I may help her now. And forgive me if she should suffer at my hands as I intercede."

He started away in his wavy black robes down a black aisle that led to a doorway into the small rectory. She pondered with disinterest how this cryptic, tragic priest could be so indifferent to the danger she had just brought him into.

In the rainbow of lightning splinters that danced with the storm, she saw the eyes of the porcelain Christ flicker alive, blinking at her, ghostly and neon.

"Holy shit," the whore called out as she started after the quiet priest with the slashed wrists, "this place is scary as Hell. Hey, hostage, wait up! I want some of that damned gin you're hiding!"

2

The whore didn't sit at tables with men very often in her world of jaded commerce. She mostly sat on their faces or spanked their asses while the carnal meter was running.

The priest glugged gin into a jelly glass for her and folded his stringy self into the straightback chair across an old Formica kitchen table. He set a kerosene lamp between them because the lights were doused by the groaning storm. The gun was between them on the table like a ballistic cupcake. Rain scratched against the ancient brownstone rectory.

She was as understated as a bus barreling through a cemetery. "So how come you tried to kill yourself?"

The gin tasted like a gulp of men's cologne, but it did the trick for her. She slipped an inch away from her recurring nightmare, a safe enough distance so it couldn't sit on her chest and pound her face like it did most times when she tried to sleep.

The priest took a velvety swerve. "Who was the man you saw do the hit and run tonight?"

She was jagged, didn't give a shit to be any other way anymore. "Some newspaper guy. A big shot type. A guy kept calling on his cell phone to talk to him about some big news story tomorrow." She shot him a testy stare. "It's not easy hearing whole conversations when the guy is using your face in his lap like a battering ram."

She didn't mean to be shocking. He wasn't shocked. He said mildly, "He's been your client before?"

She grinned. But for the gruesome makeup and the stack of nasty hair and the gold lamé leggings as tight as a three-day drunk, she was as pretty to his imagination as the Sweetheart of Sigma Chi. "My client? Jesus, you're an idiot. I ain't a damn banker. He was my trick. And no, I've never done him before, at least not in that big Jeep. That's what we remember. The cars. Not the dumb dicks driving them. The Red Chevy Blazer likes to be peed on while he does his own hand job. The silver Ford pickup wants to be called Daddy while he comes. The black Mercedes bites, the green Mustang gives it in the ass, stuff like that. No Wagoneers. I'd remember."

She slid out the gin glass. He refilled. "He didn't give you his name?"

She cackled, laughed meanly. "You mean, like just in case I wanted to blackmail him or look him up for Sunday brunch? Oh, Jesus. What the fuck is your name? Your real name, not some saintly calling."

"David. Father David."

"Well, Dave, let me school you a tad here. Never

kiss a hooker. Never come in a hooker. Never tell a hooker your name and never, ever fall in love with one or turn your back before you've put your wallet away. Class dismissed. Dave."

She put her finger through the gun's trigger ring and spun it like they were playing Spin the Pistol. "God, I'd like some meth."

"He's a reporter?"

She was woozy on the booze, otherwise she would have smacked his fair face again for the quiz biz. "Not a lowlife one, not like the guys that are at the PD when we get hauled in, the crows looking for crumbs of scandal. No. This guy's a suit type. On his phone he was giving orders, not taking them. Who lives here with you?"

Her breaths were thick enough with liquor to burn his eyes. And she smelled bad. Body odor and stale smoke and old cheese. He said, "I'm alone for now. The Monsignor lived here, but he died last week. A new priest comes soon. What did he look like? The man in the car?"

The boxy kitchen was as unadorned as a deserted campsite. The lights flickered and went out again. The gun percolating between them didn't so much as toy with his interest. The whore coiled her thin legs under herself, sitting comfortably on the ridiculously high-heeled red stilettos. The kerosene lamplight made their faces look like disembodied talking heads.

"I was walking. Some tall guy hollered to me, but he was in shadows, so I couldn't make him out too good. When I got close, he told me to turn around, and he put the blindfold on me and helped me into

the front seat. I know it was the front seat because
there was a console I had to lean over to get to the
trick. I got in and I heard the car's back door shut
and heard someone slide in, then the trick got in
front with me. He drove, yakked on the phone,
shoved my face down into his crotch. Don't go so
pale. It's out there. If it wasn't out there, this sick
shit, you'd be out of a job, asshole."

He couldn't swallow for a second or two. The gin
and tonic sat at the back of his throat like a wad of
glue. Finally he cleared his throat. "It's so dangerous for you, being a prostitute. I'm really
just . . . god, sorry as hell."

She smoked lavishly, atom bombs of poison, not
unlike her dire words. "Fuck off. Save it for the
Jerry Springer show. It's not as dangerous as that
children's prison I ran off from as a kid." She slid
into a boozy sedation, blinked dully, slurred. "Besides, I'm not a prostitute. I'm a hooker, a plain
whore. And I'm not a slut either." She crooked a
wobbly purple fingernail at him. "Prostitutes have
pimps. Hookers, we work alone, no pimp. Move
around town, you know. And sluts, you know what
sluts do, Dave?"

She was slithering at him. Hateful, and somehow
he knew that most of it spewed backward at herself.
"Sluts sleep with men they don't even like or love,
for free, so they can get married and get rescued
and not have to be alone anymore. That's a slut for
you. You don't believe me, read the society page."

He watched her take things from her carpetbag
and begin to roll a marijuana joint. Her hands were
deft at it, and they were pretty hands, he noticed.

The fingernails of course were overplayed, like bad acting, but she had a pianist's lithe white fingers.

He offered, "You couldn't have been in a children's prison. There are no such things. It must have been an orphanage."

She looked at him like a woman about to drink his blood. "Did you ever go to sleep at night, all alone in the whole entire universe, wondering what the hell you did so wrong?"

He licked his lips, met her eyes squarely. "Yes."

She saw his wrists, sat back abruptly, yanked into some brutal awareness. She said coldly, "Why would you want to die? It's all free—the house, the heat, the food. All you do is wear beads and sling incense and nod at people's pain, so sedate, so superior. Problems? What do you know. Your mama ever whip the back of your baby-fat legs with a hairbrush until your Mary Jane's were drenched in blood? Just because you were little and didn't know better and you went in and cut your own bangs, I mean, did she? Anybody ever make you sit outside in a freezing cold car while they drank there in the warm saloon, and all you wanted was just some dinner and a blanket and maybe . . . maybe a sip of Kool-Aid? Huh? No. You, they fall down and worship. So you cut your wrists and failed. Kiss my ass."

His folded hands had gripped each other white like ice sculptures. The rain intensified. The church bells pealed through the slashing rain, playing out some ancient hymn and then chiming midnight, twelve lugubrious bongs.

The priest said somberly, "Not at the children's home."

The marijuana smoke flowered. She sat back, her breasts came at him. She laughed so rudely. "No. That's right. Somebody somewhere stumbled out of some bar sober enough to see me in the car, freezing half to death, weighing about thirty pounds at eight years old, and I went to the children's home."

The words dripped disdain. She narrowed hard eyes at him. "Run by priests. I stayed two years. Then I ran off. At a seasoned ten years old I gave my first blow job to a guy I met in a motel diner. He gave me twenty bucks. The rest is good enough for ratings week. Jesus. Did that dead Monsignor leave any drugs? Pain pills? Downers? Anything?"

He tried gently. "Do you remember the orphanage?"

She leaned back again, let the pot fumes levitate her. "Just the kids crying at night. But there was food and blankets."

His chest could have exploded under the suspense. "Why did you run away?"

She kept her painted eyelids shut. "I don't know. It was time. You got any food? The stuff in the garbage can over there will be fine."

He felt his throat tighten with immense pity. He rose. He set out a placemat and utensils before her, which she stared at as if he were doing magic tricks, turning pennies into doves in her lap. She wanted the Rice Krispies, pointed at them in the cupboard, and she swooned over fresh whole milk as he poured.

She ate like a starving animal. He watched, hearing the rain chant her real name over and over to him. He knew it, of course, couldn't ever have prayed enough or died enough times to forget it.

She had milk on her chin. The pearly drop slid quietly, and he stared. He watched the drop of milk, and it reminded him of mothers and babies. The milk drop slid along her chin and was joined by another, and the priest thought of the milky pure breath of the tiny infants he baptized on Sundays. He had always thought the babies were fresh from seeing God, which is why God gave them no use of language—until later, when they had lived enough to forget Him, to be unable to describe Him anymore. So that their life's deed would be to find Him again on their own, not knowing why but knowing they should. Faith. The game. The purpose of Creation. Leaving Him and forgetting Him and then choosing to find Him again.

He said dryly, "Caressa, you can sleep here for a few days. In the attic over the chapel. Nobody knows the attic is there. Only a small stairway behind this utility closet leads up to the attic. It's part of the original chapel, more than a hundred years old."

She didn't look up, only wolfed food. He told her, "Uh, this was a convent for a while. The nuns lived here. I can find some clothes for you in boxes upstairs." He went sheepish. She finally glanced up at him.

Amazed. Amused. "Dave, boy, you are not putting me in a nun's habit."

"I have nothing else female."

"So go buy something."

"Perhaps not. A priest in a women's store? And

you can't go out. They're looking for you. The habits are plain black shrouds. No 'Flying Nun' headgear. You'll be comfortable. And disguised if anyone comes around."

She rolled her jade daggers. "God, why didn't I take Frederick of Hollywood hostage?" She sighed.

He said, "I'll help you. If you let me. You need a doctor to examine some of those cuts. They look old and infected. You need vitamins and—"

She stood and screamed at him. "Stop that ignorant social worker bullshit with me, you bastard!" She grabbed up the gun and pointed it at his face, and she kicked his shin so hard with the point of her spiked heel that he lurched forward out of the chair.

"You self-righteous asshole, here in your freak world where your pity is my glory! Stop it!"

She clutched his face, put the gun to his mouth. She was aflame again. "I . . . will . . . kill you." She cocked the gun. "I told you, don't go thinking I'm here for sunshine and salvation. You sorry excuse for a preacher, you broken-down washed-up son of a bitch! You leave my soul alone! You want to save me? Good. I want to save me, too. So get off your pontificating ignorant ass and hide me! And don't *preach!*"

He could breathe finally. He nodded, gasping.

In the depths of the hallway toward the darkened chapel, they heard the thudding and thumping noise at the same time.

They stood motionless. The kerosene lamplight made them ghoulish. She whispered frantically, "What the hell was that?"

He managed to get up, limped to her. "Someone is in the chapel. Go. In the attic there's a huge wooden Christ. He's stored there, leaning sideways against the wall. He's very sturdy. Get behind him. And Caressa, be very quiet. You'll be right over the altar below."

The priest limped toward the chapel. The whore tiptoed into the last safe place in her woebegotten world, counting on a stranger of the Lord to save her.

The priest put his hand tightly around the silver crucifix at his chest. He listened. Through the door the footsteps echoed. Slow. Deliberate. Uninvited.

He crossed himself, kissed the crucifix and gently opened the door to the chapel.

# 3

The Blessed Virgin Mary appeared to Mick Ramsey as if any moment she was going to faint in a surfeit of grief from her perch on the shadowy ceiling. The only light near her in the chapel was the ring of tiny candles that burned a blue halo around her reposed porcelain face, which very much had the expression of a sadly wilting flower. His gaze shifted to a big gaudy Christ that leered over the white marble altar. He walked to look up at it.

He said aloud to his echo, "They morphed Jesus. Should've known after what they did to poor Betty Crocker. Well, watch out, Santa."

From behind him, near a door that must've led to the rectory, a man said laconically, "That's a new Christ. The old one got his wooden feet worn out from people crying on them." The priest was soft-spoken, friendly. He reached Mick, and Mick noticed that the guy smelled of something cheap— wine, gin, dollar-store perfume.

They stared at the newfangled icon of Christ as if it were a slot machine and the fruit was spinning.

Mick said, "He doesn't even look Jewish. He looks more, I don't know, like human Spam. You know, not real but made from real stuff."

The priest grinned nicely. "He is now politically correct."

Mick mused. "Not yet. Not until they put him in a dress."

A sturdy, large hand went out to the priest. "Mick Ramsey, Father. I was walking past, and this door was open and banging. I called out, but no one answered."

"Father David Keenan," he said as they shook, and he thought to himself: You did not call out. "Thanks for checking on the door. There isn't much to steal anymore thanks to the break-ins, but I guess the vandals could have some fun wrecking the place."

The priest thought: He should go. But he's standing in the doorway to the street like an outlaw in a shootout. He's waiting for something . . . looking for something.

He would have to remember the description to tell Caressa, so he outlined it. Mick Ramsey. A fabulous fop of black hair just graying at the temples, the kind of hair balding guys cried over. Eyes the color of coffee with cream, dark skin, the kind of healthy tan that nice girls went bad for. Hit-man glare, not icy but deciphering. Big shoulders, maybe six-foot-four. The girls would watch him but never approach. The men would be aware of the boulders of shoulders and the flat belly and sense his strength. His lips curled, mere velvety ribbons that draped into an almost sinister smile. He wore a store-bought tuxedo and plain black cowboy boots.

Yeah. Father David had to grimace. Mick Ramsey. Handsome just the way women like them—tall, dark. Brooding just enough to give off a scent of the loner.

And this man would need a prostitute—no, Father David corrected himself—a whore for what reason? He rubbed his temples as the handsome devil scanned the chapel listlessly. The answer was too easy. He'd need a paid whore for the reason leading male actors and heads of state and husbands of beautiful wives need whores; nothing else in life is forbidden to them—it's all there and all theirs for the asking. Except the hooker. She's their dastardly middle finger swaying at convention.

"You're a parishioner, Mr. Ramsey?"

"I'm an atheist." His voice was phone sex.

"Why?"

He looked askance at the priest, the velvety brown ribbons of lips twirling into mockery. "Because I don't believe in God." The next remark barely floated out. "You live here alone?"

"There was the Monsignor—"

"Yeah. He died last week. I know. My newspaper did a big story about it. 'Course, nobody cared what he did while he lived, but when he died, boom. The world loves dead heroes."

The priest took slow breaths. "You're a reporter?"

"Yeah, I couldn't get into flight attendant school." He smiled, and Father David could hear a legion of women dropping dead of desire at the same time. The remark was comic relief, not cynicism.

The votives, rows of little red cups of candles that represent living prayers, waded in the dark like pages turning and making a slight, warm breeze. The reporter ran his hand through his ruggedly unkempt hair and searched the chapel with his sand-colored eyes.

"Mr. Ramsey, you seem curious. Would you like to see the altar?"

"Jeez, Father. Last time I walked to an altar it cost me a house, a car, two pedigree Labradors, and half of my retirement fund." Mick stopped right at the pew where Caressa had lingered. "Smells like somebody's been smoking right here."

"The vagrants . . ." the priest's voice trailed unconvincingly.

Mick started to speak but a small phone jangled in his breast pocket. He answered. "Ramsey." Listened intently. "Yeah, so the fuck what?" He glanced at the priest, then turned away. "Unless the dead bag lady is a former first lady, it isn't my beat. I don't do routine police call shit. That's your job. No, you listen to me—" He stopped, sighed with great annoyance. "Okay, I'll get there, but whatever this cloak-and-dagger reason you've got for calling me, it better involve me winning the lottery and you're planning a surprise party." He hung up, slammed shut the phone, said to Father David as dryly as a Texas martini, "Well, you take care. Imagine this door being unlocked like that. Here in downtown. Number three in Texas for per capita homicides, Father. Here all alone like you are, well, you could wake up dead."

Father David could feel his own pallor, a sort of reverse blush. Mick squinted, desperado style. The priest was acting weird, fidgeting, like a guy who had shoplifted and was heading for the exit. "Say, Father, you the permanent pastor now?"

"No. I just came to Texas a month ago. From Denver. I, uh, go to parishes where the pastor is ailing and the other priests need help." He shrugged, tried to be funny. It fell flat. "Sort of a Kelly Girl priest, I guess."

"You all right, Father? I'm wondering, I mean, over here it's cigarette smoke and up next to you it's the smell of god-awful cheap perfume, and you didn't know you weren't locked up in here safe." The reporter stood in the open doorway, buttoning a black trench coat against the rainy chill. "So I'm thinking," his Texas accent made it so folksy, "maybe you need help, maybe you're in trouble." He stared squarely. "Maybe you can't speak freely. I'm saying that if I didn't know better, I'd swear you're acting like somebody is holding a gun at your back. You need something? Cops?"

"I'm fine, Mr. Ramsey. Women wearing perfume hug me all day long at funerals and church luncheons and meetings." He tried to sound like he was joshing one of the boys, because if this good-looking T-Rex decided to blast by him, it would be only a minor inconvenience to break the skinny priest in half.

The reporter eased. "Yeah. Women hug me all day, too, so they can get close enough to reach me with their switchblades." He scratched at his razor stubble. Why wasn't it a surprise, Father David lamented to himself, that when this guy smiled his teeth were perfect? Standing by him, the priest felt like the "before" photo in a health club ad.

"So, Father, you get lonely in here? Just you and all these statues with eyes that don't move."

"I have many very good friends, Mr. Ramsey. And I won't worry until I begin to see that the statues' eyes *do* move."

"I mean, sure they love you, your parishioners. But—"

He squeezed the reporter's stout shoulder. Mick winced at the fleeting sight of the gory scars on both wrists. "Mr. Ramsey, I'm the lucky one. I don't have to work on relationships with people. I am not, in fact, allowed to even cultivate relationships with people. I only have to work on knowing God. It's guys like you who have to deal with knowing and loving and losing other human beings."

The reporter liked intelligence, especially mollified, understated intelligence. He grinned. "Yeah, I can see how if you don't own anything, then nothing owns you." He turned to the downpour, then back to the priest. "Do you miss the sex?"

The priest liked honesty, especially overt, intently genuine honesty. "Is the sex worth the trouble, Mick?"

He dragged a tongue across his shiny teeth, toyed with unwrapping a big cigar, plugged it in, narrowed his black eyes. "Since my divorce some years back, Father, I've learned something every forty-five-year-old divorced playboy should know: Never be satisfied with the dumb ones, and never be honest with the smart ones."

A cold breeze slapped them. The priest said nicely, "It's not the sex I miss. But I always wanted a

Ford Thunderbird. I can never have one, you know, it goes against the vow of poverty."

He smiled at the priest, the good-looking bad boy did, and the priest knew that the smile was probably all the foreplay most women needed. He said, "Still, Father, they ought to change it so you guys can get married."

Father David laughed. "Oh, Lord, I'm almost fifty. Please don't let them change it now. I do hope they let me die first."

Mick laughed. Then for a moment he looked grimly past Father David, into the abyss of darkened chapel.

Father David said, "There might be one other thing I wish for. If all this was suspended and there was no penalty, Mick, then I'd like for just one day to be in your shoes and to know how it feels to be a man who beautiful women crave instead of worship."

Mick laughed dryly. The rain absorbed him. Father David looked for a car. For a Jeep Wagoneer. But the reporter simply disappeared into the slushy night.

He sat a moment. Was it thunder or did Satan growl over his shoulder? He hurried forward to lock the chapel door against the surging storm, and then he headed upstairs to be the best hostage he could until it was time to open her up, to end the suffering.

He stopped on the rickety, dark secret stairwell that led to the attic and Caressa. When he kneeled on a stair and his hands covered his face, they were as cold as the hands of a bloodless corpse.

# 4

Lazy raindrops splatted the black body bag on the sidewalk. The zipping sound as it was closed was an eerie exclamation point that this bag lady's disparate life was a wrap.

Mick ambled—Mick always ambled, it was his male muse—toward the scene which was dotted with cops and washed by red and blue cruiser lights.

He saw the regular nighttime cop-shop reporter under an umbrella talking to two uniforms and scribbling notes for her story. The reporter didn't look surprised when Mick walked up. The burly cops straggled away.

Mick groused, "Why am I here? It's twelve-thirty in the morning on a weekend. Is this stiff somebody? I don't do street shit. This is street shit."

She pointed with her pen and said curtly, "You're here because he's here. Young Stud of Steel in the flesh summoned you."

Mick turned and instantly felt as if he could hear a guillotine sliding toward his throat.

He said flatly, "Jesse Brucker. A police lieutenant at a routine runover. Why?"

"He won't say, at least not to me." She leaned conspiratorially. "But if you get wind of it, you call me pronto in the newsroom. My deadline's 2 A.M."

"He won't tell me anything. He hates my guts."

She slung up her purse, tossed her notepad inside, and adjusted her rain-spattered specs. "Everyone hates your guts, Ramsey. The women, either because you won't fuck them or you stop fucking them. And the men, they hate you because unlike them, you aren't saddled with a conscience."

He leveled a low laugh. She turned to scamper through the rain.

Jesse Brucker turned, too, to see Mick as he crossed the street toward Brucker's umbrella. In the cascades of blue and red cop car lights, wearing a dark raincoat and puffing a pipe, Brucker looked like a black Sherlock Holmes. He was younger than Mick, meaner than a scorpion, too smart for a cop. Mick tripped on the curb heading for Brucker—seeing him there in the dark like a pissed-off creature from the black lagoon, puffing, frowning, looking for a pound of flesh to gnaw, Mick's stomach lurched. He cringed and slowed his pace when he saw Brucker spit a wad of gum out like a wrestling coach and coil another piece to grind in his mouth.

The guy, Mick muttered to himself, has the personality of a rolling ball of butcher knives.

Brucker's black eyes went frosty. Mick stepped under the umbrella. The tension was as palpable as the steam that rose from the gutters all around them in the slick streets.

Brucker's words were Ginsu daggers. "Lookee

here, boys, Mick Ramsey took his dick out of some poor woman's mouth long enough to join us."

The uniforms laughed obligingly and then managed to saunter away, out of the subterfuge. This rivalry was legendary.

"What do you want, Brucker?"

"You. In a chalk outline on your carpet."

Mick turned. "I'm not staying to hear this bogus bullshit of yours."

"Hold on, hotrod. I got a question for you. Where've you been tonight?" Brucker's black-coffee face broke into a nasty grin. "Hoo-wee, homeboy, you're wearing a tuxedo. Well, I guess you might as well look good while you're paying them by the hour, huh, Mickey Mouse?"

"Fuck you, Brucker."

"Say, Ramsey, you reckon if I'd had me a white boy's education at that big fancy Texas Tech University, reckon I could today have your stellar command of the English language?"

"Gee, Brucker, I'm sorry I wasn't brought up black and deprived like you, but think about it, without that sappy saga of yours to break the babes' hearts, what else could you tell them to get yourself laid? That sharecropper shit must melt 'em."

Brucker's nasty grin widened. His face was wet and shiny from the rain like a black jazz piano player sweating it out on a smokey stage. "It works fine," he hissed, "until I get to the part about me grad-i-atin' from Princeton and all."

"Yeah. You must thank God every day for Princeton's quota system."

Brucker laughed, threw his hand over his heart, and patted. "If I had a heart, Mickey, you'd have just broken it."

"Enough bullshit, Brucker. Why'd you call me here?"

Beyond them the body bag was loaded into a Medical Examiner's van with a graphic thud. Two cop cars pulled away solemnly. Only a uniform and a crime scene cop milled across the street where the body had been hit by the car in a run-down section of old downtown buildings, so different from the north end, which bristled with tony restaurants and snazzy nightclubs.

Brucker's smart-ass facade faded into a deadpan mug shot. "I called you here hoping you'd wrestle me for my gun and it might go off in your chest. Second to that, I need to know where you were tonight, home-ee boy."

"You don't need to know shit."

"I already know shit, Ramsey. I'm looking right at it. Tell me where you were in your rented tuxedo between ten and—" Brucker checked his watch. "Now." He veiled himself in pipe smoke.

They were weirdly alone in the rainy brick-paved walkway between two crummy buildings. Mick couldn't tell if his hands and neck were wet from rain or nervous sweat.

Brucker asked the way he might stomp a cockroach. "And where's your car?"

Mick answered dryly. "I went to the Press Association awards banquet. My car by now should be at the newspaper garage."

Brucker called out to a uniform. "Say, Eddie,

Ramrod here says his car's at the newspaper garage. Check it out." Eddie waved.

Mick saw Brucker's eyes spark, a brain flick of his hatred for Mick. Brucker said, "It's a Jeep Wagoneer, right? Custom gold trim?" He mocked. "Mattress and margarita machine in the back, no doubt, because a playboy's work is never done."

Mick bent to look under the umbrella squarely into Brucker's somber face. "To the contrary of what you said, this tux is not rented, and it's a Brooks Brothers. What the fuck is going on here?"

Brucker said, "The bag lady took it in the head fast and hard from a car that didn't stop. The ME puts her death between ten and midnight. A security guard at a warehouse just two blocks from here, over by Saint Pat's, called in a Jeep Wagoneer with a smashed windshield and grill damage, black, custom gold trim, idling, door open in the middle of Main Street by the old chapel. The call came in at twenty minutes to twelve. No license plate number, too dark, and the Jeep was gone by the time the cruiser arrived to check. First thing that came to my mind was that you used to pick up my sister for those so-called dates you all had—I preferred to think of them as Janelle's reaction to a severe head injury she must have gotten—and you picked her up in a black Wagoneer, custom gold trim."

The rain fell, goopy and golden from the streetlights, like fingers reaching for Mick's throat. He said plainly, "Brucker, you can't think—"

The uniform huffed over to them, his yellow rain slicker shiny as a brand-new schoolbus. He didn't look at Mick. "Uh, sir, the Wagoneer registered to Mick Ramsey is not located at the newspaper garage."

They both looked at Mick. Mick thought of hearing the jury foreman stand and recite the guilty verdict.

He said quickly, "Then Vic still has it. My boss, Victor Farron, he asked if he could use it after the banquet—" Mick was panting, rambling. Brucker was stony, the pipe smoke engulfing him like a menacing genie. "So I left earlier than he did, and I left the keys on the table. He said he would have my car back to the newspaper garage by two this morning. I—I—I left the banquet at ten, walked around downtown." He stopped suddenly. "Goddamn it, Brucker, you know I wouldn't hit someone and keep going and not stop to help and call the police! You know me!"

"That's right." He looked at Mick through the smoke like a cobra. "And I know that if you did hit her and kill her, you're more capable than most of lying about it."

Mick's mouth was dry, his hands clammy. He said through his teeth. "You son of a bitch. I fucked your sister so you're framing me for murder."

First, Jesse Brucker noted to himself that Mick Ramsey used the phrase "framing me for murder." And it was not a string of words that just came naturally to most citizens. The phrase stuck in Brucker's mind for some odd reason. Brucker knew instantly that Mick was scared of something. Maybe scared of himself. Maybe scared of something outside himself.

Second, in a more visceral man-to-man move, Brucker touched the big ol' six-shooter at his hip, got himself right into Mick's face. "Recite me her suicide note, you chicken-shit liar. Recall for me every chilling, tragic word she wrote before she stepped off the chair, after she decided that crushing her own throat was better than living without you." He yelled. His breath was ghostly white in the frigid air. "Say the goddamn words!"

Mick shouted, too, even louder. The uniforms kept their distance. "You're framing me for murder, you bastard! It'll get in the papers, I'll lose my job!" He took off his trench coat, slung it into the puddles. "Here. Now, Brucker. It can't go any other way."

Brucker, every solid inch of him, a rabid roadblock, came at Mick. Eddie the uniform was there in a split second, between them, knowing that he couldn't hold either one back physically, but hoping to give their heat time to cool.

Brucker shoved Eddie away. Mick walked in circles. He turned and hollered, "You can't do this. You have to take yourself off of this. We hate each other. The history is too involved, you won't work it fair—"

Brucker picked up his umbrella where he had thrown it, straightened his coat, found his pipe on the curb, and worked at it calmly. "The suicide note said 'I am so ashamed, I can't go on, I can't live without him and I can't live with his constant, horrible lying.' " His voice was hollow. "My sister loved you, Ramsey. You hurt her. And what's worst of all is that you didn't care that you hurt her."

Mick yelled, face up to the misty rain that would soon be filled with tiny bits of Texas ice, "That hasn't got one thing to do with a goddamn car like mine being used in a hit and run, Brucker, and you know it! You fucking know I didn't do this! There's another car like mine somewhere in this city, but you won't look for it, goddamn it, because your sister stopped her antidepressants and went nuts and hanged herself. So blame me, Brucker, for the fact that you watched her slide and didn't intervene, blame me for that so you can sleep at night. But do *not* work this case."

The pipe smoke was back. The cobra hissed through it. "Anybody that can account for your time tonight, Ramsey, between ten and the time you got here?"

Mick sat, head in hands on the curb. "God, I hate you, Jesse. I really, really hate your guts."

"I know. Kinda makes me proud when guys like you hate guys like me. Means we're doing something right. You got an alibi?"

Mick laughed sorrowfully. "An alibi. I left the dinner at ten, walked to the Dublin Rose. There's a girl I see—" He ignored Brucker's huff of disgust. "She met me. We had drinks, I guess until about eleven-thirty. Then I walked downtown a while. A bum was all beaten up on the corner, so I walked him to the diner there and bought his breakfast—"

"Ah, Mother Teresa lives."

Mick glared at him. "I didn't stay with him. I paid after he ordered and I left. That was just after eleven-thirty. I walked some more. Then there was a door banging at St. Pat's down in the south end, the chapel, so I went over the fence to close it, the door. I went inside, and the priest talked to me. The bells had just chimed midnight."

"So no one saw you between eleven, when you left the girl, and now. And you were in the vicinity of the old chapel at the time the call came in on the abandoned and damaged Jeep. It doesn't look good for the home team, Playboy."

"Damn it, Jesse, call Vic Farron."

"One step ahead of you, Ramrod. Farron's on the way."

"In my car?"

"Don't know. The newspaper switchboard said they reached him by cell phone and he's on his way."

He watched Mick the way a kitten watches a piece of string dangled in its face, looking for the moment to swat and snag it. "Give me the girl's name and phone number, Ramsey—if you even bothered to ask her for either one before you told her you loved her. Write down where I'm likely to find her."

Mick felt nauseous. The rain, turning to ice pellets burned his skin, which now felt way, way too small. "And the priest. His name is David. Father David Keenan."

The stark silence made him look up abruptly. Jesse Brucker, dark as a Hershey kiss and just as smooth, had gone a shade of what should have been pale.

"What?" Mick asked lowly. "You know him?"

Brucker, who never told lies, stuttered one out so clumsily that Mick sat up straighter.

"Keenan. The priest. Uh, no, no, don't know him, uh, he's at St. Pat's. Father Keenan, you say, okay, uh, I'll wait for Farron, uh, before you go, give Eddie a description of the bum in the diner, and the waitress, and don't get your tux cleaned."

"So I can go?"

He was distracted as he walked. "Yeah, Ramsey, for tonight, but don't leave town. Jesus." His breaths huffed white.

Brucker walked briskly to his unmarked car. Mick stared after him, wondering. Suddenly he lost his curiosity. He hung his head and mumbled, "Man. I'm in deep shit here." He raised his face, squinted at the angry storm clouds and muttered to himself, "Unless . . . unless I find her right now and get this fixed."

He ambled away, toward the hurdy-gurdy of the northern downtown lights.

# 5

Yollie Garcia answered easily to her street name. It was a Pavlovian response to the money that came soon after.

The voice in the dark motel room was a whisper when she closed the door behind her. There was only a dirty bed. She could see its blockish configuration swimming in the darkness. The whisper came from there.

"Velvet Comelove, chain the door behind you."

She did, hearing its metallic chomp.

"Velvet's right here, fella. I got an aching for you. You g'on put out the fire in my panties, ain't ya? Wow, you're a tall one! I bet you're gonna make me squeal!"

She reached out for the form in the dark. Her wig flew. Then there were fingers gripping her real hair, the scratch of it that a decade of drug use hadn't rotted away. She was on the bed instantly, face down, being crushed by a panting mammoth.

A drop of cold sweat fell onto her as she was jerked face-up on the bed beneath the weight on top of her. The icy pearl caught the flesh between

her breasts in the strapless bra that she wore. It was
all she had on after she slung away her coat at the
door. Excrutiating heat clamped into her salty flesh,
and she tried to scream from the pain of the knife
blade cutting her shoulder. A gloved hand flashed
under her chin, and grabbed her face. The grip
made her ears ring and sparks fly in her vision.

The whisper was a fake, high-pitched, girly
sound. If her head was jerked one more inch sideways—she couldn't stand to think of the pop she
would hear when her neck broke.

"Caressa. I want Caressa. Tell me where she goes
to hide."

"Yeah, baby, I know the girl. Let's go get her. She
hangs out, you know. I know where she is."

In the vice grip her jaw was wrenched so tightly
that her tongue went numb.

"Tell me."

She talked with difficulty. With her hand that was
trapped beneath her on the bed, she began fishing
for testicles to grab and crush. Something burned
her other shoulder suddenly, and she knew it was
not a burn. She had been cut there, too, sliced deeper than the first. The chemicals she took numbed
the physical pain, but she began to cry tears of fear.

The whisper came again, as the knife blade went
slowly and deeply into her right cheek, and she felt
the blood drain down her cheek and pool onto her
neck. She remembered for some reason the childhood terror of walking unaware into a giant spider-
web and imagining that big hairy things were
squirming all over her, crawling and oozing.

The whisper said, "She'll need drugs. She'll need

cash. And you sleazebags run traps for each other. Where is she?"

Velvet Comelove, born in the ghetto as Yolanda Garcia—hadn't really cried in years. Streetlife— sleeping in alleys under wet cardboard, eating food so decomposed behind diners that the rats had left it, screwing strangers, and doing heroin that she had left behind all her babies to pursue—all those goodies of streetlife had taught her that standing around crying didn't bring on the fix. And that was all that mattered. The next fix.

But she cried then and there, in that motel room, louder with every flat-handed slap and fist-doubled punch. She felt her teeth shatter and began to choke on the blood from her broken nose. And so she sobbed.

Terrified and hardly able to make words, she begged, and she lied. "I can take you to her. I know where she is. Stop, stop hitting me."

"She's going to ruin my life!"

"Naw, naw, baby. We won't let her. Velvet can save you."

She felt ice-cold lips right by her ear, and the whisper ran down her spine like a snake under the sheets beneath her. Behind the ski mask she looked at eyes that belonged to someone dead, like on the streets, outside the bars, when someone got shot dead, and the girls went through pockets and took wristwatches and rings before the cops came. The eyes behind the ski mask were like that. Down deep in them something was missing.

The ice-cold whisper said matter of factly, "She's a jig, like you, right? She's black?"

Yollie Garcia had spent her life disagreeing with everybody and anybody. Her parents. Her teachers until she dropped out. Her lousy stinking husband. The cops. Her public defender lawyers. The jail guards. The drug abuse counselors. But with the whisper and the dead eyes, she agreed.

"Yeah. Like me. She's a black girl. I'll take you to her. Please, let me go. Don't hurt me anymore."

The serpent lips on her ear slid down along her throat.

"Bad girl, Velvet. Lying to me. Bad, bad girl."

She called out to God in a fatal bleat, until a hand gripped her throat and the other hand raised the knife blade high for plunging.

# 6

The cubicle of a dusty attic was veiled in marijuana fog that burned Father David's eyes like gasoline fumes. The fumes were so strong they even seemed to sting the eyes of the wooden Christ on a cross that leaned heavily in a slant across the wall.

He had been discarded there, nothing more now than mournful refuse, such outright disrespect, David thought to himself, for the tender hearts that had crouched and cried at his eroded feet.

Now, He looked like an old clown slothed drunkenly, arms outstretched, theatrical frown. The whore was coiled behind Him. She spoke in a tone the priest had already become familiar with, bitter as charcoal.

He stayed in the doorway, not to wander into the fumes and get affected or dizzy and tell her too much too soon. He had fasted and prayed and traveled for decades, looking for her. In each town he walked the slums, handing out fliers that offered food or counseling or whatever resources he could drum up for the hookers on the corners. He looked closely at each hooker who reached for the home-made pamphlet, searching for the familiar little girl's bruised soul in there somewhere. The hookers sometimes spat on him, or crudely seduced him with their profanity, or ran from him, but he got a few seconds each time to meet their eyes—and to see if the special soul of a broken and brutalized little girl would glance back at him.

And always he prayed he would find her. Long after many midnights, alone in lost, lonely rural or big city chapels, until his knees burned and his back cramped, Father David prayed to find her. Please, God. Please, Mother Mary. Please, please Saint Therese of the Little Flower. He begged the first-string lineup of varsity Saints, and he even called on the B-team, the more obscure holies who prayed along with him as he begged God to bring her to him. He asked the angels to pray with him and the reposed souls, and his fingers nearly callused from rosaries.

But he couldn't ask the living souls to pray with him. They might ask why, why do you look for this girl, Father? The answer, well . . . There in the attic he looked down at the gnarled scars on his wrists . . . There had not been a day that he didn't weep over the answer that he could never tell the living. He had to tell her, the whore, what he had done to her.

He took a deep breath of the marijuana fumes in the attic, looking at the pastoral face of the wooden Christ.

In the Christ's peeling wooden eyes he could replay the night it happened at the Jesuit Home for Neglected Children.

It had been Halloween, a cold, blustery, dry Halloween. Even now he could feel the itchy chaff of his skeleton costume, and he could hear the kids swarming, giggling, all the princesses and pirates and Bo Peeps and witches and . . . the punch tasted like bubble gum amid the spiderwebs strung across the lunchroom flooded by orange lightbulbs and pots of dry ice fuming. The children sat for a scary story. They were itchy, too, and young Father David Keenan—heavier then, longer hair that was three shades blonder, no eyeglasses—had just been ordained and come to teach at the Home's school.

There, in the attic, breathing the whore's pot fumes, he went to one knee, crumpling his long black vestment, and he lived it again. The nun dressed as an angel with cardboard wings, the children's eyes all focused on her as the dry ice wisps curled through them, the nun's animated movements as she began the scary ghost story. And then . . . the ballerina scampered past him, dashed on her small padded slippers right past where he stood at the back of the dark lunchroom. He marveled a moment at how small and delicate she was, how silky was her black hair, how her eyes had glowed when she flung an innocent smile up at the priest as she danced past.

He watched down the hallway as she went alone up the wide wooden stairs that led to the classrooms and their bedrooms. In his skeleton suit, a hideously bony mask on his face, young Father David followed the tiny ballerina while the assembly was rapt by the ghost story. The ballerina did not see him behind her.

He had not known back then how deft and sure a pair of little girl's hands could be, until he stood in the shadow of her bedroom doorway and watched her manage alone to unlock a complicated window latch. Before he could blink, the dainty prima donna now calling herself Caressa Dicks had flashed onto the balcony and was darting into the moonlight. The skeleton followed.

He thought sure he was about to find their secret-most hiding place, where these troubled kids might smoke or bury stolen food or hide dirty pictures. The ballerina still didn't know the skeleton was stalking her. But a black boy, the steely eyed fifteen-year-old genius thug with the attitude who vexed the nuns constantly, saw the skeleton and the ballerina.

The black boy threw down his cigarette, walked at first through the cold and the wind, and then he ran among the trees to see where a skeleton and a silky haired ballerina might be going on such a haunted dark night.

She heard his deep breaths in the attic, the whore did, and she spoke, drunker now and dazed by whatever chemicals she had in her carpetbag.

"Was it him? Was he looking for me?"

"Caressa, the man driving the car tonight, did he have on cowboy boots?"

A shard of smoke shot from behind Christ's feet streaked with bloody paint that was fading and swirled around at the wound in his side. "Well, I told you, I was blindfolded. But there was cigar smoke. I smelled it. So? Who was in the chapel?"

"A man. A reporter. Mick Ramsey." He was sweating cold moisture all over his body, driving away the images of what had happened next when the skeleton and the ballerina got to the shed in the woods. His voice was shaky when he said, "He's very big, wearing a tuxedo—"

She gasped, "Yeah, yeah, I saw white cuffs and cufflinks. Did the guy, that guy down there, did he have a gold and diamond Rolex?"

He stepped inches, set down some things he had brought her. "No. I checked. He had no watch at all that I could see. But he did have a pocket phone, like you said."

He heard the gin bottle tilt heavily. And he could see her pathetic high heels, the sides of them badly scuffed. She moaned, "God. I hurt inside. Ha. Yeah, what the heck. I drink so I can cry it out. I do coke so I can stop crying. Man, life is fucked up."

He put an icy hand over his eyes. "I know you hurt. I am . . . so sorry. But Caressa, you don't hurt from what's inside you. You hurt from what's missing. What somebody took away long ago."

"And what's missing, Prince Valiant? Oh, shut up. I can't believe that asshole reporter came looking for me. Well. Shit. Fine. Maybe he'll kill me. Maybe that would be just fine—"

"I brought you some candles and some blankets. And some of the Monsignor's pain pills."

She slurred badly. "Aren't you going to tell me how sober I should be, Prince? Huh? All that shit about letting go and letting God? Shit. You ain't no Dick Tracy, pal."

He said lowly. "You mean Spencer Tracy."

"Well, what the fuck ever." Her thin ankles wiggled. She clicked her cruddy high heels together like Dorothy wanting to go home.

"Hey, Dave, the answer man. Talk to me so I won't go to sleep yet. When I go to sleep—which is not the same as passing out like a bag of doped-up rocks—I have nightmares. Well, a nightmare, anyway. The same one."

He cleared his very dry throat. "About what?"

She sounded dreamy. "I don't know. Hey, Dave, answer man, is it abuse to just not love your kid at all? I mean, when a grownup's not hitting you, but they're also just not bothering to get you some breakfast or wash your socks, is that abuse?"

"Yes. Neglect and abandonment of children is abuse, Caressa."

"Because I don't understand it, what I did to get that set of maniacs for parents."

He felt his throat close, so thick with tears he thought he'd choke. She sounded quite drunk when she said, "Because see, when I ran away from that orphanage, nobody looked for me. Jesus, Dave! Did I just piss off everybody by being born?"

"They looked, Caressa. They looked for you." He hung his head deeply and kissed his silver crucifix. "Caressa, I won't preach. But there is a Latin phrase. It means 'Here and Now.' That's all we have. Here. Now. Can you understand?"

She laughed, hyena drunk. "Well, Dave. Here sucks. And now hurts. Can you understand? Like one time last year during Christmas, this guy drove up and I got in, and we drove around, and as we're driving he points in the backseat where he's got his little son, you know, a kid maybe about seven. And you know what, Dave? This scum-sucking daddy, the lowlife, he wanted me to blow this sweet little kid while he watched. So me, Dave, I say to him, you sick fuck, and I bail, so he chases me into an alley and beats the life nearly out of me. Know what? Some Bubba-with-a-badge cop rolls up, sees it all, and I got arrested for solicitation. I swear to God! Man, ain't life a kick in the butt, Dave?" She cackled at him, like a witch.

Suddenly she yelled, "So, Dave, where's God when sickos are asking whores to blow their little kid? Huh?"

"God hates evil, Caressa. He wants us to choose to be good. It's free will. And our choices are our salvation . . . or not."

She struggled to sit and look from behind Christ's shoulder. Her slur was distinct. Her face was a wreck. "Good answer. You should go on *Jeopardy*. Alex, I'll take God's Lousy Excuses for twenty." She cackled again.

Like a pendulum he heard the mood swing. She was weepy now. He abided. His chest was so heavy. He could see only her rotted shoes and Christ leaning, looking onto the world with the tortured expression of Woody Allen. And here was the priest's plan crumbling again, things going wrong, like dominoes tumbling in a row. In his fantasies of reconciliation with her, he had always thought he would take her gently, tell her tenderly why she was so sick inside, and some pristine rejuvenated woman would blossom instantly.

But now, it was so obvious, she needed so much care taken of her. Somehow he had to keep her here with him, keep her a secret. The enormity of what he had done, of why she was a whore and a drug addict and a ruined, ravaged victim of life hit him, and he leaned on the wall to steady himself.

She whispered. "What's it like, Dave, to be loved? How's it feel?"

The tapered candles wafted and glowed. She drank deep from the gin bottle. Father David said, "It feels like a reason to be."

"Yeah. I like that. I've seen it on the street. A woman stopping to brush her little girl's hair, straighten the ribbon, smiling so. I've seen it. A reason to be."

She faded a while. The priest was gone then. She leaned herself forward onto the creaky floor and cried so hard that she thought the tears would rot the wood and she'd fall through, right onto that sorry altar below. The altar. Where people splayed themselves and God never had the guts to appear.

# 7

The attic door opened, and a slot of diffuse light ran across the shambles of a girl. The gin bottle was empty. The pills were spilled at Christ's wooden feet. The room reeked of stale marijuana and cigarette smoke.

A nest of peaceable pigeons in a circular covey that led onto the roof cooed at the priest. The whore made no sounds, only the compressed labor of breathing while so heavily sedated. Her storm of hair was gone, put aside on the floor like a freaky wool helmet. It was a wig.

Her real hair was long and smooth, the color of ripe black olives and the texture of liquid gold. He had known, of course, that her hair would flow in his hands like dark liquid gold.

He knelt beside her battered body. He wanted to touch her again, but he wouldn't. The head-hanging weeping came to him then, all through him. Tears came through his fingers as he covered his face and wept beside her. The pigeons cooed percussion.

The whore stirred, made some animal snort, but

she didn't wake. He crawled forward and pulled the blanket over her and collected the gin bottle and cigarette butts, blew out the candles. He wiped his wet face and spoke gently to her.

"Together, we'll go through it. I will make it not hurt you, I promise." He ventured to lay a hand delicately on her soft hair. "You'll see what's missing inside. Oh, little girl, you don't remember, but your heart knows, so much shame and anger, and you don't know why, do you? Diddia. Little Diddia the ballerina. As I begin to help you remember, forgive me. Please. Forgive us all, and become whole."

He opened a small, clear vial, touched his fingertip to its opening, pressed a spot of holy oil lightly onto her forehead, muttering a prayer. There was a plum-color bruise on her tender cheekbone, someone's vile act of hanging on too tightly while she degraded herself in his lap. He put an extra touch of holy oil there, just for luck.

In another room downstairs, the prayer phone rang. He felt his feet hurrying, the black robe flashing behind him like a shadow pursuing his feet.

The phone felt solid and cool in his hand. "This is Father David. You need prayer?"

The voice had a disguised quality, a high-pitch whisper. "So, Father David, St. Pat's is a whorehouse now? You can't hide her if you've got her. She'll run. And we're waiting. We are all around you. Satan is everywhere, Father. Evil is right outside your door. Waiting."

He was aware suddenly of the mean caverns of darkness that swallowed him, the knife-point sharp shadows of the eerie candles in his small, stark office. He was aware suddenly of the presence of the Devil in the room with him, not cold, but hot and seething.

He hung up the phone and said quietly into the stillness, "I rebuke you, Satan, in the name of God. Yes, I know you're here, to hurt and destroy. But so is the Holy Spirit here, and in that name I rebuke you. The girl is mine now."

The heat clicked on through a floor furnace. A sheer curtain rustled up and down. The priest took it as a ghostly, Godly nod.

# 8

Jesse Brucker paced the wet parking lot while he bitched.

"Damn, Eddie, I hate February. So damn cold. I came to Texas to not be cold, man."

Eddie grumbled, "Hell, Lieutenant, you've got 335 hot damn days around here. First it's hot like a damn furnace, then you wake up and it's cold as a witch's titty overnight. Then it's hot again. At least back there in D.C. where you lived, you got some seasons. In Texas we can't tell spring from shit or winter from shinola. 'Sides, I kinda like February. You get Valentine's Day, one of the two days a year my wife lets me have sex with her."

Brucker grinned. "Let me guess. The other day is your birthday."

Eddie spat tobacco juice. "Oh, hell no. My birthday present each year is that for that one day I don't have to see her nekkid. The other sex day is her birthday, 'cause she can always use the cash."

Brucker laughed easily, then glanced at his watch and frowned. "Farron's taking too long."

Eddie's rain slicker glowed. The rain had become icy. His cowboy hat made a shadow over his bleary eyes. "Now, you. Young. Single. I bet women fall for you faster than Eye-rackian fighter jets."

Brucker's grin returned. He flipped up his coat collar, blew smoke into his black gloves. He said with wise sarcasm, "Oh, yeah. They show up for the first dinner date in a damn wedding dress. Except the one I want. She could only be colder to me if she were embalmed."

Eddie got gloomy. "You mean that cute little doctor gal you brought to the Christmas party? Hell, Jess, I saw her holding your hand and all."

Brucker got gloomier. "If she was holding my hand, then she was just trying to keep it from going under her dress."

"You tried playing hard to get?"

"Kinda hard to play hard to get, Eddie, with a woman who doesn't even care enough about me to lie to me."

Eddie squinted. "Come again?"

Brucker's droopy expression worsened at the thought of it. "I call and ask her out. Sometimes she just says no." He shrugged. "Most girls, they'll string you, you know. Not Patrice, naw. She just says 'I don't think so. I think I'd rather stay here and watch paint dry.' Man, that woman is so fine; she drives me crazy wanting her. I'm only here because she's here anyhow. When she left D.C. last year, I practically broke my neck getting on the next plane after her."

Eddie was laughing. Brucker grumped, "I have no pride."

"Aw, Lieutenant, you got pride. You just ain't got no sense, is all. But there's no sense in love a'tall. Not a lick. She must like the chase or she wouldn't hang with you."

Brucker looked miserable. "Like she had a choice. After med school she got on at the teaching hospital here. She didn't ask me to move down here. And she doesn't exactly hang with me. It's just that sometimes she lets me in the door, like a stray. I'm a fool, that's all, and she knows it."

They were interrupted when Victor Farron's Lexus rolled somberly into the parking lot, splashing heavily. Farron lumbered himself out of the car, clutching the collar of an expensive overcoat and looking perturbed. His sidekick, a cowboy-booted drunken billionaire legendary for his philandering and his philanthropy, climbed out, too, smiling like the world was Comedy Central and he had gotten in for free. He lingered by Farron's car.

Brucker said curtly, "Evening, Mr. Farron. I'm Brucker. Detective Brucker. This is Officer Eddie Bettis."

They shook. Farron looked compressed, as if he were underwater. He was an inch or so shorter than Mick Ramsey and not as lean all over, about the same stature though Brucker took Farron to be older than Mick, maybe early fifties. His hair was also black, but he had much less of it than Mick, noticeably less. Right away Brucker noted the custom-made alligator boots, the tailor-made sportscoat. Touches of money all over the guy like blinking price tags.

"You're not wearing a tuxedo?"

**Farron's frown** intensified. "And why would you ask that?"

The iceberg cop wasn't duly intimidated. Farron tightened.

"You were at the awards banquet tonight? With Mick Ramsey? He had on a tux."

The big guy's eyes were watery. Booze, Brucker noted. "Why did you call me here, Detective? What kind of trouble are we talking about?"

"Well, I'm a homicide detective. That kind of trouble."

The pipe smoke twirled itself back and forth in the air like the tape in a recorder taking down Vic's every word.

"Mick's been murdered?"

Brucker said crisply, "Don't I wish, but no such luck. Did you borrow Mick Ramsey's car tonight?"

"No. I was going to, but I didn't. I left the banquet with Arthur—that's Arthur over there, Arthur Yates, I'm sure you know who he is—"

Brucker said snidely, "Sure. He's famous for all that money he was born into. We cops call it the Lucky Sperm Club."

Farron's frustration glowered. "Yes, well, I left the banquet with him instead of taking Mick's Jeep. We left the hotel around eleven, I guess."

"In Yates's car?"

"Yes, in his Rolls."

"And then where?"

Farron was smooth, wouldn't dare appear to be uncooperative. After all, he was the meister of information, running a newspaper the job of which was to invade and reveal. He said calmly, his blue gaze straight into Brucker's astute stare, "We went to Art's."

"Is that the big mansion on the hill over there or the big penthouse down here at the top of his conglomerate office?"

Farron ran a tongue into his cheek, handled the sarcasm. "The mansion, I suppose. Detective, who has been murdered?"

Brucker said dryly, "It was a citizen hit by a Jeep Wagoneer that meets the unusual description of Mick's. A hit and run. He said he didn't drive the Jeep, that you borrowed it. Why would you need to borrow his vehicle?"

"Because I went to the banquet with Art in his car, and at about ten I thought I would have to go to the newspaper for a big developing story. If I had to leave, I wanted car keys on me, but not Art's Rolls—one does not borrow a friend's Rolls Royce, of course. I asked Mick for his keys because he lives so close, right at the other end of downtown."

Jesse studied the big guy and said, "Yates has a place downtown, too. He could've walked."

Victor sighed. "It's not that simple for him. He has lead cars and cars that trail him and cars of bodyguards. He doesn't just saunter down the streets at night. So I wanted Mick's car. But I didn't borrow it after all. And I couldn't have hit her. I was at Art's house since eleven, like I said."

Brucker looked wisely at him. "Now, Mr. Farron, I didn't say it was a lady. And I didn't say what time."

Victor reddened. "I used 'her' as a generic term, Detective. And obviously it happened after the banquet, otherwise you wouldn't be talking to Mick or me because until then we were both surrounded by witnesses as to our whereabouts."

"What time did Ramsey leave?"

"I don't know. He sat at our table, but after dinner there was a dance, so everyone mingled. It would be hard to say what time anybody left the banquet."

Brucker eyed him. Farron tolerated it. Beyond them the billionaire was laughing animatedly into a cell phone. His jacket was slick black leather, the soft expensive kind, and he wore it with store-bought Levi's jeans. He was wiry thin, almost feminine, with thick, smooth, black hair that scaled down his back into a ponytail that snaked along his spine. His complexion in the dull light looked ruddy from booze, but smooth from facials and the ease of the good life. Horseback riding. Car racing. Sailing. The rigors of monitoring his portfolio hadn't stressed his skin or his hormones. He wore no jewelry, a monogram on his light blue flannel shirt just at the collar. In the streetlight overhead, Eddie could see it, a scrawl of initials.

Victor said unexplainedly, "So Mick's Jeep has been stolen?"

Brucker pulled out the pipe. "What makes you say that?"

"Christ, Detective, you're looking for it, obviously. You've asked me repeatedly if I drove it tonight."

"I asked twice. Never said it was missing. Just asked if you drove it."

Farron stiffened. "Goddamn it, I don't know who you think you are or what you think you're doing, but tomorrow when I have Sunday brunch with your boss at my club, maybe I'll ask him. Maybe Chief Garrett will tell me why you're being so invasive and accusatory."

Farron didn't like the way the cop had no reaction, no counter remark, no ire, just that bland cocksure stare. The uniform cop's eyes were too shadowed to gauge. Farron's skin was starting to glisten like he had just finished a game of pick-up basketball. His wide shoulders slumped some, then he got a grip on his usual sense of authority.

"Detective, I did not drive Mick's Jeep tonight, period. At eleven Art and I went to his home. We played pool, had martinis and—" He blew cold air upward. "Watched porno."

Brucker's grin was infuriating. "I see. Yates makes his own martinis?"

"No. He has staff—"

"So they will have seen you there with him, when they brought in the martinis. And what was the name of the movie?"

"I'm not sure if the butler brought drinks or not in Art's gameroom." He went crimson. "If you have to know, the movie title is *Deliveries in the Rear.*"

"Men?"

"Jesus, no. Straight stuff. I'm trying to cooperate—"

"So it's Saturday night, two rich bachelors and no girls? No dates for the banquet, no company for the martinis? What are y'all, like celibate? Safe sex and all?"

Farron snarled. "I resent that question—"

Brucker said, "Yeah, well, I resent people recklessly killing other people and then driving off. Besides, Mr. Farron, my job's like your job. Ask questions. And then ask questions about the answers you get. You know?"

Farron feigned boredom. "Of course. Of course. No, we didn't have dates. At business functions like the awards banquet, it's awfully difficult for an uninitiated date to have any fun. Detective, look, I left Mick's keys at the newspaper security desk, the all-night desk in the lobby. They were in an envelope. The guard who took them from me will remember, perhaps even still have them. His name is Archie Dane."

Yates was in the driver's seat of the Lexus where he had plopped, door open, light showing him with his head back and mouth open, sleeping, one pricey boot on the wet pavement to prop him up.

Farron wiped icy raindrops off his face. "I'm sorry to be testy, Detective. Congresswoman Elaine Archibald is resigning tomorrow. She has terminal cancer. It's a big story. I took a hundred calls tonight making sure the reporters got everything right, no screwing up." He eyed Brucker contemptuously. "Because you see, the congresswoman is a very close personal friend."

Eddie cracked in. "The Joy Boy there, he isn't driving, is he?"

Farron looked back at Art Yates. "No."

"Good. Take him home."

Brucker interrupted. "One more thing, Mr. Farron, where's the tux you wore tonight?"

"At home. Folded across a chair." He meant the wiseass tone.

"Yeah?" Brucker pursed his lips. "So you did go somewhere else besides Yates's before you came here. You went home. You changed clothes and got your own car. I reckon you just left that part out by accident."

They glared. Victor said solidly, "Yes. I must have forgotten. I told you. I'm very upset for my friend Elaine."

"Uh-huh. You take care, sir. Thanks for coming here."

"That's it?"

"Yep."

Farron lingered, suspicious, nervous. Then he was gone, his besotted buddy having moved to the passenger seat of the Lexus.

Eddie asked, "What'd you notice?"

"He didn't have many questions. Because maybe he already knew the answers."

"Very good," Eddie gave him a pat on the back. "What else?"

"Yates wasn't drunk. No optical drift when he stared at us. He was faking all the stumbling and mumbling. So we'd buy the martini story."

They walked to their cars, a night's work that looked like it would turn into many days of more labor. "Do we buy the martini story?"

Brucker said pointedly, "I don't know. We're missing something here, Eddie. A big chunk of logic, like we're trying to go fast and our skates are tied together. Go ahead and report the Wagoneer stolen. Until we find where Ramsey or Farron ditched it."

"You want a beer at my place? Maybe we'll get lucky and my wife won't have cooked dinner. Jesus that woman can make a roast beef into a cow patty faster than a heartbeat."

"Naw," Brucker said dejectedly. "I've got a stop to make. See you tomorrow."

# 9

Prissy was just concentrating on two things: getting down the frosty street in shoes with heels as high as guidewires, and wagging herself in case any of the passersby wanted some business with her.

From the edge of an alley to her left came hands that had hold of her faster than a last gasp.

She was a bulbous thing, so in the circus pink, filthy satin tights and sequined top, she didn't exactly look like a runway model. She had ample belly to be grabbed as she passed, and she had more than enough cleavage to sling forward and slam into the brick wall. She couldn't scream once a gloved hand clamped itself firmly over her mouth.

She squealed uselessly when her arm was yanked painfully backward.

"I want Caressa Dicks. A whore, like you. You know her?"

She struggled to nod in the fierce grip. Not too far away a police cruiser whooped, around the corner some stragglers laughed, next alley over, some of her peers were serving customers.

The gruesome whisper that came so close to her ear gave her chills. "She's a black girl?"

She shook her head no, and the grip loosened over her mouth, but those fingers like ropes held tightly as if any second they were going to twist her head and break her spinal cord.

She could see white breaths huffing past her face, bouncing off the bricks, and she could hear the desperation.

She mumbled her own white breaths, "She's white. Look, lady, I don't care what it is. She took your money. She gave you clap, whatever—"

The irritation was extreme. "Don't call me lady—"

The hooker said, cranky, "Well, you sure smell like a damn woman's been crawling your ass—"

Her face was slammed again, and this time both of her lips split open and spurted blood. She cried out loudly. At the sight of the giant shiny knife flashing in her face, Prissy made herself calm down.

Too late. The cut came then, a gash right along her face. The pain shot through her right cheek as if her face had been smashed by a baseball bat.

"Tell me where she is. Tell me where whores hide."

"Maybe jail. Settle down, sugar doll. You're hurting Prissy. Ain't no need for hurting me—"

"The priest. She's with the priest. When you whores and drug addicts get into trouble, do you go to the church, to St. Pat's?"

The hooker could feel adrenaline surging in the mass that trapped her into the bricks.

"I don't know no priests. I know Caressa. She

works farther down there usually, by the hospitals. We been busted together and hauled in, but I don't know no priest or nothing about no priest. Wait. We got something, some shit on paper from that church you said. Listen, let go. I'll blow you free."

When her face was yanked backward, she knew another slam into the wall was coming. She screamed, but it was muffled. Now she felt her nose shatter and begin to drain hot blood, and the pain in her head was a continuing vice. Her legs felt weak.

"Tell me!" And then, "Shit! You don't know! You don't know a thing about it, you lying whore!"

She was sobbing, struggling to stay standing. Her face was smashed, and she could smell and taste her own blood gushing down the cold bricks.

"Lady or mister or whatever the hell, please! Let me go! There ain't no priests 'round here and I don't know where Caressa got off to, maybe dead in the gutter, I don't know. Stop hurting me!"

In a backward jolt that sounded like a snapping tree limb, her arm broke. She howled, but only for a moment. The howling stopped when the gloved hand yanked her head backward and cut her throat.

# 10

In the Lexus, in the soft glare of all the dashboard's fancy low lights, Arthur Yates sat up, sober and lucid.

Their voices were hushed.

Arthur the billionaire had his hole-in-one smile. "So our hero is in trouble, seems like, huh?"

Victor swigged deeply from a crystal champagne flute balanced between his legs. "Imagine our luck."

Arthur swigged straight from the champagne bottle. "Does this solve our problem?"

Victor frowned. "I can't suspend him until he's arrested and charged."

"So he can still chase the story?"

Victor sighed immensely. "Hell yes. And he will chase it, until he gets the whole shooting match."

Art grimaced, his expression twisted in disgust. "Then you call this fucker Ramsey in and you ask who's his leak at Securities and Exchange—and then I'll handle that pinhead government motherfucker like a damn chained yard dog—"

Victor butted in sourly. "Art, I told you. Mick Ramsey has a wall of journalism writing awards, not to mention a Pulitzer for our newspaper." He wiped at the sweat on his top lip. "I cannot call him in and demand to know his anonymous source at the SEC. It would be unorthodox, unusual. Ramsey's very, very smart. My sudden interest in whether his source is reliable would alert him to something, and that wouldn't be good."

Yates slammed himself backward into the seat, furious. And Victor knew it wasn't good for a billionaire to be furious. He tooled the Lexus easily, but his insides jangled alarms.

Arthur said, "I'm not getting indicted because your loose cannon reporter wants another fucking award. You understand me, Vic? It's happening on your watch. Do whatever you have to do. Take him off the national news desk. Tell him that he needs some time off until this bullshit about the bag lady is handled." He had snake eyes in the green cast from the dashboard lights. At the center they were poison. "You run the newspaper. I run you. You keep me and my business dealings out of the paper; I keep your ass in your chair collecting your salary. Do you know what will happen to me if Ramsey gets the story? And fifteen minutes after it appears in your paper I'll go find me a smashed Jeep Wagoneer that will have your fingerprints all over it—"

"Art. Calm down. Jesus."

Arthur pointed. "No, Jesus can't help. But I got me a gah-zillion dollars that has many times in the past bought you and me out of shit that puts other ignorant-ass CEOs in the pasture or in the prison. The hookers. They never talk about us, do they?

The sexual harrassment suits, they just dry up and blow away in green dollar dust, don't they?"

He went cool again, gulped champagne. "And I did it all because I love you, Vic, my friend. And because I sure as hell don't want somebody running that paper who I can't control. So you take Ramsey off the story. Hell. High water. I don't give a shit. Rein the boy in. Tomorrow."

The billionaire's face was a ghoulish green. The color of his blood, Victor thought sullenly.

Victor said gloomily, "I can't. It'll set off alarm bells. He'll know that I know something."

Art smiled, and his tiny teeth looked mossy and pointed. "You know, the last person who said I can't to me would be forty-five-years-old today. If he were alive."

They drove in silence until Art said with finality, "Set up some useless bag-o'-tits reporter to fuck him at work and then sue him. Or put some goddamn coke in his desk."

"Maybe the cop will arrest him tomorrow. It'll be over. The story dies."

Art snapped. "The cop's no good to us. I had him checked after we got called tonight—while you were out I don't know where, and I don't fucking want to know where. Back in D.C. Brucker got a bunch of citations for bravery on the job."

Victor smiled flatly. "Are you saying you found somebody you can't buy, Artie?"

"Vic, my boy, the reason I'm the richest swingin' dick in Texas is because I know instinctively when something ain't worth the price I'd have to pay. The darkie cop would air me out if he even imagined I

was offering him money to make a tight case on
Ramsey. Just let me do a few things to make damn
sure the black John Wayne thinks he's doing right
by busting Mick. And you," an ominous grin tickled
Art's wet lips, "you make sure me and the guv'ner
and his brother, the former got'dam U.S. president,
don't wind up chipping golf balls at the federal
pen."

Vic heard Art pop the cork on another champagne bottle. After a long guzzle Arthur said, "And
Vic, do me a personal favor. Stay away from trouble
until I have this handled."

Victor said, "Ramsey's already got the tip of the
iceberg on you all."

Art laughed crudely. "Ramsey is toast."

# 11

It was the kind of trashy joint where the whiskey was watered down and the women were coked up. By now, two in the morning, the place resembled a psychiatric unit right before medication time.

Mick moved through the shoulders of drunks yelling over the music at Loser's Paradise—a name obviously chosen by the owners after a brew of peyote tea.

The blockheaded bartender whistled for Mick's attention, and the two nasty and lovely twins he had slopped home one recent night for a human sandwich made goo-goo eyes at him. He smiled, thinking they'd be dangerous if they could focus past the liquor and the pills.

She saw him, his newest piece, the one his respectable friends unkindly referred to behind her back as "Amazon."

And when she saw him, she squealed, not a small sound from a six-foot-two woman whose butt reminded Mick of a Palomino he had as a kid. He tried to stand still and not blush when she made the sound of a freight train stopping abruptly. She was on him suddenly, legs and all, no small feat for her height. The bluejeans were painfully tight, which was bad to look at, but she was slobbering drunk, which was good for later when he wanted to fuck and run.

As she slathered her stilts around him, moaning, he remembered the immortal sophistry of his brother upon first meeting Amazon: For a dime's worth of bullshit, Mick, that girl would give any guy a dollar's worth of fucking.

Amazon finally came up for air, her hair all wrong and her breath stinking of bourbon. He winced. From her belly Pegasus was staring at him, only instead of wings this silly Pegasus had marijuana leaves flapping.

She was wearing a crop top that revealed a road map of tattoos on her belly. Flaming dragons, two-headed gargoyles, roses (he never understood the delicate sentiments of roses among the monsters and the mutants). The tattoos continued down her thighs and up her chest onto her breasts, alarming dark-blue and bright red scenes of medieval characters. At first he had found it exotic, maybe erotic, when she was naked, but in the end it only became something he considered self-mutilation by a girl with fatally wounded self-esteem and utterly no dignity.

She squealed, "Oh! Baby!" It came out in ten syllables, and she wiggled her tits at him, the only body part she had that wasn't big.

She suddenly got a look like her panties had

caught fire. Her lips went poochy. "I'm so glad you came ... you want to ... come ... some more, baby, honey?"

He unwound his arm that she was clamped to and took a beer from the blockheaded bartender.

Amazon gushed again, and the stink of stale cigarettes and soured plaque washed at him. "Mickey, baby, huh? You want that?"

"No, Loretta, I need to talk to you. Outside. I have to fix a situation. Stop pawing me, please, just for a minute—"

It was as if the dentist hit her nerve.

She screamed, "Oh, my *gahhd*, I love this song! I love to *fuck* to this song. Let's go fuck, you 'n' me, and I'll—" She launched into something he thought at first was a liquor-overdose seizure, but as he watched he saw that she meant to do it. She bent and in a wide circle she flung her dried-out, corroding blond hair in an arc, screaming, "And while you *fuck me*, I'll bang my head on the headboard—"

"Loretta," he tried hard not to laugh, "it's time to go—"

She started to dance. "Oh, let me bang my head while you fuck me, pleeeeze!"

The crowd paid no mind. This was her cabal; nobody found her weird at all. Mick was thinking what a mistake this had been, what with this drunk biker's wet dream of a tall moll swirling and lurching at him.

"Loretta, okay, later, we'll fuck and you can bang your head. Come outside with me for now, please."

She did a sloppy, vertiginous swirl around him, using her body to beg, hunching his knee. He could feel himself sinking in the quicksand of wishing he could have his dime back and the dollar's worth of fucking could be over without incidence or antibiotics.

"Daddy," she warbled, tossing her hair and breathing out her bad breath, "I'm so horny. Drinking makes me so horny, and I've been drinking all day, you know? Hoowee! It was a bad night, but it's better now. Bad night, Mickey. Yucky-fucky night. But you're here now—"

He said dryly, "I drove by earlier and your car wasn't here. Did you drink all day here and then go out driving? Jesus, Loretta."

She did a disgusting, skewed hula number around him, squealing again like air out a balloon slowly, "Oh, I drove downtown and looked for you when you were late here. I hate it so when I can't find my Mickey."

She spun. Mick stood in one spot. His tuxedo was wilted, but he still reeked of James Bond amid the head bangers.

He said stiffly, "You're on drugs."

She pouted at him, going for his top button. He grabbed her hand. "Come on, honey. I needed it. I told you, it was a yucky-fucky night." She pleaded, unsteady on her stilts, "Do me now, in the car, then buy me please just one more drink-ee-poo."

"Goddamn it, Loretta, what the fuck are you on?"

She whined, changing her voice from the fake goddess to the little girl in the corner. "Oh, honey—"

"Please don't call me honey."

"All right, sugar. It's just a little cocaine—"

He deflated. She went back to the fake goddess voice, like a porno star in heat. "If you tell me not to, sugar, I won't use it anymore. Come on. I'll blow you in the car."

He stared. She stumbled to the left, and Mick caught her arm, and she giggled, tossing her hair in a circle again. He set down the beer, took her arm, and led her through the crowd, which was to his mind no more than a chemical junk-yard.

Outside, she whipped out a flask and sucked. He waited, then said, "You were with me tonight from ten until almost midnight, at the Dublin Rose, but you say it could've been later. You say it could've been after midnight when I left you at the Dublin."

She blinked, bleary and gory. "Well, maybe it was later. Baby, oooh, is that blood on your tuxedo sleeve? Well, that must hurt, you must need a drink. Let me blow you and we'll go get you a drink—"

"It's okay, Loretta. I got mad and hit a brick wall with my fist. That's all. You remember the times, because a police detective is going to come see you, and it's very important. Tell the cops it could've been almost midnight. Okay?"

Couples stumbled out. The bar was closed. Amazon eyed the couples hungrily, desperate for a relationship—any kind, with anybody taller than she. Mick poked her.

"Sure, sugar, maybe it was midnight. You going to

sleep with me tonight? It's time, honey—oops—I mean baby, it's time. Sleep over with me, please, just once." She dragged a finger along his cut knuckles. "I'll give you head all night, baby. And you know, all my boyfriends told me I give the best blow jobs in the United States."

He stifled a grin and said, "Your buttons must be popping over being able to say that."

"Why don't you love me, Mickey? Why won't you stay with me, hang with me, be around?"

He grinned so cruelly she had to turn her face. "No, Loretta, I believe the question is why I'm with you ever, at all, when we both know I could have a hundred other babes with just one phone call."

"Mickey, you said I was pretty, when we met, you said it."

"No, Loretta, you were whining about being ugly, and I simply said, no, you're not ugly, you're sexy. So keep it in context. Porn films are sexy. Women's used panties are sexy to some buyers on the Internet. Hell, hairy buttholes are sexy if you're into that."

She pouted. "So. Okay. Why me, and not the other hundred?"

He took her arms from around his neck. "Because you're just so damned . . . grateful. And I like gratitude, especially in a woman I'm fucking."

She frowned, just a touch, but remembered that he wouldn't stick around for any of her demands. He had said so; she had agreed to never question him.

He continued to glare at her and said, "Look, I

gave them some places to find you. Home or here. If it's here, don't be drunk and run your mouth. Just answer the questions like I told you."

She listed. One eye stuck shut. "Okay, baby doll." She came at him again, bobbing sideways in a struggle to keep her mast of a frame straight ahead. "You know, sugar, I waited for you here tonight before I went driving downtown. I just get so nervous when I don't know where you are!"

He froze, took a long, slow breath but wasn't sure any oxygen got into his chest. "You know the deal, Loretta."

She played with her hair, trying to look coy. "Her. You can fuck me, but I'm not to interfere with your love affair with *her.*"

"You took the terms."

She had a goony smile, so needy and eager to please. But it didn't soften him; it made him meaner. She swelled with a big gasp. "Fine, then, sweetheart. I told you, baby, I will do whatever it takes, anything, to keep you."

"I have to go. You tell the cops the right story." He was almost to the waiting cab when he turned to her. She was panting like a puppy under the table salivating, tongue out, eyes wide. He sighed. "Okay, Loretta, I'll let you blow me in your car. But don't take long. That cab's meter is running."

While she fumbled drunkenly trying to get the key into the car's lock, she blithered. "I've told all my friends, Mickey, that pretty soon you're leaving her for good and coming to be in my life."

They were in the car. He said, "Fine. Whatever.

Just don't cause me any trouble. You want me, you can have me, but on my terms."

She whispered—and would have blown a point three on the Breathalyzer—"Okay, Mickey, honey. Now, let me unzip your pants and be nasty for you. Let me make believe this is love."

# 12

The whore was having her nightmare, the same one as always.

When the agonizing pictures were happening in her dream she couldn't see them or stop them or wake from them. She only felt the terror when she began to wake, when her brain's safety valve shut down the memory of the nightmare because to see it as it happened would leave her insane or dead of heart failure.

She chronically woke from the dream in a choking fit of horror, always finding herself running, screaming "No! No! No!," breathless and ice cold to the touch. She couldn't remember, but she knew what she feared when she came to shaking with dread and drenched in tears.

In the nightmare, she faced eternity somehow, like a girl leaning over the Grand Canyon and knowing she was about to be pushed. In the nightmare the whore saw Forever, in what form she couldn't say, but not monsters with fangs or creepers with guns, not rape or lead-footed chases. Nothing that she could wake from and realize it wasn't real and she was safe on Earth, still human.

No. This nightmare showed her something so real, so awful that her sleeping body jumped and ran before she fully came to. The nightmare showed her Death, Eternity. The nothingness of forever. Her aloneness in the universe. And so while she slept she ran from it, and when she woke her brain mercifully shaded the whole vision. She remembered only a gagging, crippling terror, never its form, never its depth.

She was standing now in the attic, stumbling and running. She was panting, saying the only words she could ever say afterward. "No, please, bring me back!" Over and over.

She slid into a fetal position behind the wooden Christ, and she felt the insanity reach at her, some claw that wanted to take her to that airless eternity all alone. She ran again, panicked and blind, sensing again, like always, that this time she might not come back from the nightmare and she would stay this way—catatonic, tortured, wailing. From the fetal position she sat upright quickly, soaking wet but totally awake now. She was aware that she had gone insane with fear, and by some miracle she had come back one more time from it. She reached for the Christ's eroding hands, chipped by the touches of broken hearts, and she stared, gasping, into his vapid, milky glare.

She was dry from the terror, she couldn't sob as she slid down the wall at her back. "Please. No. Bring me back. Take me away from here." She whimpered. Christ did not blink.

There was no air. There was never air when she woke in this nightmare. There was only hyperawareness that after life there was nothing. A forever of nothingness or, worse yet, a Hell, a Hell for people like her, people who God had put here to be damaged and ignored and then used by Satan to wreck the world.

She ran again, her bare feet collecting attic dust. She hit a wall, spun from it. She always went wild this way, a foaming Mustang on the prairie who had just felt its first saddle. She didn't scream.

Someone had said, Don't scream . . .

Oh my god oh my god . . . don't scream, don't fight, close your eyes and go into nothingness . . .

She took some steps, her filthy whore clothes looking so pitiful, her skin shiny and smelly with sweat and booze. She was so thin, not like a model, but like a waif who had been chained and starved. Black eye circles. Colorless. Unwashed.

It passed. She felt her breathing slow. The room came into focus. The pigeons cooed. The numbness tingled away slowly from her hands, and she went to her knees. Finally she could cry.

The wooden Christ watched dully—unfazed, motionless. She didn't mean to fall against him, but she did. Her face found his shoulder. Her wisp of a bony arm and fingers found his face, and she clutched him.

She sobbed, and she didn't care if there was a killer below who heard her, or if the nuns coming for 6 A.M. Mass heard her and found her. She didn't care. She sobbed and clutched. So completely broken and not aware of the words to describe it. The misery was total, as if she were a pile of ashes or a pane of shattered glass, a bird's wing ripped off.

She could only choke out, "Oh ... god—" Not to Him, because she didn't know Him or like what she knew of Him, but to the wooden Christ because his blood streaked face was in her hands. "Please. Stop. Help me."

She lay still a while. The pigeons sensed a sunrise not far away, and they made noise while they planned going out for food to bring to their babies. And then the whore remembered a song, maybe just a notion; she didn't know. But the song was about how God took care of things. "Consider the lilies how stately they grow, they toil not, they spin not, no seeds do they sow." The theory was, of course, that God gave them water and sun and pollen or whatever it was they needed, and that the lilies just sat around being flowers, trusting Him.

She sang all of that little song that she could recall, broken bits. She had to hum some. She stood, desperate for water, weak from hunger. The Rice Krispies were so far gone by now.

Downstairs there was only a dim light over the old sink. She walked through the light to the door of the priest's silent bedroom, and slid open his door. In the clean scent of his sheets and curtains, she could smell herself, putrid and repulsive. He was cozy in flannel pajamas, every mother's good boy lying there. His hair was askew. His glasses were on his forehead and a Bible was open on his chest and a notepad was set open on the sheet. Enough moonlight ruffled through the curtains for the whore to see what the priest had written in longhand. Notes for his homily.

"Matthew 6:25—'I warn you, then: Do not worry about your livelihood, what you are to eat or drink or use for clothing.' "

Beneath that he had noted, "Also, 2 Cor.—'My grace is enough for you.' Isn't God asking us to be simple in our faith? He was talking to Jewish peasants, but to us thousands of years later, too. How much more complicated are our choices today than theirs? Cybersex. Drugs. Note—things have changed, God has not, etc. Seek Him, not material things. Spiritual riches have much more value . . ."

The whore put her lips close to the priest's face and felt nothing. She examined his nose, his skin, his soapy scent, his short, layered hair. Nothing. She watched his hands, the long spidery fingers linked as if they could come alive and slither toward her. She cocked her head. She had held hands like his once, somewhere, pleasantly, though she didn't have memories at all, no pictures, but sometimes things brought feelings. His hands had a texture she had felt before. Something about them made her back away. Something about his hands reminded her of the nightmare.

In the kitchen she found another gin bottle, took it to the attic. In the dark she took two pain pills. She offered one to the Christ, but he didn't respond, so she popped it herself and swallowed.

As the moon faded and the sun was still hidden, the streetlights blinked out on a gray, cold predawn. In the alley, someone was watching. Through the wrought-iron fence around the small chapel and rectory, light bathed the shadows when the priest's light came on. Almost time for Sunday 6 A.M. Mass, no doubt.

The whore slept. The priest peed, poured coffee, went for the newspaper on the back porch.

He stopped cold when he saw the light dusting of snow on the porch had been disturbed by footprints. Bums sometimes tried to break in the gardener's toolshed to sleep for the night. Downtown there weren't stray dogs, and anyway, he thought with a shiver, though these were animal prints, they were not canine. They were the prints of a human predator.

He closed the back door and peered through the glass pane at the top. Someone had been watching.

Across the street, someone was still watching, someone who had peered through the glass back door for a while and seen nothing, no one. But this is where the whore disappeared in the chase, where the chapel door had been open and banging in the storm.

The leather hip pouch held the sharp, jagged hunting knife. She hadn't called the cops. She probably wasn't going to call the cops. But the priest—if he had her—would work on her conscience. Her civic duty.

Tie up the whore, gut her with the knife and then fix the priest so it looked like he killed himself after all. It was at least a good plan, a much better idea than rotting in prison for a stupid bag lady's carelessness.

# 13

Under his bedcovers Mick shivered. He was not cold on the outside, but his insides were a jumble of downed power lines sizzling in icy puddles.

Things—and he said it aloud as he got up, pulled on jeans and a sweatshirt, and lit the stub of his cigar—things had suddenly gone very Twilight Zone. Rod Serling intoned: Picture a man, a writer, who holds all the marbles. At the pinnacle of his successful career. A beautiful woman devoutly in love with him. A harem of sex kittens pawing constantly for his prowess. Money. Fame. The Life. And then, his marbles begin to go. He is losing them, one colorful bulb at a time as they skitter away. So he follows the marbles as he loses them. And he finds himself entrenched, embedded—entombed—in . . . The Twilight Zone.

It was almost 7 A.M. Mick had not slept. He got up, trudged down the skylighted staircase and went into the living room of his ultra-mod downtown condo, taking up the wall phone in his dark kitchen. His cigar made a small orange sphere, like

a camera's red light recording as he played the
character losing his marbles.

Victor Farron did not answer when Mick dialed.
He had tried twice more during the night to call
Victor. He tried at 3 A.M. from his car phone, at
6 A.M. from a pay phone outside the newspaper
where Mick had gone to shower in the locker room.
And he tried again, now, 7 A.M. No Victor.

The drapes in the den showed a flimsy skimming of a sunrise coming. Snow was predicted.
With the phone cord snaking after him, Mick
walked to the wide windows and parted the
drapes. His cowboy boots stood on the concrete
patio under the awning where he had left them because the soles were muddy and wet. They looked
like a desperado had been blown right out of them.
Or maybe a phantom was watching him, an outlaw
phantasm that would come toward him in a blink
when the boots moved on their own. He closed
the drapes again.

He torched the gas jet in the fireplace to a blue
luster, tossed in small logs from the hearthside basket. He did it for warmth as much as to stall his
next move—a bad move, deeper into the depth of
reaching for another scattered marble. He dialed.
She answered. Her Dracula accent sent a shock of
sexual arousal through him. The fire made new
sweat on his face sparkle.

"Jackie, baby, don't hang up."

She could have been the queen of Transylvania.
"No, Darling."

He sighed relief. "Talk to me, Jackie."

"We have talked already. We have done it, and

broken it, fixed it, lost it. And always we talked. Now, silence is best."

He hung his head in new regret. "Please. Let me come and sleep with you. Just let me lie next to you. I want to sleep. And these months, you know, I haven't really slept well. It's more like comatose fits. Without you. I can't sleep without you."

"And the girls? The secretaries and flight attendants, the bottle washers and day-care attendants—you said you wanted to try with all of them. You needed more sex than just me. You yearned for women without my emotional rigors of creative genius, women who are simple and linear, you said, someone less than you so you could feel . . . superior."

He said, "You demean what they do."

She said, "No. I did what they do to get where I am, Mickey, to pay the bills. You demean what they want, and what they have the right to expect from a man, no matter what they do in life. They want love, devotion. And you give them only your wicked narcissism. Go to the new girl. Let her know you, so she can leave you, too, and be proud of herself for it."

He felt his gag reflex yank in his throat. "Oh god. Please. Don't. She's so repulsive." He meant it. His fervor made his voice taut. "So for a while I needed a . . . nobody, Jackie." He paced. He heard her move, felt the warm blankets rush across her bronze skin, and his mouth watered. He pleaded again. "I have nasty little drunken whore groupies fall off barstools and call it love that they feel for me, and it's okay because with you I feel so . . . unaccomplished. I have to fuck nobodies, Jackie, so I can feel like a man with you."

He sat. "I wanted a nobody. So for a while I could shine. It was an experiment, a mistake. She's pathetic. She pops diet pills. She begs for sex. Please. Let me sleep next to you for a few hours."

War drums pounded his aching head. She said mildly, "No."

"Why?"

His crackling fireplace made her silence tortuous. She answered slowly. "You are ill, Mick. You need a doctor—a psychiatrist. I loved you. We had this thing, this magic, all that love and passion for so long. And after you proposed marriage—"

He felt rage surge. "You said no to me."

"And so, now you're in the bed you made with this woman. Sleep there. With her."

"You listen to me," he lied so easily, "I haven't seen that nasty slut in weeks." The lie came out as easily as a bubble of soft gum. "She's disgusting. She's an alcoholic, and she talks filthy and begs me to be with her like a . . . like Lassie. I feel . . ." The truth, however, was harder to get out. "I feel sorry for her, is all. She hates herself. She hates her life. I just pity her. So for a while I fucked her and made her think she wasn't grotesque."

"You used her. Mick, maybe you've had a stroke. The change in you, in your ways, maybe it came because there's a brain tumor. Perhaps it is medical. See a doctor."

He growled angrily. "I want my life back. I want you back. So don't marry me. I'll get over it. I just won't ask anymore."

"My refusal emasculated you, you said."

"I'll get over it. I am over it. I wandered out there and saw what I wanted to see. Cokeheads who want to marry me because I'm an inch taller. That's what's out there. Come back, Jackie. Move back in with me. We were good. We were in love."

"I do love you, Mick."

Ah. He had cracked her, like always, like the old days. Her forgiveness was a cool pool. The image of the bleary-eyed head banger gargantuan chick was fading.

"And I love you, Jackie. Always. Only you. I'll never see her again. Come home. Let me come and get you."

It was as if the goblet was tilted, and the poisoned sweet wine of his deception was flowing so gently toward her cinnamon lips, almost wet and deadly on her tongue.

And then the call-waiting on the telephone clicked. He felt his belly lurch, felt his eyes cinch, heard himself thinking virulently, "No, not now, not now you stupid bitch . . ."

He said flatly, "Wait, baby. I've been calling Vic Farron. This might be him."

The head banger's nasty baritone hit him like cold ashes in his eyes. "Hey, lover boy, I'm all wet for you. Come fuck me."

He said nothing, clicked back to Jackie. The line buzzed in his ear. She was gone. He could feel his heart beating, the jazz of his own lies blistering inside his head.

He clicked back to Loretta. "I told you to quit calling me. I told you I could fuck you, but you can't be with me or around me. We can't date. You can't come over. We can only fuck. That's the deal."

"So I should fuck you by sending smoke signals? I can't call?"

"I'll call." He sounded furious, then he softened. "So you still want the deal?"

She had no shame. No pride. No options. "I told you. I want the deal."

"Okay. Give me an hour. I'll come do you. I have to shower and make a call. You wait." He hated this bizarre broad, but the need for sex was bigger than the disgust. "And please, bathe first."

He dialed Victor again. No answer. To the endless ringing he said, "You've been out all night, Farron. Where the fuck are you? Where's my car?" He looked down at the dangling bulge in his jeans and asked it, "What? Time for a pity fuck? Okay. You're the boss."

## 14

The priest set before her a plate of fluffy scrambled eggs, orange slices, and an English muffin. The whore thought it looked fake, like artwork.

He was in dark gray wool slacks, black shoes, and a black long-sleeve shirt with a swatch of white collar showing at his throat. She sniffed. He smelled good, like fresh laundry. She was crumpled in a bathrobe, his bathrobe, wearing black socks, his black socks, and her hair fell terribly from the two pins she had set carelessly into it.

Her mouth tasted and smelled like she had sucked a full ashtray. He moved lightly, rinsing things in the sink. The sky outside the grimy windows was not bright, but she knew it was daytime, late, midmorning. She coughed, deep and long, and fought for a breath. He set down coffee for her, stirred cream into it, barely touched her filthy hair.

She drawled, "Hey, where you going?"

His soft blue eyes studied her placidly as he stood over her, daddy of the world. "It's almost noon. I do a noon Mass."

She pushed away the food, fished a cig out of her bag, lit it, and blew toxic shivers of smoke at him.

He said, "You'll have to remove those purple fingernails."

She said, "Why? Maybe I'll say my name is Sister Mystic. Oh, relax. I'll take them off. Say, put some of that gin in this apple juice." He did. She watched, feeling her stomach wretch and her head bang on one side. She griped, "You just did Mass. I heard you bellowing down there when I sort of woke up earlier."

He spoke, footfalls on snow, "That was at six this morning. Please, take one bite of eggs. I have a towel here for you, shampoo and soap. A brush, deodorant, and a tooth brush."

He sat. She thought, taking a deep breath, how good he smelled, a mountain morning, and how composed he seemed, a lanky cherub with a heavenly secret. His hands. She glimpsed them, the long petals of fingers, and she gagged down a bite of eggs that turned out to be pretty darned buttery and good. She said with her mouth full, "What the hell do you do all day anyhow?"

He swept at his neatly cut boyish blond-gray hair. "After Mass this morning I made hospital rounds to bless the sick. I went to a meeting to help a group trying to open a free day care for the children of AIDS patients who can still work at their jobs. I visited and read to a group at the nursing home down the way. And for a couple of hours I helped the doctors going through the ghettos giving free flu shots to the homeless and the poor—"

She snarled, "Stop already. You're a regular archangel in cheap shoes, huh?" She munched toast, put her foot onto his lap and toyed.

He smiled dimly and then removed her foot from his crotch. "And then while you slept I did a morning funeral for a man I loved very much, a good man. After that, I counseled two engaged couples on nuptial commitment." He looked into his coffee steam and said nicely, "Then I went to the school and did the children's Mass."

"Yeah. Fuck 'em up early." She stared at him hard. "What'd you tell the little beggars?"

He wanted to reach and push her scraggles of hair back from her bruised cheek. Her lips were cracked. She looked like a decomposed body. He answered her, carefully, trying to sound clinical rather than pastoral.

"They're building a new Catholic school near here, and many of the children will attend it next year. So I spoke to them about building things, about how Christ came to show us how to build a kingdom. Not a kingdom of spiffy new schools or malls, of course, but a kingdom inside ourselves, a kingdom of charity and tolerance and forgiveness."

She pooh-poohed him with a coarse smile. He felt himself laugh at her.

"Hey, Dave, how long since you been laid?"

"Drink your juice, Caressa. And take your foot off my chest, please."

She did. The eggs, before she knew it, were in her belly, warming it—like he warmed her eyes. She asked again, "Tell me. Why don't you get laid?"

He rose, rinsed her dishes, spoke solemnly, "The clothes are in the bedroom off the upstairs bath. Put on the habit, the hose, and the appropriate shoes. After I say Mass I'm going to visit the jail for Bible study and then I play basketball with the kids at the Youth Correctional Center. I'll be back at four. I do another Mass at 5 P.M. Afterward, for three hours, I pray for the requests written on the prayer cards left in the chapel, and I answer the prayer phone, too. I want you to eat with me at eight o'clock. Here. That's the only time I'll insist you sit with me, for dinner. The rest of the time you can hide and do," he glanced at her bag, "whatever you do up there."

The slug of gin in the juice hit her. She slowed, saw him through a haze. She was ruthless. "I know why you don't have sex. You can't anymore. It's . . . wasted, your dick is. Use it or lose it, and you lost it. Like a flat tire."

He leaned on the sink, abiding her filth with patience that suddenly and strangely made her turn away from him. He said, "I had an anonymous threatening call. If you go out, they are waiting to kill you."

Her world was too choppy and larcenous for his concern to move her. She replied to him, "You know, Dave, I'd like to bust out crying and all, come quivering over there to you, but, let me go slow for you. Every thirty minutes of every day I get into a car with a pervert whose jollies could include strangling me. You worry about it. I'll focus on surviving—one minute at a time."

He was expressionless, knowing there was no reaching her. "Go take a shower. It's time for me to hear noon confessions."

She was in his face, pissed off, hating him. "They tell you their sins, huh? You get off on that? Hearing who fucked who and who stole money to go gamble and who's sniffing his sister's panties, all that sick stuff people do. Does that make it hard? Pretty girls can't, but sick secrets can, huh?"

He put his cool hand against her warm face, and he whispered at her. He quoted, "For thy name's sake, Lord, pardon my iniquity, for it is great."

He leaned back and said almost mischievously, "These things I do every day, girl, look how free I am to go and do them without worrying about what you call getting . . . laid. I am unencumbered to be alive for others."

She pulled away angrily. "Hey, you spooky old demon, don't touch me again, you hear me, unless you got your money clip out."

He left. Caressa looked after him, troubled and shivering and hung over.

She went upstairs and showered, lavished in hot water that she had never known without a man paying for it and putting his penis in every orifice of hers while she faked screaming pleasure. She toweled herself, found her cigarettes, and flared one in the bedroom while she slung the habit up and gave it a grim moan.

In the mirror she held it up to herself, cigarette dangling, and she said indelicately to her screwy image in the reflection, "Oh, well, here goes, Sister Sleazebag. I guess it ain't bullshit if somebody believes it."

He saw her slink into the back of the chapel behind the rows of faces rapt to his words at the altar.

No one turned to see the little nun slide into a pew. She was frowning at him so profusely that he lost a word and had to hold in a grin.

His voice resonated. A stray beam of sun crashed through the stained glass, and the organ barely made a wrinkle in the silence.

"This life, my good people, is not what counts. This chance, this life, is only a gift from God. Where we go next is determined by how we treat the gift He has given us here, the gift of being alive. It doesn't matter what we own. What we can buy or who we can defeat. God is not watching what we drive or what we wear. He is watching who we are. He watches what we give to others, how we use our blessings to bless others, whether we forgive. That's the test, my good people, that's the measure for the real life, the eternal life. Just remember out there today that you have been given another day to try. To try to love. To try to be kind. Use this day wisely. Use it joyously, and be mindful that often our greatest sins are the times when we do nothing to help. Be mindful of our sins of omission. Be strong. Be fair. Be of God's children."

The priest, quick as a . . . well, a wink, gave her a playful wink that nobody noticed. She frowned at him.

The habit itched her face. Life sucked.

An old veiled woman in front turned and said, "Good afternoon, Sister. How wonderful to have you among us."

The whore sighed. The church bells rang.

# 15

Through the glass window in his office door, Brucker saw Detective Angela Bianchi give the glass a fast rap. He motioned, she entered, and Brucker grinned.

Angie just made him grin, is all, with her Moe haircut and her Janet Reno glasses and her figure like a bull in a bad plaid blazer. The fashion king—Brucker—knew immediately it was out of season, cotton, right here in winter, and her shoes were clunks of steel-toe black concrete. But he grinned outrightly, and she frowned at him as she heaved herself into a chair.

"Don't ask me," she groused. "I don't know what happened to my hair. I did what I always do. Wash it. Comb it. Stick some goo on it." She wiggled her fingers all around her head. "Then today it had some . . . attack of something and it looks like I'm wearing a black potted plant on my head. Shut up. Quit laughing. You think I look bad from where you're sitting, you should try living in this beef-steak blimp that I am."

There was a coffeepot warming on his desk plate.

She puffed forward and poured into the Styrofoam cup he tossed her.

He teased. "You need a man, Bianchi. A good Latino stud."

She rolled her eyes. "I got a man. His name's Jack Daniels. He's smooth and quiet and he lies to me. Perfect deal."

He laughed. She said, "All I want in the world is to be able to wear a straight skirt. See. Like that gal."

She pointed out the glass pane to a slender redhead in a straight black skirt as tight as a sausage skin. "So," Brucker said, "buy one, wear it, that's all."

She smirked at him. "I tried. I looked like twenty pounds of potatoes in a ten-pound sack. Naw. As long as chicken fried steak is hotter and cheaper than a sex life, I'm gonna just eat, you see. Say, what's up? Why'd you call me in here? You have a big fat widowed brother-in-law whose dream is to meet an obese Chicano who has an anger issue and wears a loaded nine millimeter?"

She peeled off her sad plaid blazer, and Brucker thought she looked like a pug dog in dime-store pink lipstick. The lumps bubbling up in her Moe hairdo were totally weird. He said, "I need you on a case."

Her orbs of grossly magnified eyes in the thick lenses grew at him. "Can't. I'm working two dead hookers from last night. We've got a pattern. Two more and we make a task force. I'm going to work the streets tonight, asking questions."

Brucker said smartly, "You can stay on that. But I

need you because you didn't know my sister and you don't know Mick Ramsey."

"The big hunky guy? I've seen him around here working on big stories." She was quiet, but said bluntly when Brucker looked up, "And I do know about him and your sister. It was all over the division. Ramsey caused it."

Brucker pulled off his overcoat, hung it solemnly, saying, without looking at her, "I can't work it directly because of the implied conflict. But there are other suspects in the hit and run that I can work." His sterling mettle shined then. "I want the investigation to be by the book. No grudge-fucking. But he's slippery, and I know him, so I want to be part of it."

She sat still a moment, huffing under her weight, and with her peculiar succinctness, she said, "The good thing is, of course, that I'm too homely for Stud Muffin to try and fuck. So. Put me in, Coach."

Brucker talked to the cold windowpane, his face awash in dim white sunlight, his toasty eyes hardened. "On my desk there is a name and some locations where an alibi of Ramsey's might be found today. See where he was between ten and midnight last night. There's some other names there, people he knows. Shake 'em down about Ramsey. At the Dublin Rose, find a bartender named Brian. At the parking garage of the *Tribune* find a security guard named Archie Dane. See if there are surveillance tapes of cars going in and out. Also, Ramsey's car is missing, a Jeep Wagoneer. The license tag number is on that list, too. I think he used it last night in a hit and run. Old lady died."

He sat, fiddled with his pipe. Angie watched him and was quiet out of respect. Finally he said forcefully, "The other angle is Victor Farron, the newspaper mogul asshole. He had the keys to Ramsey's car for a while. He's got an alibi, Arthur Yates of all people, this town's fucking Santa Claus. So I'm working Farron. Let's talk again in a couple of days."

She sighed and closed the notepad. Her bulging lenses penetrated him. "So, Lieutenant, what else?"

He said dryly, "The crime scene team picked up his tuxedo from last night. It's at the lab. Farron's too. It came in this morning. Follow the evidence, the fibers. The window was busted by a shopping cart, so maybe glass, maybe blood specks. You know. Just do the drill."

The phone rang. He took it up, and a look came over him like he had just seen Paris come up through the clouds from his window seat in a 747.

"Hey, babe, oh no, you're not a bother. Important? Naw. We were just talking here, nothing important." Angie smiled. Brucker winked at her. Then he went dark. The 747 crashed. "You can't, huh. Well, sure I understand. Your parents are coming? Yeah. That's nice. No, no, babe, it's okay. It's just a dinner honoring me with an award. No biggee. Yeah. Sure. Bye."

Angie said, "There's a song. So quiet in here you could hear a heart break."

"That girl's never going to love me." He ran his hands across his face in great frustration.

Angie said, "Maybe you should, you know, give up. Get another woman. Preferably one who wouldn't rather chow with the folks than see you get a Commendation for Bravery from the Fire Department. I mean, you did get there first. You did go in alone and bring the kid out alive. Doesn't this Ice Queen gal of yours watch the damned TV news?"

"No. She just watches me twist in the wind. That is, when I'm not doing Fido tricks and buying jewelry to get her in love with me."

Angie was on her way out. She stopped at the table by the door. "Hey, Brucker, can I have one of these doughnuts here?"

He nodded, she laughed. "See, I'm not going to eat them. I'll just open my underwear and stick them to my ass. I mean, that's where they end up, you know?" Her pug face became serious when she added, "Hey, Brucker, this prick who fucked-up your sister, how'd he do it?"

"He laid it on thick. Seduced her, opened her up. Taught her to love him. Then he said there was a woman in his life, Jacqueline Sofiya, the movie writer who lives here, so he tells Janelle that if this woman marries him, he'll still be willing and available to fuck Janelle." He found himself chuckling grimly. "I reckon she couldn't live without him by then, but she also couldn't take the deal he offered, not her. Too good. Too honest. Not sick enough. She hanged herself."

Angie seemed crestfallen. "Good Lord."

"So he plays good games, our Ramsey. Watch him, Bianchi."

She had a weird sparkle. "Oh, I'll watch him, all right. First I'll catch him, and then we'll watch him hang. See you in a few days. I've got your back, Lieutenant."

She waddled out, shoving a doughnut into her mouth.

Brucker picked up the telephone receiver and then slammed it down as hard as he could. His dream girl's picture, that glamour image of Patrice, toppled onto the floor, and the glass cracked, just like his heart every time she ditched him again, which she did often and effortlessly.

# 16

Cocktails were at six, which meant that for an hour Brucker had to live out his worst nightmare. Mingling.

The ballroom was draped in low light, thick with low-cut evening gowns. The real guys—the firefighters—wore button-down shirts and pressed jeans and boots. Their wives came in off-the-rack sequined stuff that only true-hearted working girls could afford. The anorexic designer bitches paled by their sides.

There was another tier at this annual ball, the society crust, who found it quite genteel to go around saying that they weren't firefighters but that they did however donate to the Firefighters' Burn Victim Recovery Fund. Leading the brigade, of course, standing there like a spruced up young Geronimo, was Arthur Yates. Brucker watched how the crust collected around Yates, like hundred dollar bills were going to fall out of his pockets and they could dive for them.

Yates gushed when he saw Brucker lurking in a corner, far away from the lavish buffet for a thousand people that Yates had paid for with pocket change. He was on Brucker in a heartbeat.

Tonight Yates wore a deep chocolate western-cut tuxedo, sandy colored boots, and a bolo tie. He was pure Dude Ranch Deluxe, dripping class and money.

He put out a hand, smiled like a swindler. "Detective Brucker, my man. How the hell are ya? That drink looks pee-kid, boy. Let me get you another one—"

"No thanks, Yates. It's just ginger ale."

Yates rocked on his heels. Everyone who passed whistled or called out or reached over to pat him. He was a touchstone of the proud and the privileged.

"Well, hell, boy, I'm giving you your award tonight. And I'm as proud to do so as a prize pony."

Brucker coughed. "You're—"

Idiot Yates beamed. His cheeks were too rosy. Drunk again. "That's right, son. I fund all the civic awards events for the Firefighters' Associations in this county, so's y'all don't have to go selling ign'ernt little raffle tickets and show up to eat cold cuts and drink warm beer. I mean, hell, Brucker, when your house is on fire, who're you gonna call? Your fucking banker or broker? Naw! You call a fireman! This here buffet and the band and the door prizes and all this—" He upended a scotch rocks. "This here is my . . . fucking . . . duty."

"I'm not a firefighter, Yates. I'm a cop. I was a block away from the scene when the call went over the 911 dispatch that there was smoke from a house on Evans Avenue. I circled the block, saw the smoke, and went in. The little girl was home sick from school, that's all, and I carried her out. I don't deserve any award. It was just my ... fucking duty."

Yates took the bold, drunken move of putting an arm around the taciturn, stony Brucker. "You're too humble, my man."

"Yeah. And you're too close to me right this minute."

Yates belly-laughed, but he stepped away, surveying the room, doing silly little waves at people who were dying to come and fawn over his billion-dollar stupidity. He mumbled something. Brucker leaned forward.

"What did you say? What the hell did you say, Yates?"

Yates looked square at him, eyes like a viper, showing the confidence of a man who isn't joking when he claims to own the damned world. "I said, I see your girlfriend didn't make it here tonight."

Brucker straightened. A tingle went through him. He smelled the threat. It stuck in his chest like an iron rod.

Yates slapped Brucker's shoulder again, looking forward but talking sideways. "She's an intern I believe, over there at the County Hospital. Let's see now, what's that hospital called ... help me out here, son."

Brucker wanted to coldcock the motherfucker. He said profoundly, "Arthur Yates Medical Center."

The viper eyes ignited. "My granddaddy, my namesake. Yep. He built that place a hundred years ago. I reckon I've got, oh, 'bout forty or fifty million in endowments going there right now. Whoo-wee. I'm sorry your little doctor gal couldn't get here. But hell, ain't she just lucky as all git-out, Brucker, just to have a damned internship after all? I mean, what a competitive dog-eat-dog-shit arena that is, trying to get accepted today at a good teaching hospital. That gal of yours, she is one lucky little filly. Now. Y'all take care."

He swaggered away. A busty, aging docent nabbed him in a flaming embrace. Lieutenant Brucker sipped his ginger ale and stood very, very still so that he wouldn't let loose and go kill the son of a bitch.

With a phone call from Yates, Brucker's potential murder suspect's alibi—Victor Farron's only alibi—could take Patrice out of the program at Yates Medical Center Teaching Hospital. It wouldn't be overt. It would be rigged and wrangled, but it could be done.

Brucker went toward the bar fast to get some whiskey put in his ginger ale.

# 17

At 8:05 P.M., just as Hero Brucker rose from the dais to the thunderous applause of a huge, eclectic dinner crowd and took his commendation meekly, death stood up to meet one Miss Hipjive Clitfella.

On the corners of the jittery, hurdy-gurdy old avenue in the commercial district where the girls peddled their pussies, Hipjive staggered, cursing the world's woes. An anemic snow dusted everything, symbolic of the white dust that Miss Hipjive would soon melt and shoot into her scarred arm there in the alley. The alley stank of pee and pot. When Hipjive swished down the empty alley, walking like a Chinese princess and smelling like a brewery, she didn't notice the sudden, eerie quiet, as if something evil had scared off all the cats and bums.

Her beaten-up suede boots had fringe on them. She wore silver leggings under a gold fake-leather skirt so short and tight it barely covered her ample buns. Flicks from her cheap pink feather boa were stuck in her gruesomely red hair.

She was stoned blind, stumbling, needing to keep

one hand on the wet brick wall to steady herself.
She was cussing.

"Shit. Eighty dollars. Shit. I owe eighty dollars? So
I gave the motherfucker forty and a blow job. Ha.
Don't cover it, he says, so's he can smack my face
for the 'balance,' shit, he says. Looka here. I got another busted tooth. Shee-ut."

She was close enough and in just enough muddled streetlamp light to see that her face was covered in blood. From a covey, a dank, filthy doorway
that led into a deserted building from the alley,
black-gloved hands reached for her.

With her face jammed into the cold rust of that
rotting old door, she struggled to answer the
growled question.

"Fucking A, I know Caressa Dicks. Bitch ran off
two days ago with my fucking stash that she took
from my fucking locker at the bus station. Let me
go, asshole cop."

"Where is she?" Something to muddle the voice,
she thought, a handkerchief, maybe a scarf, something that made the voice a scary, deep, dark buzz.

"I 'ont fucking know, bitch—" Because through
the vividness of all that pain, something bizarre lilted, like noticing the bright stars in the sky just before you sink and drown for the last time. Perfume.
Cheap perfume. "Let me go, you bitch!"

Miss Hipjive Clitfella never heard the horrendous
popping sound of her arm being wrenched backward because the pain wave hit her full force like a
cannonball. She started to scream, but a hand was
clamped so hard against her mouth and nose that
no air could go in or out.

"Stop screaming. I'll kill you if you make a sound. Tell me where she is. If she took your drugs, then you've been looking for her. Tell me."

She could not speak, only bleat. Her left shoulder felt like it had knives through it, knives on fire, and it was almost impossible to breathe through it.

She came to wildly, a shock of adrenaline, when her other arm was taken up and bent painfully backward. "Okay, okay. I been—oh god it hurts so bad—I been asking. She took my shit. So—god, please, not my other arm, oh jesus—"

"Where is she?"

"She got in a Jeep—"

"I know that. Where is she now? You stupid sluts know each other. Same methadone clinics. Same pimps. Tell me."

She had passed out from pain. When let loose, she fell like a costumed paperweight.

The feather boa became a tool, pulled completely tight around Hipjive's neck until she stopped convulsing. No pulse. Something under the boa protruded oddly, out of place and lumpy under her tattered crop top showing huge bosoms. Moving the crop top up made it all almost laughable. Socks. Her bosoms were socks. And beneath them was the hooker's chest hair.

The insane chuckle was cryptic white breaths through the ski mask mouth hole, thinking, damn, I just killed a male whore. What'd'ya know.

It was a short, brisk walk down the backstreets, back toward the chapel and the rectory, back to where the little whore in the car got lost after she ran. The neon streets of the whore district were crowded with so much dazed human circus tragedy. Nobody noticed the masked stranger in the dark alleys.

She hasn't told yet. The whore hasn't talked to the cops. But she's told the priest. No doubt. And he'll talk.

A cop cruiser passed but the shadowy figure ducked, sliding and hiding in the dark crevices of doorways and under rusted fire escape ladders.

The rectory wasn't far. Where she got lost, the little whore, where she bailed. Where she no doubt had taken refuge. The rectory wasn't far.

# 18

Brucker drove slowly on the slick downtown streets. People flooded everywhere, bundled up and laughing, out of the bars or into the movies. His plain sedan moved cautiously. But he wasn't contemplating caution for the pedestrians; he was thinking of the best way to get to the rectory without attracting attention.

He had been planning it since Saturday night when Mick Ramsey mentioned Father David Keenan. Even now, lo these decades later, Brucker had to drop his head and sigh heartily at the thought of Father David Keenan.

Across the street from the church, he thought, sure, the Water Department, just across the wide avenue from the wrought-iron fence that circles the little pastoral oasis among the skyscrapers. He had it, the plan. His car with the city tags wouldn't look funny parked among the other city vans and cars at the Water Department parking lot. He wheeled in.

Two lights were on in the rectory. Kitchen. A bedroom upstairs. The chapel was dark inside completely. Brucker's black skin and black trench blended in fine. He moved around the building and found an outside intercom button.

Man, what a risk. He swallowed cold breaths, let his finger linger near the call button. Emergencies only, please, the sign screamed. Brucker wiggled his finger, drew up his nerve, banged the button and waited.

He wasn't hidden well enough by the darkness to be invisible to the shadowy figure who rounded a corner and spotted him instantly.

Brucker—in the rectory courtyard. Shit. Crap. No, no. She told them who I am, the stupid little whore bitch told them, oh my god. A description. The phone calls in the Jeep that night of the hit and run. I must've said my name when I answered the cell. Whore. Priest. Brucker!

Furious panting broke into a consuming sweat. There wasn't time to think, only to turn and skulk away. The meeting was in one hour. There should've been time to skim the rectory and find a window to crack the next night, time to find a way in during the dead of night and skulk through each room, knife out, find the whore, cut her throat before she even woke to make a sound. Find the priest, cut his wrists again, along the old scars, put the knife in the priest's hand.

But Brucker. There. Ringing the bell to get in. Holy mother. It was definitely cocktail time, time to think, get-a-grip time. If the whore had already talked, they would have come to make the arrest. It was pitch dark. A thought. Go in, kill them all. The whore. The priest. The goody-goody cop. Yeah.

With a knife. My knife and Brucker's Beretta. Maybe not, huh, asshole? Get a gun. Go get a gun. Right, you fucking genius, so shots can echo through downtown like the fucking Rifleman Chuck Connors is in town.

"Uh, Father Keenan? Uh. It's . . . Jesse."

Not a sound came. Brucker licked his dry lips. A door buzzed. He reached, and it opened, and he was faced with the darkened altar of the chapel where only Christ's face of frozen despair looked down on him in a rain of eerie candlelight. He stepped inside.

## 19

The players escalated their game of treachery. It was almost midnight.

Jesse Brucker slid into the soundproof safety of a confessional in the church.

Across town, Mick Ramsey took a cab to meet a stranger who called on his cell phone while he was at the White Elephant Saloon and said to Mick, "The sky is falling." Mick paid for his two beers and bolted.

Victor Farron guided his Lexus into the pristine stateliness of Art Yates's boulevard of a private driveway, pulled up to the back of the mansion, and used Art's personal code to enter through the private quarters where Yates lived alone.

The confessional door didn't squeak as Brucker went into its cushy interior and kneeled on the padding in front of the opaque screen. When the priest slid a panel back from the other side, they could hear but not see each other. One mute light shone on Brucker's left in the tiny cubicle.

"David."

"Jesse." The priest sounded older, tired.

"I'm sorry, Father. Sorry to come here, to contact you. I know we agreed after that night never to—"

The priest said diffidently, "It's all right, Jess. I knew from the TV and newspapers that you live here, you're quite a hero. But I honored our promise that night not to contact each other after you graduated from the Jesuit school. I wanted to. But I would never complicate or jeopardize your life."

Brucker remembered the incident every day, like remembering being in a horrible car wreck. How surreal it seems later when you're safe, how the fear tastes like rusty water in your mouth. Some days, sitting alone, Brucker would play it in his head, walking into the shed, hearing the little girl screaming, seeing the priest he loved so much doing something so hotly violent and wrong. In those moments, Brucker would sometimes tremble and have to pace. Now, in the cubicle, hearing David's voice, he found himself breathing too fast.

"In my job, Father, I was able to check. I know you got . . . treatment. I know you were hospitalized."

A fluttery sigh. "Yes, it took a long time for me to recover from my . . . from what I did."

"From what we did, David."

"No, Jess. You were not accountable. With the girl . . . with Diddia . . . it was my fault."

Brucker leaned close and whispered. "We can't talk, David. We can't talk about it. While you're in this town, we can't look at each other like we've met. If they connected us, ever, in any way, it would bring up questions." His voice trailed. The cubicle felt like a tomb. "And the answers would come. Don't care about me, David. Don't worry or wonder. We can't—"

They breathed together, silently. The priest said, "I came here a month ago. I won't be staying long, until the new priest comes in spring. We won't connect."

"No, David. Never. But soon a detective has to come here. She has to ask you about a man, Mick Ramsey. He is a murder suspect, and he says you saw him at the time of the killing. She's smart, Angie Bianchi is, so please don't . . . look aware of me if she mentions that I'm the lead investigator. She might say that, might say my name. Be cool."

"Jesse. I've looked for the girl. There is something I'd like to tell you, because I need help, but it could, no, it would put you right where you mustn't be—involved with me. Jesse, I prayed for that girl to come to me and—"

He felt his body tense to a hard ball. "No. Don't do that. Why?"

"To tell her I'm . . . to apologize."

"No, David. You didn't mean it. You were lost."

"I can help her remember, Jesse. I can stop her pain."

"Father, no, please, don't speak of it or even think of it. You'll go to prison."

"I'm imprisoned now by my memories."

Jesse put a hand on the opaque screen. "I'm leaving. Don't find me. Don't find the girl. Don't open those gates. Hell's gates. You know, Father, suffering isn't the same thing as courage. You can suffer a whole bunch in a short time and then get over it, past the guilt, and you get just as much relief as a lifetime of hurting a little every day. Let it go. Let it be."

He went out softly. Father David hung his head in utter remorse.

Mick Ramsey stepped into the gas station urinal that was drenched in stench. The light switch, as planned, didn't work. In the dark he felt his way to the appointed toilet stall.

His confessional door, a corroding stall, was scrawled with obscenities. The man in the dark stall next to him was ranting, maybe drunk, maybe just nutty. Mick was writing the best he could in the dark on his notepad.

"You got a tape recorder, boy?"

"No. I use shorthand."

"Good. 'Cause you get every word."

"Why can't you tell me your name?"

"Because I ain't stupid. I'm pissed. And I'm gettin' even with the bastards, but I ain't no friggin' hero. I been waitin' ten years to drop this bomb on the lyin' bastards and watch them boil in oil, but I couldn't, until my friend at the SEC said you was the right guy, says you wouldn't back down from writin' the story. 'Sides, now's the time, before the goddamned cheatin' guvnor makes his bid to be the goddamned cheatin' president."

"Are you with Securities and Exchange? I have to attribute even an anonymous source. A high-ranking state official. A member of the Senate. The governor's relative. What?"

The guy's voice seethed with contempt. "I'm a

fucking former millionaire who is now a broke old bum. I'm a oil man, boy, was anyhow. Until I went and invested in the eighties with an outfit called Haslon Oil Company. Now you listen, 'cause you first ain't gonna believe me. And when you check it out, and it's all true, you're gonna shit your pants . . ."

Mick wrote. A couple of times he had to stop, cock his head or shake it. The story was unfathomable.

"Our pretty-boy Guvnor Green. He wasn't governor then, but he was the majority stockholder in Haslon Oil, he let us all buy into some oilfields he was gettin' ready to drill in Bahrain worth a sure gusher and worth well into the double-digit billions of dollars. I reckon we each five of us threw in about six million, which was literally all I had besides walking-around money. Anyhow, hearing that Haslon is in the deal, the stock prices for a piece of Haslon goes the next day from ten dollars a share to thirty, because ever'body knows Haslon don't dick around with losing deals. You with me, boy?"

Mick's hands were cold. He knew where it was going. His fingers felt numb. "I hear you. Go on."

"So, lo and behold, that goddamned nutcase Hussein up and invades Kuwait, and the whole world is shocked dead, and nobody can believe the crazy camel jock had the gonads. Looks like we're eatin' shit on our prospective oil wells in Bahrain. Stock price drops like a mule turd, all the way down to six dollars a share over-fucking-night. With what I paid for my stock at the outset, I and my fellow investors lost everything we put in. The stock is shit. The oilfields are dead—"

Mick said, swallowing the suspense so he could get it out, "Everyone lost everything. Except, let me guess, the governor."

He felt the old man lean on the stall door, crushed by the weight of the treason. "You win, boy. Seems that a couple'a days before the camel jock invaded, Mr. Guvnor Harding T. Green and one other of his cronies sold all their stock. In the nick of damned time. At thirty dollars a share. And didn't bother to tell none of the rest of us about it, neither. I hope you're doing the math, because I have a hun'ert times in my head. Two days before the invasion of Kuwait, when he sold his stock, the guvnor of this great state made a profit of almost $200 million, free and clear. Him, and his buddy."

"Insider information. About the invasion." Mick slid. His knees felt funny.

"Who'd know, boy? Who'd have the word a week before a secret military invasion into a foreign country by a foreign militia? Think out loud for me, please."

It came out as sucked air. "The CIA. Only the CIA."

"And who would the CIA tell faster than a whore counts cash?"

Mick stood again. He wanted to run, to write so fast the keys smoked. "The president of the United States," he said flatly. "The governor's brother."

"Bingo, Ringo. These Texas traders weren't nothing but a bunch of goddamned un-American traitors."

"Fuck un-American," Mick almost laughed it. "It's a crime. A federal crime. Insider trading."

The old man snarled, "So you've put your right

foot in, now shake it all around, why don't you. Follow the smell of shit to who was going to drill them damn wells and make a billion bucks."

Mick closed his eyes in gritty anticipation. "Yeah, the production company who did the drilling. You say it. I want you to say it."

"Yates. Arthur Percival the third."

Mick sighed. "He was the other person who sold just before the invasion."

"No. Not directly. He wouldn't dare. He's smarter than any pinhead politician. He bought his stock and sold it through someone else. A buddy of his."

"Vic Farron." Mick said it and let out a long breath and left his chest empty for a moment in total terror. "I told Vic. I told him I had something cooking with a high-level source at the SEC about insider trading that would rock the world. Jesus. He knows that I know."

"Boy, whatever you're gonna do, do it. 'Cause until you put it out there for the world to see, you're the only one besides me who knows, and they won't never suspect me of telling you. Sleep with the lights on, boy. 'Til you verify and the story runs, you're as good as dead."

Mick rasped, "The other investors?"

"All dead within six months of the deal. Think of the odds, boy."

"So why not you?"

The man chuckled godlessly. "Me? Why didn't they kill me, too? Because I'm stark-ravin', snot-slingin' in-fucking-sane, boy. Just ask the doctors at the state hospital where they put me when I lost everything. Shit, boy, I'm locked away. Court orders signed by the guvnor himself. Guess I'd better get back before head count time in the psycho ward."

He left, just like that. But first he spat, and Mick heard him uncock the gun's hammer. The stall door squeaked after the guy was gone, squeaked like it was haunted.

In his beautifully upholstered, quiet den, Art Yates leaned forward into Victor's deadpan face. The ice in their glasses tinkled. The fireplace popped.

"So," Yates whispered, "you have someone with Ramsey."

"Yes."

"Somebody we trust?"

"You're paying off gambling debts for her."

Yates smiled, his tiny teeth like some hissing varmint. "Tomorrow's Monday. He'll start making calls on the story. Damn, we need to know who the leak is. And the hit-and-run thing? It's progressing?"

Victor rubbed his weary eyes, downed his drink. "I'm watching it through a source at the PD. They consider Mick a strong suspect."

"Good." Yates stood by the fireplace, dashing and suave until he spoke, then he became nothing but a rich, crooked, conniving punk. He looked accusingly at Victor. "Where you been tonight? And where'd you go last night, after you left here?"

"I'm your pawn, Art. Not your pet pony."

Art came, stood over him. Victor was bigger but not nearly as mean or powerful. He didn't look up at Art.

Art put a hand on Vic's shoulder; it felt like it was

dipped in gunpowder and could detonate. "So, we'll know what he knows before he writes it in a story."

"Yeah. My snitch is with him."

"Who is it?"

"You don't know." He looked up at Yates. "If it comes to it, someday under oath, you don't know."

Yates smiled like a dog snarls. "Looking out for me. That's good. You keep the snitch on him to see who he's got at SEC. Things are going fine. Pretty soon we'll look back at all this and laugh. Don't you think? I mean, imagine our luck, we're trying to kill his story and he's suspected of killing a bag lady. My, my."

Victor couldn't fake it. He said sullenly, "Oh, yeah, we'll probably look back at all this and . . . die laughing."

From behind him Yates whispered sinisterly into Victor's ear. "You keeping something from me, Vic? Don't try it. Because I can smell it. There are four things I can smell like a wolf smells death. From a hundred miles away I can smell oil in the ground, money in the bank, and pussy on its way."

Vic looked up miserably. "And the fourth thing?"

Art smiled like a dog showing its teeth. "Liar's sweat. You keeping something from me?"

Without the right conviction Vic answered, "No."

Arthur Yates smiled wider, the smile of a sick, bad boy who had just lit his kitten on fire and was enjoying the screams.

# 20

The priest slept. The whore wandered.

She was greatly medicated. Pain pills. Globs of gin. In the Monsignor's cabinet she had found Seconal and vials of Demerol. She blended them, mixed them into a killer cocktail, downed it all with a shot of gin.

The rectory was the most silent place she had ever been. She sat at the priest's desk and fiddled with his things. It was all so perverted to her, and she didn't get it, but she fingered it all.

A stack of opened envelopes was too tempting, so she ungraciously pulled out the cards inside and read them. It was an assortment of sap. "Dear Father David: Thank you for getting the banks and grocery stores to give enough money so our school can buy new wheelchairs for all the kids who need them . . ."

Caressa dragged on her cigarette, said, "Yeah, yeah," and tossed it. The next one said, "Dear Father Keenan, thanks so much for the things you said at Daddy's funeral last month, and for the hours you sat with him at the end . . ."

She tossed it, swigged gin. She found his bifocals on the desk and slipped them on, just for fun, and she giggled because she was looped. The next envelope said thanks for doing the wedding vows for somebody's damned kids, and it had a hundred dollar bill in it. Caressa whistled, stuck the money in her habit pocket and opened another envelope.

The prayer phone rang. She glared at it, wobbled an arm toward it and answered clumsily, "What."

The voice hesitated. "Uh, I was calling the prayer line."

She blew a gum bubble, then a smoke ring, then said, "Okay. Shoot."

"Uh, you're a, uh, a nun?"

"Sister Mystic. Prayer queen and psychic."

"You don't, hmmm, sound like a nun."

She winced. "That's what my parole officer says, too. So, tell me the dirt."

He cleared his throat. "Well, I need prayers, I mean, I need a job badly—"

"Got canned, huh?" She was nodding stupidly. She had pushed the habit's hood away from her face, so her hair fell long.

"No, Sister, I didn't get . . . canned. What kind of nun are you?"

"Well, what kind of Christian are you, anyhow? Like God is a supermarket and prayer is a coupon. Honestly. You don't need prayer. You need the want-ads, which are jam-packed with jobs, so why are you calling here at midnight and whining to God?"

He tried. She blurted, "What kind of job do you want, anyhow?"

"I was a CEO. They downsized, and I lost a salary of nearly a half-million a year. My wife and I have these huge debts—"

She guffawed. "Hey, so you don't want a job after all. You want God to waltz you in there as the Big Boss and you're all scared that they might repo the wife's Jag. Oh, please."

He said, "I'm calling the Bishop."

"Besides, how the hell do you get in debt when you make a half-million a year? I can see living beyond your means when you're knocking down, say, seven bucks an hour. But outpacing a half-mil? Please. Don't pray for a job. Pray for the good sense to know when to quit buying junk you don't need." She hung up and spun in the chair, laughing wildly.

She was reading more of the priest's personal mail when the prayer line rang again. She felt practiced by now, inflated from drunkenness and high joy. "Prayer line. If you've got the dime, we've got the time."

The woman hadn't heard. "Sister." She was weeping.

"Yeah. That's me."

"My daughter died."

Caressa sunk. "See how they are? That's the thanks you get."

The woman sobbed. "She's dead. My darling Annetta. Oh, sister. I'm terrified. She wasn't . . . good. She was . . . bad." Between heaves, she got it out. "She was eighteen, and she'd had an abortion, and she didn't know God. She was wild, with boys, with drugs. Oh, god, Sister, I'm so afraid. Please. Pray."

Caressa shrugged. "For what?"

"I have to know." The pain dripped. "I have to know if she's in, oh god, if she's in Hell or if God took her. I can't sleep. I can't eat. It's been a month, and I'm dying of this grief. Please. I can't live if she's in Hell—"

Caressa squawked, "In Hell for what? Screwing up? Shoot, there's no room in Hell for people who didn't mean to be lousy. Hell's for lawyers who mean to screw us and developers who wreck the land and politicians who ride in limos while children starve in this country. Hell's not for gals who make crummy choices."

The woman gushed. "She didn't know God. She wasn't ready for eternity. Oh, oh, Jesus. Not my girl in Hell. Please."

Caressa said, "Look, calm down, okay? You're freaking me." She lit a cigarette. "Here's what I can do. There's these saints." She looked around the room, bleary, sloppy. "Here's one. Saint Therese of the Little Flower. You pray to her. She looks real nice, real serene. She's got all these flowers all around her. See? That sounds good. Ask her to pray."

"And you, too?"

Caressa pouted. "Me? Pray? That's a new one."

"Please." The sobbing again. Caressa sighed. The woman begged.

"I came to you tonight, Sister, in such agony. I am dying of grief. And if she's with God, I can live again. Please. Your prayers to Saint Therese and mine. We'll ask her to pray."

Caressa was not a liar. Whore, yes, thief, certainly. Addict, of course. But not a liar. "Lady, I'm not a nun."

"I don't care who you are. God put you on this phone for me. Give me your prayers whoever you are. I hurt. I'm breaking. Ask God to tell me if he has my sweet child."

She felt small suddenly, and wrong. "Okay. But see, the saints don't much know me either, I mean, not at all really, and God, well, he wouldn't know me if he saw me."

The woman in agony was gone. Caressa poured holy water from the urn into her gin glass and took another pill.

The prayer phone rang again. She yanked it up. "Sister Mystic's prayer line. First three minutes free."

"I'm homosexual. Can I go to Heaven?"

She rolled her eyes, sat, and began to go through Father David's desk drawers shamelessly. "I don't see why not. Television evangelists do, and they screw everybody straight up the ass."

His despair drowned out her sarcasm. "I was gay—am gay. A few years ago I tested positive for AIDS." He started to weep, and Caressa sighed loudly. His words were broken; his voice quivered. "My parents, they hate me. For being gay, for getting sick. Sister, I didn't choose it, I fought myself for so many years. Oh god, my mom, she knows I'm dying slowly, and she tells me over and over that I'm going to Hell." He cratered again in sobs. "I'm scared. I'm lost. I want the love of God, that's all. Please pray for me."

"The special of the day, it seems, sir, is Saint Therese of the Little Flower. Ask her to pray. That's all I know."

"And you'll pray, too, Sister?"

She was thumbing through stuff, personal stuff, tossing it aside without thought. "Sure. And to be safe why don't you also ask Charles Manson and Tim McVeigh to send one up for you. They're as connected as I am."

He started to sob. She hung up.

"God. What losers."

She had the hundred dollar bill in her pocket. It weighed like bricks on her. She needed cocaine, badly. She could be back before dawn. She could do two or three "customers," maybe just BJs or some regular stuff so the priest wouldn't see bruises at breakfast. And in the nun get-up no killers outside the door would know her. She had her street-hooker clothes in the carpetbag. She had her locker at the bus station.

She had a need for cocaine.

She stood silently, Saint Therese did—over there in the corner like a porcelain bloom, bathed in robes and flowers and gentle eyes. The whore looked away from her defiantly.

## 21

From the cubby of an alley between office buildings across the street, the nun could be seen silhouetted in the window.

The street was marooned in darkness. No sane person would be wandering on this blistering cold night around this dark end of downtown. Even the way-cool clubs and restaurants up at the other end would be mostly empty by now.

Through the front bay windows of the rectory it was clear that the nun was bending to use a telephone on a small table just next to the glistening fireplace. She looked like a witch, so thin and sheathed in the colors of death. Her face was obscured, but it seemed heart shaped, and she seemed very fragile under the heavy woolen robes, almost elderly and bent.

The church's heavily shaded lawn was perfect for hiding. The image crossing the street in black slacks and a black parka was nothing but a shadow. The buck knife bounced at hip level in a plain leather pouch. Hopping the low wrought-iron fence around the rectory yard was easy. A line of shrub-

bery that stood high against the old brownstone was
thick and tall. The vines were lacquered with a
shiny coating of ice, but there was an opening perfect for slipping through. Just above, close enough
to see lost moonlight in her eyes, stood the nun.

She was inches above. She was . . . smoking? She
looked down where her slayer was hidden and
would have seen the horrible crouched figure clearly if not for the night and the black mask and clothing. The nun's eyes were worried, but not because
she had noticed anyone lurking; she was looking
past, waiting for something.

It was a strain to remember the whore's face from
the hit-and-run night. The nun blew smoke at the
frosty glass like a fiend, sucking in hard and blowing out hard. It gave her stalker pause, but then, it
wasn't so strange that nuns were humanly flawed,
too. In the old neighborhood the nuns who ran the
school down the street had actually come out sometimes and played basketball and drank beers afterward at a pub.

The whore had been in gobs of makeup like
a . . . well, like a hooker. She had major tits, too,
though playing with them in the car had been impossible with one hand on the steering wheel and
another driving her chin over and over to the magic
rhythm. The nun. Could it be a disguise? There was
no way to tell in those robes.

She had a huge bag at her side as she stood there
worrying. Did nuns worry? Squinted eyes discerned
silently, hungering to find the nasty whore—and
hopefully not have to murder a nun along the way.
There had been spears of fingernails, some horrible

purple jobs that clicked. The nun's hands were thin and delicate, no purple daggers.

A car trudged past on the wide avenue that ran the length of downtown. At the traffic light that led up onto the freeway ramp it skidded on a patch of sheer ice. The skidding sound caused shivers of anger, rage. The goddamned whore. She could ruin everything. She *saw* what happened, blindfold be damned, she had to have seen when she ripped it off and took off running. Prison. Maybe even the death penalty because solving the hit and run would lead to solving who killed the hookers. Multiple felonies. Jesus. Now a nervous sweat broke inside the ski mask.

She came from nowhere that night, the damned bag lady, pushing her shopping cart like it was a Trojan prize. The damnable moment when the car rounded the corner was emblazoned in slow motion, the blindfolded whore assailing the interior with cigarette smoke and yakking about how much money she needed—extra to keep on the blindfold—yak, yak.

A glance in the rearview mirror started it all, the whole dastardly nightmare. Sour resentment filled the memory of looking forward again and seeing the headlights hit a string of metal in the rain. The shopping cart first, and then the bag lady in the ratty overcoat and huge men's shoes, a straw cowboy hat over grisly white hair. She had stepped right off the curb into the Jeep's beams.

Drumbeats and screeching tires and the bag lady's bloated face crashing against the windshield, both eyes bleeding and her mouth opened into a black hole of a terrifying scream. She lingered there and then flew away. The whore screamed, yanked open the door, and then yanked off the blindfold and ran.

The whore ran screaming like a maniac in a King Kong movie.

## 22

The little nun passing through the bus station was an oddity, but somehow a welcome one. The unwashed and washed-up who were cramped inside out of the cold either lowered their eyes away from her humbly or searched her face for miracles and answers.

Caressa ignored them. She found her locker, spun the lock, and opened it so her junk fell out. She cursed. Liquor bottles, full and empty. Ridiculous shoes with spikes so high she could leap tall buildings. Bottles of dime-store cosmetics, cigarette cartons, her jam box was in there, stolen prescription drugs, some silly clothes like sequined halter tops and short-shorts.

She dragged some of it out, picked out a cherry-red wig, and headed for the bathroom. She didn't see a tiny girl about six years old follow her in. But she saw the girl behind her in the mirror, the comely little cherubic face, blond curls, chocolate on her chin. The little girl only stared like kids do, like they're watching chimps fly kites, wide-eyed and trusting. Caressa turned, shoving the red wig back into the carpetbag so as not to scare the kid too much.

"What, kid? What is it?"

With a voice like a sweet violin note, the baby-face blond said, "Hi. I'm Madison Renee Fitzgerald. I'm going on the bus to my grandma's burial in Mississippi." She blinked, sweeter than honey in mint tea.

Caressa stared, confused, all her meanness momentarily twisted backward into curiosity.

Madison Renee Fitzgerald said, "My dog, Cinnamon, that was my dog's name, Cinnamon ran off."

Caressa smiled. "Must've been a male."

"Well, my mama out there, she said I should come in here and ask you to pray because you're a woman of God, she said, and God will hear you and I'd like Cinnamon to come home. Mama said you and I both pray and it works faster."

Caressa fumbled. Shit. A big sigh left her. The big blue eyes and the pink cheeks were killing her with their trust and innocence.

"Look, little girl, I'm not a nun. This is like a costume, you know, when you play dress-up. Get it?"

"You're not a Sister of the Lord like my mama said?" The bottom lip came out and Caressa wanted to die.

"Okay, I was joking. Okay, so don't get sad. Besides, you can pray, you know, you don't need me or somebody else to do it. God hears you just as good as me, all right?"

She took a step forward in her shiny patent slippers. Her blue ruffled dress touched Caressa's black robe.

"Yes, ma'am, I know. But my mama, she saw you come in, and she told me a story about a woman in the Bible who wanted to get healed from being real sick. So she went over and she touched Jesus's garment, which I guess was his old-timey dress like men wore. And the woman got healed just from touching his garment."

Caressa turned away to lean on the sink. Her hands and face felt cold. She held herself at the waist and stared at her face in the mirror. And she wondered which was worse—the trouble you get dressed as a whore or the trouble you get dressed as a nun. "Little girl . . . oh, Jesus . . . all right. I'll pray."

"Now?"

She wheeled, horrified. "No! I can't just fall down and pray, for heaven's sake! I need my . . . miracle beads and all. Look, maybe the dog's dead. Did you think of that? If God wants your dog dead and He wants you to just deal with it. What if it's that, huh?"

Those blue beams lit up in an angel's smile. "Oh, but Sister, he won't be dead. Not if you and me pray. Because what my mama said, she said you're like that Bible story. She said you're not God, but that you're like the hem of his garment."

Caressa put a cold, trembly hand to her warm mouth. The kid looked like a hologram and sounded like an echo.

"Thank you now, Sister of the Lord." The little voice lilted as the girl turned to go. Then, like a kid's game, she darted back, touched the hem of Caressa's black habit, yelped a giggle, and stopped long enough at the dirty bathroom door to blow the whore a kiss.

Caressa looked upward. "Do me a favor, would you, Lord in Heaven? Leave me the hell alone."

# 23

A long dark hallway led from the chapel into the rectory. There were no lights on, except the dim light in the two distant rooms. The killer walked softly in plain black boots.

The church bells pealed 1 A.M.

The first room on the right was a small office. Over the desk a weak lamp glowed onto cigarette butts in what appeared to be a priest's silver chalice. One butt still smouldered. Faces of unamused, tightly laced saints glared, their eyes frozen in expressions of some grim search into nowhere.

A bathroom on the left side of the hall was empty. In the kitchen a soft light shone down from a greasy old vent hood over the stovetop. Water dripped lamely into the stained sink. More cigarette butts were crushed in a saucer on the small Formica table. The sniff of a glass on the table caused a jolt. Gin. The fucking priest is a lush, and the nun chain smokes. The discovery elicited a cruel smile from behind the ski mask.

Off the kitchen on the right was a living area

where the fireplace had showed through to the outside, where the nun stood gazing at the sinking nighttime. Along the hallway to the living area, the dangerous intruder passed two closed doors. One was a closet. The other—the eerie shadow slung backward immediately when the door pushed back silently—was the priest's bedroom.

The priest didn't stir as the gently breathing figure loomed over him, breathing so shallow he hardly stirred the air, watching with eyes so hard and black they could be granite. Streetlight shining through sheer curtains bathed the room in muddled gray. The buck knife made a tiny slap sound as it switched from hand to hand.

A clock chimed. A silver crucifix on the bedside table glinted once as the light through the curtains caught it. The intruder backed away and hid in the dark shadows of the bedroom.

In fifteen minutes Caressa Dicks was back on the busy streetcorner, jangling with the other hookers who had not so much as noticed her absence. She wore a crotchless fake leopard skin bodysuit, shiny red knee boots, and a wig the color of cherry Jell-O. They congregated, the nasty girls, and the talk was of nothing but three murdered hookers found in two nights within the same six block area where they worked.

But nobody cared. They talked about it sensationally, with no sentiment because, after all, a bunch of weird murders didn't mean they didn't have bills to pay and drug habits to support. The whole gaggle of them together didn't have as much emotional warmth as lukewarm blood. Life meant nothing. Death meant even less.

Caressa's first customer was a businessman in a suit so cheap it would have walked out on the check at a diner all by itself. The suit had a gelatinous sheen and was jittery, and he wanted Caressa to get naked in his backseat and pee on his face while she pulled his hair and called him vile names. And so she did. He paid in all coins.

She dug into the cocaine vial that she had bought outside the bus station and snorted, licked her finger, sniffled, sighed. The next guy, in a pickup truck with a bumper sticker that read, "Tailgate me and I'll flick a booger on your windshield," wanted Caressa to straddle him and scream that his big penis was too much for her until he reached orgasm, which luckily for her turned out to be about forty seconds later, but he liked it and thanked her. She thought he was probably an okay guy out in real life, even if he didn't have front teeth.

Two eighteen-year old boys—she checked their IDs—wanted to do her at the same time in a camper. So they did. They each paid twenty. A woman in a Lexus, some horny society babe whose rich husband would've croaked, she said, if he knew she liked girls, wanted Caressa to use fingers and tongue on her, so she did. The crisp fifty practically still had the husband's cologne on it.

She went down on a guy in a work truck full of his roofing or electrical supplies—Caressa couldn't tell which. And a fat preacher in a church van wanted to take her from behind while he played a cassette tape of himself spewing from the pulpit about how the way to Heaven was by tithing, and, during all this, he wanted to gag Caressa with his daughter's panties. So he did. He paid with money still in the sealed church envelope dropped in the basket by a congregation member.

She took a break in a Dumpster behind a coffee shop, drank from a vodka bottle she took from the preacher's car, and wiped herself down with some napkins she found in the dumpster that looked cleaner than the rest.

The inside of the Dumpster stank bad. She had never noticed it before. She counted the money, climbed out and went to find her dealer who'd no doubt be lurking somewhere near one of the bars with the doors propped open, bars where the owners toted shotguns and the patrons did, too.

She stumbled once along the way, held a building and couldn't stop laughing—until she heard the cop car's siren give one whoop, just around the corner. And she heard the collective bitching of the gaggle as the cop car descended among them like a nuclear battleship.

"Aw, fuck you, Bianchi, go on, get on outta here, bitch. Please. No, we ain't getting in your damned car." A pause. The cop was talking, bargaining. And then, "Pancakes? Hot syrup? Shit, I'm in. Scoot over, I said, yeah, me too. No bust? You swear? Just food and bullshit talk? Let me in. I'm hungry. Man, Bianchi, you getting fatter by the day, girl, ouch! Don't you thump me! Hey, Bianchi, let me in, too. Girl, you stink. It ain't me, must be Bianchi . . ."

They all laughed, even the woman cop, and Caressa heard the car full of hungry hookers roll away

in the slush. She was alone then, frightened where
she had never been scared before—on the streets,
her streets. She walked, and when she got really
scared she hummed. Men whistled for her, but she
didn't stop. It was almost 2 A.M. The priest would
get up in a few hours and find her gone. Not that
she cared what that spooky old bastard thought
about how she lived. But he did make good French
toast. And the rectory sure did smell better than
that flop motel she used to call home.

Quickly as she could she shoved herself back into
the nun get-up at the bus station, wiped the goo off
her face, and wondered what to do about the smell
of human flesh all over her skin and her hair.

Her big bag slapped at her side. Her need to find
her dealer forgotten, she scurried down the dark
streets, looking like a flying apparition.

24

The priest had not stirred. The shadow was retreating out of the room, and hit a lamp table. It jangled.

The priest snorted, lifted a hand and then dropped it unconsciously. Moving ever so slowly out of the room was crucial.

There was a stairwell that led to some musty, stark bedrooms upstairs. Empty. A small bathroom smelled like . . . like a woman. Nail polish remover and crappy perfume and that other scent, not like a man's, the scent of a soft neck when you nuzzle it.

On the exposed shelves there was no girl stuff. No powder or lipstick. No shampoo in the shower, no flowery soaps or pantyhose.

A powerful light beamed suddenly through the bathroom window, and the intruder ducked, went down the stairs crouched. In the kitchen there was nothing but small cabinets and a half door that seemed to lead into the wall. Damn. A hiding place.

Outside, Officer Carrie Ann McCormack shined her big light across the rectory and said clearly into her radio, "This is Baker Two-six, uh, dispatch, I have an unlocked door at St. Pat's in my routine night check. Have you got word from the priest here that the door is supposed to be unsecured? Could you check for me? Sometimes after dark he leaves it open for meetings, but not this late."

"Ten-four, Baker Two-six, you want back-up or canine?"

The cop's blinding spotlight scanned the brownstone ruthlessly. Inside the utility closet, the beam snaked under the crack in the door. It pierced through the darkness inside the wide windows like hands groping for the black boots.

"Uh, not yet, dispatch."

"No notice from the priest that the door will be unsecured tonight, Two-six. Advise, please."

The female cop opened her car door and got out, talking into her hip radio as her thick cowboy boots crunched in the snow.

"Okay, advise please send canine to stand by while I try to roust Father Keenan. He might answer. Stand by."

"Standing by. Okay. All officers in vicinity be advised, Baker two-six out of vehicle in perimeter check at One Thousand Main, St. Pat's Chapel. Requesting back up and canine."

She knocked heavily.

A voice crackled. "Canine in route. Two-ten A.M. Three minutes out."

"Ten-four."

She knocked again.

The priest was rumbling. The knocking at the front door was louder, not frantic but insistent.

The priest called out loudly. "Caressa?"

Beneath the ski mask, it was a grin like the devil's. The little door to the attic went unnoticed in the heat of escaping from the kitchen when the priest left, but the name Caressa came through loud and clear. The whore was here.

The cop insisted the dog search the premises. The priest gave her coffee and asked all about her new baby whom he'd just baptized a few months before. The dog got testy and nutty at the half door, so the priest opened it and they all peered in.

"See, nothing."

The canine officer said, "He smells something other than your clothing."

From outside Officer McCormack opened the back door and looked pale. "Father, somebody was here. Inside. Footsteps lead from this back door down the steps and into the alley." Her gaze was alarmed. "Anything stolen?"

"I've been through the rooms and the chapel," he said, feeling his own dread rise. "No, nothing's gone. About the footprints, Carrie Ann—"

"Big. A big guy. I'm calling for the chopper. He's sneaking through alleys as we speak, because there were no tire tracks."

Using her radio she called for a chopper to scan the area with searchlights.

The canine officer asked mildly, "You got enemies, Father? Somebody who doesn't want to steal but might want to hurt you for other reasons?"

Officer McCormack snapped, "Perverts. I hate

perverts. Wanted to get in here and assault you. God. How sick. Assaulting an innocent priest."

Father David sat on the cold porch while they searched the bushes and the helicopter thundered overhead as if in a war zone. The police dog had rigors when the skinny nun all in black sailed around the corner of the rectory as if she were on air.

She stopped. The priest stood.

"Sister . . . Elizabeth. I'm sorry the commotion woke you over at the convent. Thank you for coming, but everything's all right now."

Officer McCormack smiled and put out a strong, firm hand. "Sister, sorry about all the noise. We had a break-in here tonight. Big guy, too. Big cowboy boots."

She peered in at the nun's stoic face. "Say, don't I know you?"

You've busted me twenty times, you snotty Annie Oakley, Caressa wanted to say, but didn't because Father David yapped up.

"Sister Elizabeth is new here, Carrie. You may have noticed her at Mass lately."

The girl cop relaxed and smiled. "Oh, sure. Nice to meet you, Sister. Call if you ever need me. It's my beat around here. Anyhow, we're calling off the chopper—no sign of the creep. Lock up, Father. And Sister, you take care."

They were gone. The whore and the priest stared at each other forlornly.

She said, "He came here."

"Yes. And in the utility closet that leads to the attic, there is melting snow. So he found it. Worst of all, I said your name when I thought the noise was you. If he was still hiding, then he knows."

She was too stoned and woozy. "Well, to hell with him."

He took her arm and led her. "Sleep for a while, Caressa. In the daylight we'll talk."

## 25

The priest had made coffee and then laid on his bed to rest a few minutes while it brewed. The whore came into his room.

She had showered, and her glistening black hair was wet. In his mind she was Diddia the ballerina again, delicate and charmed.

She sat and barely imprinted the thick quilts with her light weight. "I'm sorry I went out."

She was drunk, but hyped. Her fingers twitched when she played with a piece of quilt, and her eyes were nervous.

"Don't apologize to me, Caressa. Don't ever apologize to me."

"Why?" Now she was childlike, drunk enough to be guileless for once.

"Because. What you are, the things you do—they're not your fault."

She chuckled and lay down beside him. Her warmth seeped at him like perfume. "Well," she said so Texan it made him smile, "I got to pray. Tell me how."

"Just ask Him."

She flopped. Her long, wet hair touched his warm pajama sleeve.

"Asshole. If I asked you how to type, would you tell me to learn to spell?"

He smiled again. "Probably. I'm somewhat of a moron."

"I answered the prayer line last night."

He cinched his eyes. "Oh, Lord . . ." And then he had to laugh loudly.

"You're not mad?"

"Oh, child, no, no."

She sounded sad, if good and blasted. "I don't sleep at night. It gives me nightmares. This thing comes for me, I don't know what. But I wake up all sweaty and just terrified. You ever had a nightmare?"

He looked over at her kindly. "They're not real."

"This one is. This one is about, you know, me being in Hell and nobody can save me. I think. I never remember it. God, I wish I was normal. It's so exhausting to be screwed up."

He lay very still. She said in a girlish whisper, "You know, one time I did this married couple in a fancy hotel. They paid good, too, almost $200. It was pretty sick, him wanting to do me while I was down on her—"

"Uh, Caressa—"

She flipped onto her belly beside him, a kid at a slumber party, and in the soft lamplight she looked pink. "But after all that, I came out into the lobby, you know, and there was this giant wedding reception in this giant room, so I stepped over there to look in. And all these fancy people, beautiful clothes and stuff and pricey shoes, they were dancing. Up at the front there was this fabulous girl, my age or so, man, she was so . . . fine, all sophisticated like a, like a debutante or something. I watched a while, and this woman who looked just like Lady Bird Johnson, only it wasn't, I know, because she said her name was Mrs. Obermayer, well, she said to me, 'There's just a ton of food on that buffet, sugar, now you go get yourself a big pile of it.' And she said it was her daughter's wedding reception and that since there were about a thousand people nobody would care if I got some food, so I went in."

She put a cigarette in her mouth. He yanked it and tossed it. She shrugged and went on.

"Well, this beautiful bride, the debutante chick in this gorgeous violet going-away suit, she asks at the microphone if her daddy will come up and dance with her. So this big tall Texan hero in a tuxedo, big ol' drink of water, he was, he saunters up there and they dance. And the band—there was an actual orchestra, not a band—they played a song."

She sang. He lifted his head at the sound of her lovely singing voice. ". . . the radio and the telephone and the movies that we know—may just be passing fancies and in time may go, but oh my dear, our love is here to stay . . ."

The priest said, "Caressa, you can sing."

She slapped at air. "Oh, pishaw. Hush. I'm telling you a story. Anyway, I heard her say while they were spinning, her daddy and her, she says, 'I love you, Daddy.' That's the story."

He turned on his side to face her. "No. There's more."

She was a creamy little bony thing, all hopped up and stretching for feelings that did nothing but hurt.

The whore said, "Well, I wish, you know."

"Yeah. I know."

"That I had a daddy, and he loved me, and I wasn't just a pile of shit, that whatever hurts so bad would stop. I wish I could have friends and get some reading glasses. I wish my mother called on my birthday and my sister and I went shopping." She looked right at him. "If I had anybody. You know?"

He got up wearily, found his specs and slid them on, then took up something from his bedside drawer. "It's a Bíble. It's got in it the very perfect words for someone who wants to pray but can't." He opened it, dog-eared a page for her.

"Yeah? Why's it perfect?"

"You'll say I'm preaching."

"So just tell me without all that hoopla."

"Okay. It's perfect because it's Christ at Gethsemane, just before they took Him away to kill Him. In the first half of His prayer He's human, He's scared. He asks for it all to go away. But then, He accepts what has to happen to Him. He says okay, I'll do it. At first He's fallible, like you and me. But at last He's something better than human. He gives in to God, no matter how much He doesn't want to do it."

"Do what?"

"Die."

"I can't say all that stuff." She spoke softly.

He held out the book. "You don't have to. It's

been said for you. You can't stay here, Caressa. We have to move you."

She settled herself under his cozy quilts, the first bed she had been in in so long, and she felt herself drifting. "To where?"

"My friend Brucker. He'll have to take you for a while."

She was dozing. "So you'll be alone again. When this killer comes back for me, he'll find you. Like feeding yourself to the sharks." She was nearly gone. "Big mistake, Dave."

He turned out the lamp and sat by her for a long while, quietly listening to her breaths. The skeleton face came at him in a fit of hideous memory of the shed on that awful Halloween, as he saw her clean skin and shiny hair so close up.

He hung his head and sighed. "Oh, God, how could I have done such a thing. What kind of monster was I?"

The whore mumbled, "No, no, I won't scream."

The priest took up her frail hand and kissed it lightly.

He said wearily to the framed Christ lamenting silently on the wall, "What a great daddy I'd have been, given a choice in all this. And anyway, why don't they ever paint you smiling?"

# 26

Mick's first response to the glaring national implications of what he had just learned was to go and get laid.

Loretta of course obliged, though he didn't call first and opened with the line that has never been known to make a woman wet:

"I can't stay long."

Dawn was less than an hour away, but Loretta was in last night's clothes, there on the sofa of her little house where she passed out from drinking the night before. She looked rugged, and she felt worse than she looked.

Mick, on his mission through the living room to the bedroom didn't notice her. He took off only his pants and boots—not to bother with the shirt or socks, he figured, for this gal. And he lay down.

She was frantic, flapping, combing down the wild mane madly and talking stupidly from the bathroom while trying to repair her wretched face.

"Oh, baby, I'm so glad you came over." Swack, swack at the mane with the brush. "I told my parents last night that they can meet you this weekend. Oh, Mickey, it'll be so great. They'll just luuuuv you. I told them that you're just so wonderful—" Blah. Blah. She chattered, though her head banged and the pasty inside of her mouth felt stuck together.

He said flatly, "You almost through in there, or what?"

She came in, towering, a look in her eyes that screamed a pathetic plea for his approval. He looked away. "Turn out the light, Loretta. And put that old dog of yours out on the porch. He'll bark and it'll screw up my orgasm."

Loretta reluctantly said, "Well, Mickey, he's so old, and it's so cold outside, honey—"

"Fine. Leave him in and I'll go."

She flapped again, her long frame jarring even taller in panic. "No, baby, no, don't go. I'll get him and put him out. I'll make coffee afterward. Would you like that? Gourmet coffee? And I have bagels. We could sit and talk and—"

He was in the dark. The edge of his voice made her ashamed and somehow aware that she should stab him in the chest and claim self-defense.

"No. No coffee afterward. I have to go. Now put out the stupid mutt and come lie down."

She did. The sex took fifteen minutes. And in it she was reminded of why she didn't stab him in the chest. It was good sex, not romantic or emotional in the least or even slightly loving, but he could do things to her in a way other men hadn't.

He started dressing immediately. In the dark she heard his belt clanking and his cowboy boots make a sucking sound as he put his feet into them. That was that. He headed for the front door. She followed, panicked again, begging.

"Mickey, honey—"

"I asked you not to call me that. I told you, Jackie called me that. Which is it, Loretta, are you just forgetful or plain retarded?"

She hung her head, felt the adrenaline of first seeing him and thinking it would be different fade away in disappointment. "I'm sorry, darling." She tried perky, pretending she wasn't awash in repulsion by herself. "But you are coming to meet my daddy, right, darling?"

He was as icy as the treacherous winter wind singing against the windows. "I'm going out of town for a couple of days, but I should be back by then. If I am, I'll eat with your dad."

She felt a sigh of relief and said cheerfully, "One cup of coffee, baby?"

He didn't feel sorry for her. He felt contempt, enough to stay for the sick pleasure of watching yet another woman degrade herself for him.

He deflated. "Sure. One cup."

She squealed and ran for cups and the cream. Back in the living room she curled her immense self at his feet. He moved sideways, away from her.

"Mickey, where are you going out of town?"

He sighed as if she had just pried into his personal finances. "The state mental hospital."

She poked a bottom lip at him. "Can I go? I'll be quiet, and . . ." she licked the knee of his blue jeans and made moaning sounds, "and I'll be so horny for you."

He squinted at her, almost laughed. "Loretta,

have you ever been to that horrible, dusty, godforsaken town? There are only two reasons to go there.
To check into the mental institution or to ask for directions somewhere else. It's horrible there. Cold.
Depressing. No, forget it. You'd be bitching in an
hour that you're bored."

She sounded teary. Her coffee cup wobbled and
she slammed it harder than he preferred. "Well,
Mickey, you just never take me anywhere. Bars.
That's all."

He said cruelly, "You never seem to mind as long
as I keep buying."

She whined. "Just last night at that bar a guy tried
to pick me up, but I wouldn't do it because I
thought you might show up. And he liked me."

He butted in. "And how long did you have to play
him and flirt with him before he thought it might
be worth it?"

She scoffed. "I want to be part of your life, Mickey, and I want you to be in my life—"

He set down the coffee. "I think this is where the
cowboy rides away, girl—"

More panic. "Oh, Mickey, please, I'm sorry. You
misunderstood! Please don't be angry. It's not fair
for you to be angry about things I do when you've
never told me not to do them. It's so unfair!"

He glared, standing over her. She started to cry.
"Loretta, I have to tell you not to get blind drunk
and throw yourself at me like a sleazy shotput
every time you see me."

She sobbed. "Please. Just take me out of town
with you. Anywhere."

His smile widened. "Even the mental hospital?"

"Anywhere, baby, just let me sleep once overnight with you. Please. You slept overnight with *her*
for years. Why not me, just once?"

He stepped over her and said coldly, "Fine. I'll
get you tomorrow afternoon at four. Don't be late.
And don't give me shit when we get there that
you're bored. And don't bust my chops over Jackie.
She's none of your business. In fact, I'm none of
your business."

"I'm sorry, baby. I was out of line. Don't go."

He bent to her face. She closed her eyes to the
gritting of his teeth. "I told you, in the beginning,
I'd been with her a long time."

Her sob fell like an anchor. "Yeah. And then you
told me it was over, you hated her, she chased you.
And you said I was so sexy and you wanted me so
much and we had to do it and be together. You said
all that bullshit, and now I care about you and now
it was all lies! Oh, god, Mickey, you just wanted to
seduce me. I'm just the flavor of the month."

Mick sighed, "Look, I said I'll take you, okay?
Just . . . stop bitching."

He closed the door. She steeled herself. The sun
was trying, but could only make the gray morning
a blanch of unpolished silver. In the kitchen Loretta put bourbon into her coffee. She sat quietly at
the table and began making a list of what to take
for her romantic adventure with this man of her
dreams.

She chewed the pencil, then wrote. "I'll need new
panties, some real sexy ones from Victoria's Secret,
and a hot bra, and some nasty little thing to sleep
in. A scented candle or two for the motel room, a

book to pretend I'm reading. Let's see, lots of perfumed soap and powder."

She let out a dreamy breath. "Finally. All night with him. Wow." She lit a candle on the table, basked a moment in its glow. Her liquor breath fueled it to a sizzling flare. She remembered then, and let in the decrepit old dog who was nearly frozen to death on the porch.

She said to him, "Puppy, got to remember to pack a flask and my diet pills. All night with him. Just like it's for real. Me and Mick!"

The old dog glared at her from beside the fireplace, and he growled deeply enough to show the few teeth he had.

# 27

Mick drove, gripping the wheel. Jackie's house when he pulled into the driveway was completely dark. He sat a moment, then dialed on his cell phone.

"Hey, sweetheart, can I come in? If you look out the window, you'll see I'm already here. I'm driving my truck this week, for a while maybe. Can I come in, baby?"

Jackie felt warm and rested. Her sheets and hair smelled soapy and sexy. She wasn't fully awake from a long night's sleep.

"What do you want, Mick?"

Through the window he saw her bedside lamp come on. He needed her woozy to manipulate her better, so he spoke softly. "Coffee, sweetheart. I stopped and got gourmet coffee at Starbucks for us. I'll make a fire for us, we can sit by it. There's stuff I need to tell you. My Jeep's stolen. I'm in a little trouble with the police. I need you, Jackie. Please."

The phone almost grew warm in his icy hand when she said with her voice like an orgasm, "All

right, Mick. Use your key. I am worried about you,
and I care for you, but I won't do that to myself. I
won't be used."

He closed the phone, juggled the coffee mugs,
used his key. Her house smelled like her—sweet,
exotic, spicy, like fresh eucalyptus. He found her in
her lush, textured bedroom, sitting upright on the
lavish sheets and blankets, looking at him as if he
were aiming a gun at her.

"Jackie, oh my god, hold on to me." He put down
the coffee and went to the side of the bed, where he
kneeled. Her hands in his hair were as wonderful
as a warm tropical waterfall.

He kissed her juicy mouth, and she sank back.
"You've been with her. I can taste it, foul and foreign."

He cuddled her. "Why did I leave you?"

"It was about you, Mick. It was all about what you
needed and how you could get it. It had nothing to
do with me, or the other girls. Only you, getting
what you wanted." She stroked his hair tenderly
and whispered, "Mick. Are you losing your mind, or
are you just now finding it?"

He said sadly, "I swept her away in the beginning, I said things to her that other men never say.
You know me so well, and she didn't, and I had a
chance to . . . be somebody else for a while." His
gaze vibrated pain. "Jackie, I'm in trouble. This girl,
she won't go away unless I hurt her so much she
can't stand it, and I keep trying, but she won't go. I
keep saying and doing things that no other woman
would stand for, and she doesn't go. She calls. She
cries. And the police. Jesus, I'm in trouble with the

police. And now, there's a story I've got to write, but it'll get me killed, I swear to god."

She said smoothly, "Mick, women stay for the lies. We leave when you say the truth. When you say good-bye." She looked wisely at him. "Mick, you must always write your stories. They anchor you. This big story, you steel yourself, and do it. Tell me the trouble," she whispered, and she pulled him close.

He began. She didn't interrupt. She only kept him close to her chest and patted his back gently.

He told her about the Bahrain oil fields, the insider information. He put his trust and his life in her hands.

# 28

At 7 A.M. the unthinkable happened. The entire detectives' area of the downtown division went silent.

The normal zest died. The clanking typewriters that churned out hundreds of standard homicide reports stopped. The yakking into telephones by more than twenty of the day-shift cops fell silent. The mindless and often antagonistic banter collapsed into total quiet. The dirty jokes went unfinished.

Brucker, in his glass office, felt it first and then heard it, and so he looked up. There in the doorway to the detective division stood billionaire Arthur Yates in a sheared calfskin coat, elegant suede black slacks, cowboy boots, and a beaver-skin Stetson the color of his pants. His black braid twisted over his shoulder and down his left arm. His eyes were clear, even vivacious. He removed his hat.

"Mornin', boys," he blurted, breaking with a smile that glistened. "I'm looking for Lieutenant Brucker."

One fat detective who was by now so impressed he was mute—not many actual billionaires dropped into the joint—pointed. Yates nodded and strutted past the cops, their eyes riveted to his clothing, which was worth more than all the cars in the parking lot.

Brucker stood, felt himself growl. Yates popped in, hung his hat on the hat tree, and sat.

"You rang, Lieutenant?"

Brucker chewed a lip. The showmanship was sickening. "Yeah. I left word on your secretary's voice mail that I needed to see you today."

"And here I am." There was mischief all over this cat like red hot paint.

Brucker sat, cleared his throat, found the papers and wrote on his notes. "Mr. Yates, last night I spoke with your butler, Mr. Anson Noble. Between 11 P.M. and midnight Saturday he doesn't remember seeing Vic Farron in your private den. For that matter," Brucker paused lethally, "he doesn't remember you there, either, or bringing in martinis, or even hearing your Rolls pull into the garage, over which, I might add, he lives."

Yates sat back arrogantly and smiled again. "So?"

Brucker felt his jaw tighten. "So, Mr. Yates, I also spoke by telephone with two downstairs maids who live at your residence, and your chef. The chef left your dinner in a heated buffet in your private den by 10 P.M., per your instructions, and the next morning he found the buffet and the food untouched. From what I hear, it doesn't look like you came home at all Saturday night. The night of the hit and run."

Yates pulled from his breast pocket a long, skinny

cigar—Cuban, Brucker figured—and started to light it. Brucker spoke.

"You can't smoke in here."

Yates laughed easily. "Sure I can. I own the building. Aw, don't look surprised. It's just real estate. When y'all boys wanted new digs a few years back, I had this big old place just cultivating cockroaches." He lit the cigar with a solid gold lighter, heaved out, very relaxed. "Lemme see, here, Lieutenant. I'm thinking. You know what I used to do on all those homey, cozy weekends I used to spend with my granddaddy Arthur Percival Yates the Very First at his ranch or at his French villa or in his cottage up in Vermont or sometimes even at his flat over near Trafalgar? I was knee-high to a whippersnapper back then, and first thing Arthur the Very First taught me to do was make martinis. You get me? I'm good at it, too. Making martinis to me is kind of like jacking off. Don't need help, because nobody does it better than yourself, you know?"

"You didn't touch the buffet."

"Just come from a dinner, you see."

Brucker stood. "Your friend doesn't have an alibi for the time of the hit and run. And neither do you."

Yates stood, but he was maddeningly composed. An ash fell on the floor. "It's not Farron's car. Or mine."

There was nowhere to go, and yet Brucker hated this swishy, cocksure asshole. "Would you be willing, Mr. Yates, to authorize me to see your cell phone records from the night of the banquet?"

He took up his beaver-skin Stetson, twirled it like

a pool shark with a wad in his pocket. "I got eight of them. Sure. Help yourself. Plus I got two car phones, six lines in my mansion, a car fax, and about 200,000 phones down there at my office building. You knock yourself out, Brucker."

The picture frame on Brucker's desk came into focus. Yates bent to it. "Pretty girl. Even for a sister, huh?"

Brucker's belly broiled. "How do you know that's Janelle?"

He plunked on the hat. "Aw, I just figured, is all. That whole story about you two being separated in a bunch of foster homes, and then you finding her and uniting with her after all those years. Then that cocksucker Ramsey gets her all nuts and she kills herself—"

Brucker, without a thought, came over the desk and knotted the skinny Yates's shirt into his fist. His nostrils flared and his teeth gritted and he felt the sweat. "You checked me out, you goddamned trust fund fucking trash—"

Yates laughed, wasn't afraid. "Boy, are you retarded enough to wrangle me or just too crazy not to know better. Huh?"

They were there suddenly, staring into his glass office like Mafia dons with rippled muscles and earphones connected to an army of more goons. Yates's security people. Brucker let him go.

He asked Yates, "And them. The goons. They go everywhere with you, all the time, no matter what?"

He had an idea; the security people would know where Yates went. Yates was ahead of him.

"When I want them to."

"Did you want them to Saturday night? Were they on you and Farron the whole time?"

"Kidnappers don't rest, Lieutenant. I am a billionaire, and the ransom would be sweet. I have bodyguards."

Brucker bristled. "I asked you a question—"

Yates for the first time didn't smile. "Simmer down. No, they weren't on me Saturday night."

They glared. The goons flexed. Yates straightened his shirt.

"So, Yates, nobody knows where you and Vic Farron were at the time of the hit and run."

His hat brim shadowed his eyes. The cigar smoke coiled around the brim as if scarves were dancing. "I reckon not, boy. Not even you. I got home between eleven and eleven-thirty. Victor Farron was with me. I don't need an alibi. I'm not a suspect."

"Farron was with you? He made some stops, Yates. Where did you take him? He said he changed clothes and he got his car."

"You already know where he changed clothes."

He came toward Brucker, fearlessly, some blistering rage surfacing suddenly. He said very softly, "Little man, do not fuck with me. If Texas wasn't a state, we'd be the fourth most powerful nation in this world from pure assets. Gross National Product. Military. Oil. Land. Shipping at the coast. Hell, even international trade. They say California would be number three, but I don't know. They got the fruits and nuts; Texas, we got the guns and the ammo. Most of all, we'd rule in money. And guess who'd own the most of all those prize assets and have the most money in this new, powerful sovereignty called the Nation of Texas? Me."

Just as softly Brucker said, "I'm going to knock the fuck out of you in two seconds, Yates."

Yates smiled again. "Just what I'd expect from a Princeton man. But see, at Harvard, we learned to say I'm going to knock the fuck out of you in two seconds, and then do it in one second. You have yourself a nice day now. Any more questions you call one of my hundred or so personal attorneys. They ain't got shit to do all day anyway, me being so squeaky clean and all."

Brucker said coldly, "If you're lying for your friend, you're obstructing justice. It's a crime."

Yates twirled his ten-gallon hat and grinned so his eyes lit up. "Boy, billionaires don't have friends—except other billionaires. The rest of you, we just let you call us your friend, so we can use your little brains to do the tedious chores. That's how we stay billionaires. Run the game. Never play it."

He went. The goons followed. The whole room of detectives drooled as he passed.

Brucker sat, aching to sucker punch Yates and knowing that a cool head was his only real weapon in figuring out who killed the bag lady. One of them. Ramsey, the reporter. Farron, the boss. Yates, the billionaire. He hung his head, sure that things couldn't get worse that day.

His phone rang, and he knew not only could things get worse, they could get downright unbelievably bad. The receptionist outside the secured area said, "Uh, I got a priest here to see you. Father David Keenan. He's on his way back."

Lieutenant Brucker picked up his cup of cold coffee and threw it as hard as he could at a picture on his wall. It splattered all over the framed face of former President Lamar Green, but Brucker personally didn't give a damn.

## 29

$V$ictor Farron's office door was open, as usual, by 8 A.M. Things looked normal. Classical music lulled from his big stereo on the shelves. Steam pirouetted up from his coffee mug set in the middle of a pile of out-of-state newspapers on his desk. Drapes were open on his expanse of windows that scanned a drizzly skyline. Nothing seemed out of sorts.

Except Farron, when Mick found him. He stepped in, and Farron looked up like a man who had just read his own obituary and felt a pitchfork in his butt. His suit was good, but his visage was wan. He was slumped and haggard at his desk.

Rain slathered the tall, wide windows and made eerie prisms on the walls.

"Vic, I've been calling you all weekend."

Farron said hoarsely, "Come in, Mick. I phoned you, too, at home and here and at your health club." His throne of a leather chair sagged under his weight suddenly as he sank in it. "I'm sorry about the mix-up with your car. Seems you and I are in a maelstrom here. Pour yourself some coffee."

Mick did, then set it down and stood at the span of windows, watching the rain, hands in his blue jeans pockets. "I called Brucker early yesterday morning after some crime-scene guys came for my tux." He stared at Vic, who seemed to be hypnotized by the lugubrious music and the gore of rain prisms. "He said you didn't use my car after all."

"No. I didn't drive it. I gave the keys to Archie Dane down at the twenty-four hour security desk, for you to pick up there when you came back."

"Uh, Vic," Mick went purposefully to the side of the desk and stood stoic, wanting a clear gauge of reaction. "Archie Dane died yesterday morning. Full-blown coronary."

"Well, we all knew about his heart problems—"

Mick tightened. "It was under control, his wife said."

He pierced Vic's silence. "Seems Archie went for a walk yesterday afternoon before coming to work, and collapsed in the park. No symptoms. Nothing. Just sudden death."

Victor cleared his throat, messed with opening some of the newspapers he read daily. "Well, Archie was sixty and—"

Vitriol ignited. "And, Vic, he was also the only person who knew if you really turned in my keys to the desk."

Thunder rolled gently. Victor stood.

"Wrong, Ramsey. I know I gave him the keys."

They faced off. Words didn't count on this battlefield of the wits; cunning did.

Victor said, dripping contempt, "I heard the lab found blood on the sleeve of your tux."

Their face-off became a step closer when Mick moved up. "Yeah? Who told you that?"

"We have a reporter on the hit-and-run story, of course, but we're not naming you as a suspect. Until you're arrested."

Mick fumed. "I was walking when I left the banquet. I found a bum some assholes had just beaten up in the alley. I took him to a diner, cleaned up his face, and bought him some breakfast. He must've bled on me." He grinned. "And anyway, I have people—the bum, the bartender, the priest—who saw me during the time of the . . . accident—"

Victor squinted. Accident? A word of such convenience, he realized. He sat again, but kept an eye on hothead Ramsey.

Mick went on. "And you have only Yates, whose servants never saw him come home that night."

The phone rang on Vic's desk. He let voice mail get it. The seconds ticked as the phone jangled and made them each twitchy. The rain percolated on the windows.

Victor said, "Brucker will polygraph us soon, next week. And they'll find the bum, test his blood. What bartender?"

"Brian. At the Dublin. The one who has cut you off so many times and driven you home."

Victor sighed dismissively. "Well, we're lucky, Mickey. There are stories popping like crazy out there, so we're down the food chain for the hit-and-run story. We've got dead hookers, a dying local congresswoman, a sheriff who it turns out is a pool hustler, plus we've got mavericks and cowboys and rangers in various stages of indictment or indignance. So. What're you working on today?"

Mick held back a crafty grin. "Don't know. I'm dropping the SEC thing. It didn't go anywhere."

"What do you mean?" Vic asked sharply, his eyes calculating over the top edge of a page from the *Milwaukee Journal.*

Mick shrugged, sipped. "I mean the leads were cold."

They stared again, harshly, with venom. Vic shrugged, too. "It happens."

Mick sizzled a moment and said, "You saved my job a year ago, Vic. I thought we were friends."

Victor didn't look up. His dislike was fizzing like the rain on the windows. "Fifteen years as my best reporter, and then bang, two sexual harassment suits inside the company. I had them paid, but not because we're friends." When he did look up finally it was like the cock of a pistol. "And I didn't cover you because your midlife crisis evoked empathy, either. I saved you, Mick, as one good ol' boy to another. We can't let the bitches have all of us."

Mick arced a brow. "So it was hating women for you, not brotherhood with me."

"Brotherhood is all about hating women, Ramsey." Victor chuckled rudely.

Mick stopped at the door and turned back. "Yeah, Vic, I know. I just wonder if you hate me enough to frame me for murder."

Vic chuckled again. "Mickey, along with sex addict, pathological liar, dirty rotten slut, golden bullshitter, and the best reporter I know, add paranoiac to your resume."

# 30

Rain swirled sideways at him, but Brucker didn't care. He was mesmerized by the trains, staring from under his ten-gallon black hat like a train robber mulling his choices.

From where he stood on the high, long, sloping bridge he could see the entire switching yard, hundreds of freight trains down below him, a moving, screeching web of huge rail cars. One by one the mammoths lurched up a small incline and stopped, while a worker uncoupled them from one another. Their air brakes whistled—whale sounds, so exotic, as if calling out hello or good-bye to each other. The endless lines of rail cars came here from all over the country to be separated and rejoined and rerouted. Brucker liked to stand, to imagine them jostling through the countrysides at night while boys in farmhouse beds dreamed of journeying. He loved to watch each car peak the incline and then sail downward to one of the fifty or so tracks that spiraled outward. And then came the squeals, the whales laughing, as the mammoth's air brakes slowed it to an almost precision crash to the car it was to join.

Brucker stood just to the side of the sprawling bridge over the railyard, impervious to the slashing rain as it banged his umbrella. The switching of the rail cars made him centered and sane, somehow, just reminding him that the world is big and his problems were merely fleeting . . . adjustments, was the word he picked.

Angie Bianchi came bitching through the tall grass toward his perch, cursing and swacking at weeds that clung to her too-small raincoat. Her Moe hair was drenched, and she was vastly unhappy with the whole scene when she reached him.

"One question, Lieutenant. Why did they say I'd find you here?" She took refuge under his umbrella. "Are you like working on a merit badge for weirdness?"

He puffed his pipe sedately. "I come here a lot. I like the trains. They're romantic."

She huffed, "My granddaddy worked down there for forty years, coupling those cars. He lost two fingers and got skin cancer from the summer sun."

"Don't matter, Bianchi. He was happy, doing a job like that. Moving the earth, promoting commerce. Good, honest, hard work."

She slipped in a mud spot and cursed again. "All right, Brucker, what gives? I'm up here on a mud hill in the pouring rain watching trains go by, and you're being cryptic."

He smiled through the pipe smoke. Didn't look at her, just kept focused on the wailing of those air brakes. "Tell me what you've got."

She struggled with her boxcar of a frame to find her notepad, flipped it, cursed the rain again, lost her footing and then caught herself. The massive train engines chugged, power in motion.

"Three dead hookers—"

"No, the hit-and-run first."

"Here?" Bianchi squealed. "You want a case briefing while we stand in mud and get drenched by—"

He turned at her, not pleasantly. "Bianchi, talk to me."

She composed herself. "First, there are no surveillance cameras in the newspaper garage. Never have been. So we got no films of anyone driving Ramsey's Jeep off the lot. The lab found blood on his tux sleeve—none on your boy Farron's, by the way—but Ramsey says in his statement to me that he found a bum who'd been rolled, washed him at a diner john, and paid for the guy to order food. So I look for a bum based on the description, which fits every toothless reprobate in every gutter downtown, except our bum wears corrective shoes, Ramsey says, so I'm looking. The diner waitress remembers a tall, dark guy bringing in a bum. It caused commotion when he dragged this loser into the john all bloody, but the bum came out cleaned up and sporting a $20 bill. He ordered eggs, pancakes, coffee, two sweet rolls and a bowl of red beans with rice—"

"The guy who brought him in?"

A fat raindrop gouged Angie's eye and she squeaked at it. "Ouch! Shit! The tall dark guy didn't wait around. The waitress couldn't ID Ramsey from his file photo I got from the newspaper because when the bum came in bleeding everybody got all upset and confused. But she remembers thinking at the time that the tall guy was way good-looking and real built. So it sounds like Ramsey. The only problem is, Ramsey said he took the bum in just before midnight. Before he went to the rectory and while he was out walking and our bag lady was becoming road kill. Our girl, Rosie the waitress, who remembers the bum and the big hunk, can't say the time because she pulled a double shift, 11 A.M. to 2 A.M. that day to earn a little extra money. She has no idea what time it was when the bum and the hunk came in. Not even a guess. She was cranky and tired and didn't give a shit at that point."

Beneath them, in an open boxcar that sailed below, a hobo lying under a filthy blanket waved up at them as the train sped along on an outside through track. It wasn't stopping here.

Brucker asked, with his black eyes seizing her almost meanly, somehow angrily, "So you'll be requesting a blood sample from Ramsey. And you'll cross it with the blood on the tux, as well as the blood from the bag lady."

Angie studied him. He was too sad, too distraught. "Well, hell yes. I'm on it, man. What's with you?"

"Don't hammer the waitress. If Ramsey's got no alibis, that just gives me a major boner. But make her be honest."

"Okay."

Cars sped over the bridge beyond them and made foam sprays that rose up and swirled madly. Brucker asked, "How about fibers on their clothes?"

"Nothing unusual. Their own hair. Are you aware we're standing out in the lightning, and holding a metal umbrella rod that begs for a bolt? I have one pair of work shoes, Brucker, and lightning will melt the bottom of them. Anyway, we don't have the Jeep fibers to compare to their clothes, but Ramsey's statement says he has leather interior and common car carpet, so I cross-checked at the auto dealer's place. Ramsey and Farron both have standard Jeep fibers on their cowboy boots, but just that day Ramsey drove Farron to a business lunch, an editorial board think-tank thing, I don't know—"

Brucker contemplated aloud. "So I need the tux Yates wore that night. Yeah. Because he was at the table, and maybe he took Ramsey's keys and went to get a hooker for after the porn film at his mansion." He puffed. Rain sogged the smoke instantly as it drifted. "Mick doesn't sport Art Yates around to luncheons, goddamn it, so one Jeep fiber on Farron's clothes puts him in the Wagoneer, and no servants remember him home at ground zero time."

Lightning screamed. So did Angie Bianchi.

Brucker seemed to regain consciousness. "Okay, all right, let's get coffee, out of this stuff. Can you make it down the hill?"

"Yeah. Just put a sign on my butt that says 'Wide Load.'"

He took he arm. "So. Don't eat so much."

She griped and slid. "If I didn't eat anything but my words for six months I'd still have my mother's ass. Genetics sucks."

Brucker struggled her down to their cars parked by the roadside. He closed his umbrella under the bridge, and they could hear waves of cars clattering above.

He said somberly, "We've got to talk about your dead hookers. I, uh." He stopped, took a breath, looked at Angie as if he were identifying her body at the morgue. "They're not being robbed, are they, Bianchi?"

She blinked. "No. Just—"

"Tortured," Brucker said flatly.

"Yeah. Like somebody's trying to make them talk."

Brucker took off his black Stetson and tossed it into his car, turned back to Angie, and asked cautiously, "You talked to the priest yet?"

Angie felt befuddled, out of the loop. "No. Not the girlfriend either, Ramsey's so-called alibi, and not the bartender yet. And what? The priest and the girlfriend have what to do with my dead hooker cases?"

He felt his heart thud. "I saw the priest this morning. He came to me. I know why your hookers are being killed, and I know who your killer is looking for." She felt him swallow before he asked, solemn as a death knoll, "Detective Bianchi, do you ever look the other way?"

She smiled and it fattened her already fat cheeks. "You mean like one for all and all for one, us cops? Sure. I saw *Serpico*."

Brucker tried a lame grin. "Follow me then," he said.

They pulled away in separate cars.

# 31

At noon the whore slammed into consciousness. She sat bolt upright, gasping, pale as a tombstone. Her hair and skin were hideous. She had to think.

She was in a bed—swatting through cobwebs and nausea—the priest's bed. My god. She looked at the brazen sun slashing the room through the thin curtains. I had sex with the priest? Oh god. And then, it came, no, he got up as she got in.

In his small bathroom she went to her knees and vomited blood. The gagging hurt her whole body through, and she stayed on her knees, skinny arms wrapped around her sunken middle, panting and wanting to weep. She flushed, rinsed her mouth, staggered weakly back to the bed. Last night—she couldn't remember it, and the waves of belly pain that wracked her caught her off guard so that she doubled over into a brittle, skeletal ball in the bed. She went out. She remembered leaving. There were muddled visions of the streets, the cocaine, the men who smelled like putrid garbage humping her.

The noon Mass ended. The church bells pealed. The whore cried like a baby.

The priest came straight into the room like an emergency ward doctor, rushing at her. He sat, took her shoulders and turned her toward him. She saw pure panic in his eyes.

"Caressa, you have to dress in the habit. I'll get you some soup and bread, and then I'm taking you somewhere else, somewhere very safe."

The blood taste in her mouth was horrible. She answered in a whisper. "I went out. I fucked some guys—"

He got up, brought her a damp washcloth and set it on her aching face. "Don't think about it. Listen to me. And look at this."

A newspaper rattled in her face. She opened her eyes, and the priest took pity with a sigh and put his glasses on her. The headline screamed that three hookers had been killed in the downtown area between early Sunday morning and early Monday. They had been tortured and variously lacerated, stabbed, strangled, bitten, and had their bones snapped. She pushed it away.

"The price of doing business, Dave—"

He cursed, and that got her bleary attention. "Dammit, he's looking for you. He's trying to get them to tell him where you are! Caressa, he came here last night, don't you remember?" Then he sighed mightily. Of course not, she wouldn't remember, she was drugged to dementia when she came back. "A friend of mine is taking you, to hide you. He's a policeman—"

She was out of bed, feet on the floor, an explo-

sion of mangled hair and flapping arms and
naked, bare legs out from under his long black
sweater that she'd slept in. The energy seemed to
have come from nowhere, some survival rush that
waylaid the hangover and malaise of moments before.

"You motherfucker." She came at him, flailing,
and he caught her wrists when she went for his
face. His glasses flew off her face. She spat on him.
"You goddamned asshole. Let go of me!"

She struggled, but he held her wrists, so she
spat again and tried to slap him. Her feet went
suddenly, flying at him from all directions until
he spun her and flung her down on the bed. They
were tangled there, he on top, she facedown and
blurting more profanities than he had heard in all
his life.

He was panting. She was raging.

"Cocksucker, bastard. Let me up and get my gun
and shoot your lowlife ass you—"

He was stronger than he had known, with this
wild pony fighting beneath him. He had her
pinned. "Caressa, we need help!"

She spewed at him, "There's no *we*, asshole.
There's me, and you aren't shit to me. And I'll cut
your balls off and boil them and eat them before I'll
spend ten minutes with a fucking cop! You busted
my confession. They'll arrest me! I hate you, let me
up!"

Her nose was bleeding on the sheets. He could
see the warm red ooze, and she was crying so hard,
so angry and animalistic. His grasp was bruising
her, he could feel it happening to this scrawny

thing under him. And he knew the most awful thing—he knew that day by day, now minute by minute, the whore was dying.

"He's not helping me as a cop. He's helping us as a friend, my friend, oh god, you're bleeding everywhere, Jesus." His voice was bereft, and he felt near tears. "God, Father, please be here, come here, let us feel you." His words broke, his tone cracked in sadness, so he whispered, "Holy Spirit, bring us your comfort and love and wisdom. Please, come."

She screamed with force he didn't imagine that she had left beneath him. *"You make me so fucking sick with this sick fucking religious shit! Let me go!"*

So he did. He lifted himself. She was tiny and decompressed and mangled on the bed. She was sobbing uncontrollably.

The priest said, "He is my friend."

She sat up and shook her fists at him. "Why? Because you forgave him for butt-fucking his mother once, and so now he owes you enough to hide a drug addict whore in *his* attic? A cop? Goddamn you. Cops don't have friends. A cop. You told a cop and now he's coming to get me." She fell and sobbed more. "Oh, what you've done to me."

Her agony washed over him like the blood dripping from her nose and staining her chest. He put on his glasses and sat by her. "Caressa, the world is not orange."

He patted her face with the wet cloth. She let him clean her while she said sadly, "Fuck you."

"The drugs make it look orange to you, or slant-ed or cratered, but it isn't. There are people who care."

She swatted away his hand. "Oh my god. A cop. Why didn't you just call a firing squad?"

He wiped some more, and she let him again. Her blood stained his hands. He said to her as he swabbed gently, "It's real, little girl."

She looked at him, so battle fatigued. "Do not start. And anyway, how do you know, you stupid old fart. You liar. You busted my confession. People like you, always busting me and lying to me—"

He was finished cleaning her. She was a sight better to look at without the gore on her face. Her eyes were pretty, and he could see the ballerina scampering through the woods, the moonlight dusting her so that she became a fairy hardly touching the ground as she skipped the wet leaves. The skeleton stalked. The priest could see himself darting through the trees and the moonbeams behind her, toward the shed.

He said to her, his heart so leaden with guilt, his hands smeared with her blood, "Someday, Caressa, I'll get sick. And they'll put me in the hospice for dying priests, and I'll be alone."

She cracked, "So fucking what." But her baleful eyes stayed on his.

Outside, the sky darkened as a cloud drifted, and a cold breeze played the wind chimes like teeth chattering, like fingers tickling her hair. She could feel spirits and spooks whispering around her. The priest's hands, his long fingers. She felt something sinister and sickening, something that made her want to run screaming.

But his voice was a salve. His eyes were so soft and blue.

"When I'm there, and I'm dying, there'll be no abiding wife, no grieving children, no mournful grandkids. Just me. Already my eyes are going, and too soon I'll be nearly blind. My life, my choice, you see, to never be a husband, a father, to give everything over to the vow of serving God—it hits me some days, days when people like you scream that it isn't real."

Another cloud drifted, and the room went darker. She could not stop watching his lithe, slender hands.

She said dryly, "I know you. Don't I?"

Their gaze lingered, penetrated. He said, "Not yet. It's not time."

She said, very hushed, "In my nightmare. There are hands in my nightmare. Hands like yours."

He said, even more hushed, as the breeze became a squall that twisted leaves and tapped the windows, "It's got to be real, Caressa. All of it. God, eternal peace, the plan."

She whimpered at him. "Why?"

"Because I've bet my life on it."

She watched him, less testy but just as cynical. "So this lousy stinking cop, why does he owe you? What horrible thing did you forgive him for anyhow?"

He stood, touched her hair, helped her up. "I'm not here to forgive. I'm here to remind the people that God forgives."

She leaned on him as they walked, "Yeah. So, oh holy one, maybe sometime you'll remind us that we should forgive God for the sunken wrecks He makes of our lives down here."

He led her to the shower. At the kitchen table he sat down on legs so wobbly with dread and horror that he almost fell.

# 32

Angie's lunch plate arrived at the table and Brucker groaned. "Man, Bianchi, why don't you just order a coronary with extra gravy?"

The chicken-fried steak was smothered in it, and so were the mashed potatoes which also were pooled in extra butter and salt. The two giant biscuits were like pillows of baked lard.

She dug in and said with her mouthful, "Once, I tried this diet, eating six to ten small meals a day instead of three big ones. Turns out, my idea of 'small' rivals Dante for the term gluttony. I gained eleven pounds on that one."

Brucker sipped his coffee and smiled at her. Her cheeks bulged with food. She pointed a fork at him. "I'm healthy as a brood mare, kid. And I'm happy as a pig in mud, too. I see you looking at these gals, the skinny ones who look like they've never so much as seen a picture of a burrito, but me, screw it. I want lots of everything. Excitement. Food. Beer. Sex. Kids. Money. You go to bed with Miss Concentration Camp queen if you want. I'm going to find a man who likes me, my gusto."

He laughed. She said flatly, "By the way, I can't find a cabbie who picked up Ramsey's girl—uh, Loretta, is it—at the Dublin anytime Saturday night. Ramsey said she left in a cab and he started walking downtown and came upon the rolled bum, but the cab companies don't jive that the chick took a ride."

Brucker went serious like a Buddha. "Well, we may as well get to it, I reckon."

The young black waitress poured him more coffee and gave him the come-fuck-me eye. He may have blushed. When she was gone he said, "The priest, Father Keenan, he's hiding a girl. She's a hooker. And she was with the hit-and-run driver Saturday night. In the car. She can't positively ID anybody, the priest said, but she's got info."

Her spoon stopped just before it hit banana pudding. "Brucker, most excellent! Let's pick her up."

He frowned. "No. It can't go down like that. It has to be on the QT, she can't be involved."

Angie stopped chewing. "She's a material witness—"

"I know that," he said harshly. "But the priest, I owe him. I'm going to take the girl home, question her, get all I can, and then I want her to bunk tomorrow night with you. Wednesday I get her anonymously into rehab. Father Keenan says she's real sick."

Angie stared, stony. "You're going to hide a material witness? And obstruct justice? And suppress the prosecution's evidence? God, Brucker, what do you owe this priest? And by the way, I don't owe him a damn thing, but now my career's on the line, too, if I go along with you."

They leaned in. No one could hear them in the clattering, noisy diner, but they felt secretive.

"Bianchi, look what it brings together for us. Your hookers are dead because the driver was trying to find the girl who's hiding at the rectory. He got a call after midnight, the priest did, threatening him if he had the girl. I'm checking suspects' phones already, but I'm sure it was a pay phone. If it was Mick, maybe this big gal, the alibi, didn't take a cab because she was with him, maybe they're sicko and wanted a sex sandwich and maybe the big gal is covering for Ramsey. You can go there in your questioning of her. The hooker saw a gold and diamond Rolex and the guy used a cell phone and talked newspaper business before the hit. We've got that. And the guy shot at her as she ran, so we can find bullet chips in some of those old brick buildings and match the gun to its owner."

She screeched a whisper. "But it's dick without her testimony in the trial!"

"We'll have the physical evidence!"

Angie squealed. "Brucker, it's a crime. If she's scared, we'll put her up in a place and get a unit outside and she can go into witness protection after the trial—"

The tension mounted. He said, "No. Look, there'll be physical evidence from one of these guys all over your dead hookers. We don't need the girl. We'll get what she's got and then ship her out—"

"Would you tell me why?"

He sat back again, surveyed the bustling joint, looked square at Angie. "Look, Bianchi, it's nothing to you. It's all to me. The priest, Father Keenan. I

was a kid. He was there. That's all. I was going bad.
Father Keenan, he worked with me. I was in high
school, I was real tough. And the priest, he was not
so tough. He threw the ball with me every single
day when other people wanted to throw away the
book on me. So I got through Princeton on a baseball scholarship." He looked into his coffee like it
was an eight-ball and the answer floated. "Yes. Because David Keenan taught me. He got into some
trouble later, the year I left the school, and he put
himself into a treatment program, an asylum, for a
long time. He had his own demons. He fought
them. Okay, Bianchi?"

Angie evaluated and said, "And the hooker? She's
what to him and to you?"

Brucker blew air. He leaned forward again and
she saw a man about to implode. "Bianchi, please,
trust me."

She said sourly, "Brucker, I don't know you. We're
not friends. We're just two cops slushing through
the sewer. Why did you pick me? You knew I'd go
along, but why me?"

He had pulled out his pipe though he couldn't
smoke it here. But he toyed with it, and his face
when it met hers was painfully honest. "When I got
home and I found my sister hanging there, like
a . . ." He lost a moment, and then regained it.
"When I found Janelle dead, you answered the call
first. When the crime scene boys got there and they
cut her down, you talked to her, to Janelle, like she
was still alive. You said 'It's okay now, Miss Brucker,
we've got you, easy now . . .' And she was dead, but
you cared about her, my sister."

"Jesus, Lieutenant, she was still warm. Dead for sure, but I thought, you know, even though her soul was gone maybe her body could still hear us—"

He put a big black hand over his eyes, and Angie Bianchi wanted to look away, to spare him the invasion of privacy, but this was not a private talk, this was talk of cops obstructing justice.

"Bianchi, you were good to my dead sister. And the hooker, she's just as dead, inside, with drugs and poverty and human degradation. But if you help me, we can save her. Please."

Her coffee was cold. Bianchi sipped it anyway, just for the moment to think. Then she said, "When you talk to the whore tonight, ask her if she did a blow job. Because Victor Farron is and has been completely impotent for two years. Rubber snake, baby. You told me to interview everyone who sat at their table at the press banquet, so I did, and two of them were women he used to bop—or want to bop, anyhow, but he couldn't."

Brucker's jaw dropped. "So maybe he could only get it up with hookers?"

Angie smiled like a five year old faking it, but her retort was interrupted by her beeper. She used her pocket phone and said a whole bunch of times, "Yeah, okay, yeah, okay." Then to Brucker she said, "Well, Lieutenant Jesse James Brucker, if you and me weren't friends before, we are now. Archie Dane is dead."

"The security guard? The one who could have told me definitely that Victor Farron turned in Mick's keys long before the time of the hit and run?"

"Dead, Lieutenant. Heart attack, walking in the park. He wasn't jogging. His ticker sucked."

Brucker cursed. "Shit. We'll never know—"

Angie's smile widened with an arc of a suspicious eyebrow. "Now, not so fast. That was the medical examiner. Archie died suddenly and unattended, so they did an autopsy. Seems now it's a police matter. Seems I'm going to have to make a run by there and make a report."

Brucker finished irately. "So now we'll never know if Victor Farron dropped off Ramsey's keys."

Angie put her five bucks down on top of the check that the waitress left. "Oh, Brucker, that's not the strangest part."

She laughed. She loved this cockeyed job of hers, thinking like killers and not being one. "The strangest part is why Archie Dane had in the back of his right ankle a set of puncture wounds that the ME has now determined are dog bites."

Brucker plunked his hat on and said succinctly. "So he's strolling, and somebody lets loose a dog, and it chases him, and Archie Dane with the heart problems is scared, so he runs and his heart—"

Angie Bianchi, the fat chick with no thin skin, held the door for Brucker, out into a weird afternoon squall of wind and churning clouds. "Could be just a coincidence, Lieutenant, just a testy old yard dog that got loose and chased a guy and scared him to death."

The wind flapped their trench coats. Brucker set his black Stetson over his black eyes. He said, "Only reason anybody would kill Archie is if Archie saw somebody drive out in the Jeep just before the hit and run. They made sure we didn't ask."

Bianchi said, "If Farron did leave the keys, then Ramsey might have wanted Archie gone."

Brucker played it. "And if Farron didn't leave the keys, then Farron would want Archie gone. Okay. But we still don't know who was driving the Jeep. I mean, it could have even been Yates!"

Bianchi's Moe hair blew upward like a Mohawk. She said playfully, "About Yates's tux . . . I got it. I am in charge, cowboy. I took a subpoena to the cleaners for his custom-made laundry bag with his tuxedo still in it."

Brucker laughed, "You got a subpoena for the tux of a man who isn't an official suspect?"

"Sure. The judge owes me poker money."

The first cold raindrops hit them as they stood on the street corner. The sunny day had gone rancid into bleakness.

Angie said, "I'll get the hooker tomorrow. It's my day off."

Brucker asked, "So, Bianchi, how do you feel about what I've asked you to do? Can it fly?"

She popped her sunglasses on and said wryly, "I don't know about flying, but we'll bend it until it breaks." She pointed at him like the grade school detention monitor. "And if it does break, Brucker, you'll say I never knew anything about her. You hid her from me, too." Brucker nodded to her crisply.

# 33

Mick rolled off of Lola the fat girl. He had done his magic; she was panting like a hot puppy. Along her cheek, he stroked one of her fallen curls with his finger.

She panted, "I should go back to work. My boss goes apeshit if any of us secretaries are even five seconds late."

He oozed at her, "No. You should let me make you come again, baby. You are so beautiful."

Mick began his slide down her billowy belly with his tongue. She giggled. "Oh, I'm not beautiful. I'm fat."

He said the way a sorcerer casts a spell, "No, baby. Not fat, just a little overweight. Ten pounds less and you'll be perfect. Tell you what I'll do, I'll sweat if off you. Be with me every day at lunchtime like this, and in a month you'll be skinny as a skeleton."

She giggled again. Mick did more magic, having let down the hook and watched her slippery, shiny red lips chomp it like he was doing now to her most vulnerable private parts.

* * *

Victor Farron gave a luncheon speech to the Kiwanis Club and received rousing applause for his comments on media responsibility in the millennium. He looked ashen and weary, sort of stooped over for his big stature. Some in the crowd wondered if he was working too hard.

Arthur Yates basked and beamed in the wash of endless television cameras and radio microphones and newspaper flashbulbs as he dedicated the new wing of a cancer hospital that he had built and paid for with a simple bank draft from his account. He bent next to some balding children in wheelchairs and let loose with a grin that would blind like the sun.

Brucker drove through the thick downtown lunch bustle toward the rectory. He gave pause to the thought of meeting a whore dressed as a nun. He gave a shudder and a shiver of thought to the idea that somehow, in some dreadful wake of events, the night in the shed with the ballerina would surface.

# 34

The whore was slightly drunk. She sat right down in the face of the wooden Christ, and she swilled the gin bottle.

With a breath that would've blinded a real person, she said to his listless gaze, "I'm not gonna bow my head because if I do I'll pass out. So. This is me. Praying."

She was in her nun's habit, but by now it stank of gin and marijuana so badly that fumes almost rose from it. She had her things packed in her ratty big bag, and she sat cross-legged in the dusty attic, hearing the choir practice below.

She leaned at him, peered heavily, listing sideways a few times. "I got this card, see, from the priest's desk, this card with a picture on it of this Saint Therese of the Little Flower, and it says alls I gotta do is read it to her and then tell you about it. Oh, well, I'd tell you my real name except I don't know it, so I'll just be Caressa Dicks, if you don't mind and all."

She let out a ballistic sigh, glugged a deep swig. The habit was a wrinkled pile.

She slurred through the card. "Little Flower of Jesus, Saint Therese, ask God to grant the favors I now place with confidence in your hands for intervention . . ."

She stopped, wondered.

"Funny I don't remember learning to read. Or tie my shoes. Or pee in the potty. But I must have. Somebody must've taught me. I don't remember anything, you know. Like, today, when I woke up, it was the first day. People, they have places they were. They know stuff about themselves, but me, I don't have places or people to remember."

The wooden Christ stared obliquely. Caressa wobbled at him.

"Anyhow, I told that old lady with the dead daughter, and the fag and the little kid, I said I'd do this, so I'm doing it. I wonder if I ever cared about anyone? Did I?"

His chipped lips were idle.

"Well, the old lady wants to know if you have her daughter or if Satan got her. The fag wants to know if he can come to Heaven. And the kid wants her dog. That's the prayer, if that's how you pray, I don't know. I don't care."

A pigeon cooed. The wooden Christ's eyes followed Caressa as she walked around the attic for a last look. But she knew they weren't really watching her. She knew about the illusion, so many illusions, mainly the illusion of Christ loving her.

"Father David, he said there's a story about a son who was gone for a long time, and how the other son stuck around and did all the chores, and then when the runaway bum of a son came straggling

back, the father was glad. He said that most in the
world you love prodigals. Well, I'm not a prodigal.
I'm a whore. And I'm not straggling back, because I
never knew you to begin with. Like I said, I don't
know anything. Or anybody. Or any place. But I
said I'd pray. So I did.

"And you said you're God and you answered
prayers, so you should."

She stood, rickety drunk, her vision spinning.
The wooden Christ was focused into oblivion.

The whore said pertly, pointing with the gin bottle, "People, you know, they get comfort from me
and you for the same reason. Because they think
we don't know what they really are. But we do
know, don't we? You 'n' me, they bring us their total
worst. We know all about their little sins, and we let
them think it's okay, like they got away with something. Well, they pay me with cash. You, I guess
they pay you with their burned butts in Hell. What
do I say now? Amen?"

She patted the wooden Christ.

"No, P.S., one more thing. I'm not so good and all.
I'm sorry about that. I'm kinda sick. But that crazy
Father David, you know what he says? He says
there's not a doctor or a shrink or anybody anywhere who can fix us until we're ready to give it all
up to you and let you heal us."

She smiled, patted the wooden Christ again.

"He wasn't talking to me, of course, he was talking in his office to some bulimic little punky
teenage girl who was wearing $300 shoes, for heav-
en's sake. Anyhow. I was eavesdropping. And then
he said the most amazing thing to her. He said,

whatever her stupid name was, Muffy or Cherry or something that sounded like pastry. He said to her: God truly loves you."

She had to look away from his peeling, wooden eyes because they pained her.

"So, thanks for not striking a dope addict whore with lightning when she had the guts to talk to you. And you know, I'd give it all over to you, maybe, the pain, if I knew what it is. Well. Good-bye, Lord Our Father. That's what Dave calls you, anyway."

At his wooden feet she set the gin bottle.

The whore dressed as a nun turned and walked away. The sunlight in the attic faded.

# 35

Angie snarled and bitched her way through the noontime swell of traffic and found the bizarre bar where Ramsey said Mick's alibi could be found if she wasn't at home. The joint had to be waiting for either relief supplies to fall from the sky or a bulldozer to put it out of its misery. It stunk. The floor was cold concrete.

Loretta didn't look too good; Bianchi wrote as she strutted herself over to the bar where the big gal was slumped: "Rode hard, put away wet." Two empty beer mugs made sweat on the metal bar, behind which the bartender was clipping his toenails with one shoe and sock off to his side.

Angie said, "Loretta?" The girl looked up, and Angie thought of root rot. "Detective Bianchi, ma'am. Got a minute?"

Her hair was gross, the color of stale beer, the texture of stale pretzels. She sucked long on a mug of brew, pushed it toward the bartender, and said in a voice as mannish as athlete's foot, "I was with him until eleven-thirty. It could have been later, maybe midnight. We had drinks at the

Dublin. He got there about ten. He left walking. I took a cab."

Surly. Angie scribbled it. Too seasoned, boozing at noon. Angie put her porky self onto a stool, told the bartender, "No. just coffee, thanks." Then to Loretta she said easily, "But Ramsey lives downtown, I mean, not far away from the Dublin. Why'd you go all the way home? Why not his place?"

She guzzled, rolled her eyes. Not a friend of many women, Angie figured. Six-two and pissed about it and especially pissed at gals who weren't tall. She said drolly. "I don't go to his apartment anymore. He won't let me."

Bianchi cocked a brow. This person had a sloshed washerwoman look, and the clothes were incongruent. All black. Black slacks and flat shoes, black sweater and blazer, against skin the color of one who has just vomited profusely. No color, really.

Bianchi offered, "Well, honey, maybe you ought to raise the bar in life on your idea of true romance. You think?"

The big gal chuckled dryly, dragged fingers draped in fake red nails around the rim of yet another full mug of beer. "I thought I was going to marry this man." The cigarette flared from her lighter.

Angie fired up one, too, for the posture of bonding. "Known him a long time?"

"Few weeks. Six, I guess. He lays it on thick at the start, I'll fucking tell ya', man." She shook her head miserably, and Angie saw the first sheen of tears.

Liquor was not this gal's friend; it ruined her tough-bitch act with the other chicks. "He says, 'Oh,

baby, you gotta go here with me, be with me, you
gotta give in and make love to me, meet my friends,
be my girl, you're so sexy, oh, baby! And he says it
all with his hand up some girl's dress at the next
fucking table. Jesus. Then you're hooked. Then he
gets to the good part, the part where you agree to
just fuck him and not ask questions, which means
not ask if he's seeing Jacqueline Sofiya."

She didn't look at Angie, just smoked hard and
fast between glugs of beer. "So I said okay, because I
wanted him, and I thought that if I gave him
enough ego strokes he'd stay with me."

The bartender set out a cup of coffee. Angie doc-
tored it with cream and sugar and said blandly,
"Trouble with that is, honey, it's not about how you
make a person feel. That ain't love. Naw, love is really about how you feel about the other person.
That, my friend, doesn't go away so easily. Maybe
he just plain loves her. Maybe he used you to make
her love him again."

Loretta wiped at a tiny escaped tear. "The world
according to a fat cop," she said, saucy and pissed.
"Finish your fucking questions."

"Okay, first question. Why do you put up with it?"

She looked over at Bianchi with a scowl. Drunkenness was fogging into her. "Because I'm like you. All
wrong. I can't be choosy. And he's two inches taller."

Bianchi shrugged. The jukebox played something
that should have cracked the mirrors. The big gal
bobbed her head. She was good and loaded by now,
feeling five-foot-five and precious again.

Bianchi asked, "How'd you meet him?"

"Right here on this barstool. Then some friends

set us up, and we went to a Mavericks basketball game. He told me how Jackie is crazy and he wanted away from her, how I was the answer to his problems—"

Bianchi laughed. "Ha! Boy, that's what I want in life. A guy who arrives with problems! Whoowee!"

Loretta half smiled. This time the drink was scotch and water. It was, after all, past noontime. She said, "We started right off having long romantic talks. Turns out both of us had just left love affairs that went bad. And both of us had real deep problems from the religions that were shoved down our throats as kids. And we both had screwed up in our careers and were searching for a change. It was very romantic."

Bianchi wanted to knock this silly slut into the next room, but she played along. "Wow. That is romantic. Both of you so equally screwed up. That's got to be in the vows somewhere."

Loretta said as dully as a chant, "It goes on like that, me eating the crumbs, him chasing Jackie. And him telling me she's chasing him and begging. Yeah. Fucking yeah, man."

Bianchi watched the new scotch and water come, frowned at it, but knew it was truth serum and would only help the situation. Loretta's voice got deeper with every swig and toke.

She told Bianchi in a slight slur, "So I say to him, Mickey, how come you won't hang around, you know, baby, like lay on the couch and watch movies and drink beer and screw? He tried. Like a caged animal. Twitching. Bitching. And me. Shit. I took the deal."

Bianchi asked, "You ever known him to be with a paid whore?"

The cackle was crude. The hair slung and she slipped on an elbow. "Paid whore? No. Not Mickey. He's got too many of us dimwits throwing it at him. But he doesn't want us. He wants the one who makes him feel inadequate. He wants Jackie."

"There's no record of a cab pick-up at the Dublin at the time of the hit and run, Loretta. I need you to be up front with me."

The drunk big gal cackled again, listing badly. Angie felt bad for her, sad for her, like God had done an injustice to make this girl who looked like a freak take up with men who also made her feel like one.

Loretta yelled over the vibrating discordance of the metal music, "He hates kids. So I faked, you know, like I don't want kids. I faked orgasms, man. I fucking even faked like I don't smoke! I faked like I didn't mind or worry about the times he can't get it up, I say, it's okay, baby, honey."

Bianchi had enough. "Jesus, girl! Why?"

Eyes like cesspools of booze came at her finally. "Now look at you. You're short. You're fat. Your hair's . . . bad, honey, real bad. And those eyeglasses of yours. But you've got self-esteem, see. Now how'd you get self-esteem looking like you do?"

Bianchi grinned. "I reckon I've got self-esteem because I don't wait to get it from men."

Loretta peeled at the dewy label on a dirty beer bottle next to her. "That Jackie, she called me, you know, at the beginning. She said she wanted to save me the grief. See, I thought he was fucked up because of her, that with me it would be different because I'm different than her. It didn't occur to me that I was really just getting some other woman's abusive, lying son of a bitch. Until it was too late."

"It's not too late, Loretta. You didn't take a cab Saturday night from the Dublin. Did you?"

"No. Mick left, and I felt the shame in my gut of knowing that he was running to Jackie. I was really drunk. A guy, he took me with him and we . . . had sex. Next day I told Mick about it, because I wanted to hurt Mick. Only it didn't hurt him at all. So I went crazy, crying and apologizing and begging. And that's when Mick Ramsey feels loved by a woman, Detective—when he can sit and watch you be crazy."

"I need to know his name and description, an address maybe, your Saturday night sport fuck."

This time a double scotch hit the deck. "Yeah," the big gal sniggered. "Me, too."

# 36

Angie asked, "What's your occupation, Loretta? You said you had screwed up and are changing."

"I design cubicles in office buildings, big companies. I figure out the best way to get the most rats into the maze. How'd I screw up? I had a good gig as a stockbroker for a while. Then—" she stared sadly at Bianchi.

Bianchi nodded. "Random drug test. You got caught. You also need to get off the diet pills, girl."

"How'd you know?" She was suspicious, snarly.

"Your purse is open on the floor there. I see all the pill bottles. It's bad shit. I bet you're a stimulation junkie, huh. I bet you can't stand to be alone at home. With yourself."

"It's worse to be fat than eat diet pills. Mick hates fat women." She glared at Bianchi. "You should try it."

Bianchi didn't care about the insults. It was only to her advantage to look like a troll. Girls like this one wouldn't open up to a beautiful babe, but they'd talk openly to one of the cabal—one who was also Less Than.

"Say, you got a key to Mick's Jeep, Loretta?"

She blew a smoky laugh. "Honey, I don't even have his zip code. He won't let me. Why?"

"You mad at him about that?"

The big gal shrugged. "I don't stay mad long. I'm not vindictive. I hate trouble. I just wanted somebody to care about me, you know, and he said he did. And I believed it. Because I fucking wanted so bad to believe it."

Bianchi set out some money on the bar. The blockheaded bartender had the shoe off the other foot now and was sawing away at his icky, curled claws.

The big gal asked directly, "And anyhow, how come you need to know all this personal stuff about Mick and me?"

"Oh, the personal stuff. I don't care about that, really. I'm working a profile of you. It's an old trick. I mean, what are the chances of you two sick wackos finding each other?"

The big gal, now a big drunk gal, eyed her rudely, asking, "And what's the profile, Cagney? Or are you Lacey?"

Bianchi grinned. "The profile is that Ramsey goes into a bar and looks for gals like you who are standing around with nothing else to do and nowhere else to be. Because a woman with a life wouldn't take his bullshit for a New York minute."

The big gal stood and towered like Godzilla with Bud breath. "I'll have you know that I'm the niece

of Congresswoman Elaine Archibald. I'm not a nobody. I spent half of Saturday evening reading out
her press release statement for all the reporters
who called about her resignation. She picked me to
be the family spokesman because I'm her favorite
in our whole family."

Bianchi said sincerely, "Well, I'm sorry about her.
She's a good egg."

The big gal stumbled forward, pointing the scotch
glass. A barrier. "I love Mick Ramsey, and nothing
anyone says or does is going to make me get upset
with him."

To the blockheaded bartender Angie command-
ed, "Come over here, boy." And she whispered to
him as Loretta stumbled back to a barstool, "You
let her drive from here, I'll personally run every
vice officer through here like Turista every weekend until the place is a ghost town, you got that?
Why the hell do you let her drink so much in
here?"

He shrugged, and she got a sense he wasn't normal, a sort of pitiful mutant. "Hell, Officer, she's
just lonely, is all."

Bianchi went back to Loretta. "Honey, let me take
you home."

Loretta ignited at her. "Arrest me or go the fuck
away. Anyway, I am home."

But Bianchi missed the salvo. She was intently focused on something, remembering what Brucker
told her the whore said about the Jeep driver.

To Loretta she said with a peculiarly icy mono-
tone, "Hey, Loretta, nice gold Rolex. Stay in town,
why don't you."

She left the bar. At the first gas station Bianchi got out and waddled into the bathroom and stood for too long a time washing her hands and face. The grime of reality seemed smeared on her skin like warm manure.

# 37

When Brucker loomed over her in the rectory kitchen, the whore was astonishinly sedate. The priest thought with a sigh of relief that he might not have to wipe up after a bloodbath after all.

Brucker sat and took off his hat and trench coat. The priest took it and then set down a cup of coffee, and he slid it away from the whore's reach in case she went off and wanted something to sling on the cop. She was messed up; the pristine little black habit couldn't hide the fact. Her eyes were droopy, her speech halting and she slumped like a barfly at closing time.

Brucker glanced at the priest curiously and then said, "Caressa, what is your real name?"

"I'ont fucking know. Give me a cigarette."

The rectory was hauntingly quiet. Only an occasional traffic sound filtered through from the front windows. The tree limbs that they could see in the small backyard were barren and looked like crippled hands.

The priest snapped up with a pack of cigs and

ashtray and lit one for her. Brucker watched cautiously, deciphering that she likely did remember her childhood name but she certainly didn't remember the priest or him . . . or the shed in the woods. He felt a tickle of sweat sweep lightly over his forehead.

He said, "What are you on?"

The priest said dully, "Only wine. No drugs today. Yet."

Brucker leaned at her. "For my friend Father Keenan, I'm going to take your statement about the hit and run and then help you leave town."

He saw a flash of rage in her eyes that made him sit straight back in a jolt. She hissed at him, "But you're going to fuck me first, right? For free of course. Like all your cop buddies do when wifey's at the mother-in-law's."

Brucker blew air. The priest stood at the sink, feeling the sweat at his white clerical collar. The whore glugged wine from the bottle and clanked it down with a hard stare at Brucker.

He said, "You're free and clear after I check out what you say to me. No head games. No favors owed."

It hit him that he was talking to Diddia the ballerina. He had a weird series of heartbeats and asked for a glass of water, which the priest brought with heavy steps. The whore was oblivious to their simmering glances at each other.

Brucker said calmly, "Tell me first where you got into the Jeep and what time."

"Give me twenty bucks, asshole."

He did. She rolled it into a tight tunnel, a cocaine

pro. "The Jeep came to Rosedale and Hemphill, there by the old burned-down drugstore. It was almost eleven-thirty."

"And you know the time how, please?"

She cackled insanely, "Because I can read a goddamn wristwatch, you cocksucking cop." She put out her skinny arm and showed him a crumbling, cracking leather band with a Timex face.

He said dryly, "All right. What happened?"

She saw it in her mind. Parts of the street were still brick and they were uneven on her high heels. The breeze was crispy and made her bones cold through the thin leggings. She was alone on a corner near a pile of charred two-by-fours that had fallen when the building burned. She was smoking, and she spat blood from a hole in her mouth where she had used pliers in a gas station bathroom to pull out a rotten tooth.

From around the corner on a dark side street she heard a whistle, and she followed the headlights that were blinding her. A man's voice said, "Stop," so she did, perplexed but too lost in pain pills she bought on the street that night to be scared.

The man's voice said, "Stay in the headlight beams and walk this way."

A rat ran across her path, and then a near-death old dog chasing it. From the beams she saw only a silhouette, tall guy in a black coat and some kind of boots, maybe cowboy boots. But she was seeing the world through a deafening sound like a loud dial tone in her ears, so she couldn't focus. He told her again to stop. So she did. He said turn around, so she did.

The blindfold made her gasp at first, but the guy said quickly, "I'm just taking you to the car, that's all, no one's going to hurt you. Just a blow job. Here. Walk with me. What's your name?" She told him.

The car's interior was high, she had to step up with his help, and it smelled like cologne and something else . . . maybe food, or people breathing food they'd just eaten. She remembered for Brucker that there was a whisper, slight as a ripple in dark water, and the whisper said, "I'll walk to your place downtown just in case . . . you know. Bring her there."

A door slammed, the back car door, and footsteps clicked away. The driver said to her, "I won't take my pants off. You can't touch me. Just rub hard, around in circles, and I'll hunch your face until . . ." He had taken her head and run it into his lap and started doing just that, and many times the cell phone rang and he spoke commandingly into it.

Somehow, in a blur, he screamed something and at the very same instant there was a metallic crash and the car slid, fishtailed into a curb, and bounced back into the street. The rain was loud on the windows like troops marching, and the guy was cursing over and over, shoving at Caressa so hard that she hit her head on the passenger window. She yanked at the blindfold and could barely hear the driver's open door dinging for the waves of folding rain. She clambered out and stumbled and fell onto her knees, which the pain pills had numbed, and she began to run.

At the back of the car she stopped dead. A woman in ratty clothes was face-up in a pool of bright red blood swirling into the gutter beside her head. Her face was crushed as if it were a red watermelon, and the bottom half of her body was twisted so she was face up and knees down. Caressa ran, and heard the gunshots but never saw the guy. He chased her. Father Keenan's chapel door was open.

Brucker had his eyes covered with his immense hands, seeing it. Seeing that there were two suspects now, and that the vehicle was high like a Jeep and four-doored like Mick's Jeep. He saw that the driver didn't or couldn't use his penis, so he was impotent like Victor Farron or maybe just a kinky snob like Arthur Yates. And he saw that one wheel at least had run over the old woman's head. He calculated that the driver—like Ramsey and Yates—lived downtown, walking distance from the Jeep, and that the passenger didn't want to be in the car with a hooker if . . . in case they got pulled over by a cruiser.

He asked solemnly, "Where was the shopping cart?"

She glared. "Twenty bucks, dick."

He said, "No, Caressa. Twenty years for the drugs I'd find in your bag. Answer me."

She blew an acrid cloud at him. "In front of the car. All mangled."

He closed his eyes again, seeing it all, hearing the pounding rain and stodgy thunder, feeling the blood swirl into a gutter with such symbolism for the poor bag lady that it caught in his throat. "Caressa, when did you see the gold and diamond Rolex?"

She had lain her head down drunkenly on the table and raised it, looking like a beaten-up, pale relic in a habit that a street walker stole from a church bazaar.

"He was hunching my face, I told you, you moron. It kind of jarred the blindfold up on one eye. I saw the watch, and I noticed because I wondered if I could get him fucked up afterward on some pot or coke and get the watch off him." She put her head down again.

The white crime-scene van pulled up across the street. Brucker and the priest saw it at the same time through the wide front windows. Brucker said, "They're looking for bullet chips in buildings around here, or whatever they can find."

The priest said lowly, "I'm sorry, Jess, for involving you like this."

Brucker touched the girl's arm. "Caressa, there may be fibers from his clothing on what you were wearing. Did you touch his hair? Did you hear a name when he talked on the cell phone?"

She didn't raise her head. She stayed slumped over. The need for uppers was sinking in. "I didn't see or hear anything. I only smelled money in my pocket. God, you're a dumb fuck. I don't know if he touched my clothes, but my wig touched his clothes, his pants for sure. And no, we weren't exactly making out. He didn't let me run my fingers through his hair, idiot."

"What did he say into the cell phone? Sit up." He pulled at her. She swung at him like a wrecking ball, but his hand was quicker and he twisted her arm onto the table while she squealed. The priest started forward in alarm but Brucker held up a hand.

"Look, little girl," Brucker shouted, "I got dead people, people like you, down and out but by god deserving every minute of every chance to try and make themselves better!" He was panting. He let go of her arm. "Now I told you, I'm going to grease your wheels out of this mess, so you grease my wheels to catch this bastard. We don't have to like each other. We can do it out of mutual hate. I don't care."

She said furiously, "A bigwig was dying or something, a woman had cancer. I don't know. He kept talking about it. The phone rang about three times while I was bobbing his hump."

She came up flying and swinging toward the priest, and she landed one good one on his cheek before Brucker leaped and had her arm twisted behind her back. The priest was mortified. The whore was sobbing and cursing and sinking to her knees.

She screamed and tried like a cat to get away. "Who gives a fuck who's murdered? I want out of here—"

She fought. Brucker held, gritting his teeth, gripping her as hard as he needed to, reminding himself why she was a banshee and why he was partly responsible. He wanted to snap his fingers and make it all go away, but he was sorrowfully aware that what happened to her meant she would never know fantasy from reality. Diddia the ballerina would always fight like a banshee, until somebody helped her understand.

The priest knelt to the whore. "Caressa—"

She spat in his face. Brucker said, "I'll take her now. Later I'll get her stuff." To Caressa he said, "One more swing and you're cuffed. Grab your bag. Let's go."

He hauled her away, her feet dragging while she screamed obscenities at them both. It was all so bizarre, the burly cop overpowering a fragile young nun, as if he were a black bandito kidnapping her from a remote frontier mission outpost. The priest went straight to the chapel and sank to his knees, crying madly, the way he had the night the pain drove him to cut his wrists almost to the bone.

# 38

The whore blitzed Brucker. There he was, driving along a rural road to his place in the country, thinking the whore beside him in the car was finally calm—when she coldcocked him. The first wild kick busted his Ray-Bans and made his unmarked unit slice sideways across the lonely road. The second blast from her feet to his chest and face really steamed him so he almost shot the bitch; she messed up the crease in his prized Stetson.

In half a second he was out of the car, yanking open her door to handcuff her, screaming curses at her, and by the time he jerked her door open she had her gun. She popped off two crazy rounds at him, and he hit the deck, facedown on the cold street, feeling her leap over him and head across the muddy field.

He was on her faster than a leopard on a baby goat. Her arm almost broke when he took the gun hand and wrenched it behind her. Then, like a rocket to the moon, she spun at him and her knee found his balls. He went down. She ran.

He tackled her full force in the mud, and down

they went, cussing each other and mud wrestling. She'd get a break. He would slide and stumble and leap her again. When the cuffs were finally on her—when Brucker hauled her through the mud and realized this wiry little tornado had almost whipped his ass—they saw the old farmer bundled up on his tractor, stopped, staring at them like he was waiting for their spaceship to land nearby.

Brucker stopped. He was mud covered. The little bitty nun he was dragging by one foot through the mud was screaming words the farmer probably hadn't heard since Christianity began. Brucker fished his muddy hands into his pocket, pulled out his badge, and flashed it.

He was panting at the whore. "Shut up, you street-brawling whacko." To the farmer, "Uh, howdy, sir."

The nun screamed, "You son of a bitch asshole . . ."

Brucker tried a smile. The farmer frowned, one eyebrow up.

Brucker saw it all then, the mud, the nun wallowing in it, handcuffed. His bloody nose. Her bleeding bottom lip. He shrugged at the farmer and said, "Sometimes in the apprehension of dangerous fugitives, sir, you have to speak their language."

He hauled her to the car and opened the back door, but he decided better, went around the back, and shoved the kicking, screaming nun right into the trunk. The farmer chewed straw and shook his head and remembered why he was glad he didn't have to live around city folks.

At Brucker's quaint little one-story wood cabin on

a plot of several nice acres, he marched the whore inside. He opened the cabinet under the sink and locked her handcuffs around the U-shaped pipe underneath. He stood back from her.

She was a wreck—a muddy, furious eel wiggling and whimpering. She growled at him, "I hate you."

He peeled off his muddy shirt slowly, cursing. "Oh, I don't know how you could, me being so fond of you and all." She kicked at him and missed. To fix up the crease in his prized cowboy hat, he put a teakettle on to steam. In his bedroom he changed clothes. In the kitchen, where the muddy little whore in the nun's habit still flailed on the floor, he poured himself a beer and went to work on his hat in the billows of steam from the kettle spout.

She stopped making noise. He looked down at her by his feet. She spewed at him. "What do you care if some whores and a bag lady were murdered anyhow? Why can't I just go?"

He worked on the hat in the steam and said quietly, "People got a right to do what God put them here to do. You murder somebody, you've taken away their right to find God and do his purpose."

She cringed. "Oh shit, I got me a damned born-again spook."

He said dryly, "Yeah. And I got me a damned drug-crazed slut. I hope there are some experts standing by as this thing unfolds. You ruined up my hat crease."

She said, "Unhook me. Give me a beer. I'll be still."

"No." The wall phone rang. He answered and the whore watched him go all dreamy on the line, like it was fifth grade and Susie Q had just showed him her panties. He said into the phone, "Hey, sugar, thanks for calling. Yeah, you sound real tired. I'll be over in a little while. I'll bring you some dinner, wash you real good in the shower. We'll—" His face fell. The whore watched.

"Oh. I see. Too tired. But look, sugar, I got wine for you. I rented some movies for us tonight. Come on, baby, I'll make you feel good and then you'll sleep good." The low voice on the other end floated. Brucker's sigh was twisted with disappointment. "I know. But you're off tomorrow from the ER and I thought we might have lunch, you might let me take you down and buy you that necklace you saw when we walked around the shops last week—" The chick on the phone, the whore figured, was either heartless or had a better offer. Brucker concentrated again on the hat, and the steam in his face seemed to be coming from his ears, he was so upset.

Caressa said, "Want some advice?"

"Shut up."

"Do you have sex with her?"

He looked down angrily. "I said shut up, girl. You tried to wreck us in the car, then you tried to shoot me, and then worst of all you messed up my hat. So stow it. I don't take advice from gun-toting street whores."

She was lassoed by the cuffs to the pipe, but she managed to sit up against the cabinet doors, uncomfortably. She said, "It's a trade secret of mine. I never told anybody else. But since you didn't gun me down in that field, I reckon you're an okay guy.

The way I survive out there is, I try to get repeat customers, the safe ones that I know about."

He turned on some lights and sat back down in the steam, saying harshly, mostly to himself, "He'll start killing hookers again when he finds out we moved you from the rectory. I should get a cruiser outside the chapel for a few nights, until we flush him out—"

The whore interrupted. "So here's the technique, and nobody knows it but me. You should bond with her, this cold chick, when she's coming during sex."

He squinted at her, his big ol' muscles flexing inside his sweatshirt, his onyx face shiny from steam. The whore went on blithely. "See, it's like a mind game. At the most pleasureable moment in a person's life—during orgasm—when you feel their most breathless moment, well, at that moment you say something softly to them. Like . . ." She whispered seductively. "Good girl or . . . give me more or . . . come home for me, baby."

She shut up. He stared. She said girlishly, "And it works, see, because when the johns see me next, like on the street corner, I remember the bonding words, and I say them, and the moment I say them they start feeling all that breathless pleasure. Just from me saying 'Hey, there . . . good boy.' Get it?"

Brucker cleared his throat, set aside the steaming kettle, and stood over her. She looked up at him, those guileless eyes that he knew could rip out a man's testicles and gut him.

She said to him, "My theory is that while you're giving someone an orgasm, you say the same bonding words every time, and pretty soon, just the words when you say them in conversation will stoke him good. Try it on this ice queen. Next time she's squirming. Say at the right moment . . . you're my girl, you're my girl, yeah, you're my girl. When she calls to break the date, like tonight, say it on the phone. Say 'It's okay, sugar, you're my girl.' She'll be over here lickety-split."

They heard a car door. The early afternoon wind and bright sun were diffuse inside his tidy cabin.

Brucker reached to uncuff her. The cop and the whore were eye to eye. He said plainly, "I'm going to let you go. And if you run I'm going to shoot you."

She asked for her bag. He went to his car, fished it from the muddy trunk, took the bullets from her pearl-handled pistol. Bianchi was trudging up his gravel driveway, hand over her eyes in the brightness. When they went inside, the whore was over the sink, washing mud from her face and tending her cut lip. Bianchi gawked.

Brucker said, like he was pointing to a turd in the Kool-Aid, "This is her."

# 39

The two women laid eyes on each other listlessly, no banter. Bianchi said, "She's covered in mud."

The whore said, "Wow. You're quicker than gunpowder."

Bianchi ignored her and answered Brucker's question about why she had come to his home. She said slowly and flatly so he would fully understand, "I went to see Brian Connelly, the bartender at the Dublin. But the cops were already there. His landlady had just found him in his garage apartment. Naked and dead. They've ruled it autoerotic. No sign of a break-in."

Brucker sat heavily in a wooden kitchen chair. "Mick's other alibi. Two out of three. Holy shit, man." He gazed at her ominously. "Get a uniform on the rectory tonight. And tomorrow early come get this girl. I'm going to Austin to see the governor."

From her bag the whore pulled a full bottle of whiskey, uncapped it, and swigged. They watched. Bianchi said blandly, "I've already called him, soon as I found out he also sat at Ramsey's table at the banquet that night. He's here on business tomorrow, meeting the editorial board at the newspaper. You can meet him in Farron's office at six."

Brucker grinned. "Angie, you're aces."

Bianchi grinned, too. "Yeah? So maybe now you'll stop thinking of me as just another pretty face."

In the slant of crisp afternoon sun, Brucker looked lost in the desert. "I want to know if Governor Green saw any keys on the table."

Bianchi took the whiskey bottle from the whore, swigged from it, handed it back and said stoutly, "Well, I'm going now to talk to Ramsey's long-time hot affair. Jacqueline Sofiya."

Brucker said miserably, "God, I wanted Ramsey to be guilty. I salivated to put that son of a bitch away for life. But why do I get the feeling that all this is just too perfect—Brian, the bartender—nothing could make Mick look more guilty—or more set-up."

She said, "He could be killing them, you know, because the alibi stuff is bullshit and he doesn't want us to talk to them." To the whore Bianchi said without inflection, "I'll pick you up in the morning, kid. We'll have chick chat."

She left. The whore showered. Brucker cleaned mud from the floor, and he only looked up once from his mopping, when he heard her singing, as lovely and pure as a silver flute, wafting around his barren walls.

# 40

In one of Brucker's dusty spare bedrooms, the whore did two lines of cocaine and sat looking out the window, contemplating her escape. Nowhereville, man. Fucking desert outpost. I'd need a camel to get through that field, and the first person who picked me up on that road out there would be a sheriff's deputy with a toothpick and a stun gun. She could hear Brucker showering. She could see no way out and no place to go once she got out. She sat wearing one of Brucker's long T-shirts and drinking one of Brucker's beers.

In the shower, Brucker was thinking. Let's see. Ramsey. Wows the babes with a heavy onslaught of love at the beginning and then starts twisting them with lies they want so much to believe. Ramsey. Picks the damaged ones, the ones with no confidence, the mental cripples. Ramsey can fuck anybody he wants. Was the heat that thrashed through him caused by the hot water or hatred for Mick Ramsey? Brucker couldn't tell as he leaned on the shower wall.

The whore went through his wallet. There were guns locked in a glass cabinet. She sighed. Shoot him? Jeez, didn't that involve the death penalty? The phone rang. She stared at it mischievously.

Brucker lathered his skimming of coarse, dark hair and let the water ladle over his face. Yates, he thought. Yates has two sides, the good guy billionaire who builds hospitals and funds technical research programs and could buy the world twice over with the interest on his personal accounts. Yates, with the dark side so well encased behind his public image. Could be gay. Could be kinky, maybe S and M. Surrounded by security people and powerful enough to ditch them when he wants. Arthur Yates could buy anybody and anything he wants.

The whore answered the phone with her lusty voice, her Texas accent dripping Southern summer rain. The woman on the other end hesitated. The whore grinned. Brucker's grandfather clock chimed loudly, mellifluously. The woman said in a tone suggesting she had just found a package ticking on her porch, "I'm sorry. I must have the wrong number. I was looking for Jesse Brucker." The whore's grin stretched. She said, "Yes. This is his number." And then nothing, so the ice queen was stuck with it, stuck with finding out that if she didn't want him, maybe someone else did.

Brucker used the sponge on his back and his groin. He was enveloped in steam, a black ghost in graveyard white fog. Farron, what do we know about Victor Farron? Runs the biggest newspaper in town. So Farron can pull our mind strings. He can slant the truth, or obscure it or outright hide it. Farron can tell us whatever he wants us all to hear and make us think it's reality. No steady women. Best friends with Yates, or maybe just Yates's puppet, but he keeps at it because the perks are good. The limos. Suites in the four-star hotels Yates owns worldwide. Investment capital and information.

He turned off the water and stood immobile. Water dripped down his face—just as his mind jelled to a crystal clear revelation. Investment information. They would frame Ramsey if he knew something, if he discovered something suspect on the financial end, and maybe Ramsey asked the wrong people all the right questions. He asked himself, What do people kill each other over most often? Jealousy. Revenge. And, at the top of the list in Yates's arena, money. Brucker toweled himself, energized by the idea of a new direction to go in this game of Stump the Dumb Black Cop.

The woman on the phone said—and the whore could hear the blush of contempt, "Then may I speak to him please?" The whore sat on his bed, fingered his old quilt and smelled his cologne everywhere. "Well," she feigned sweetness, "we're—I mean, he's in the shower." She wanted to scream hootenanny style when the ice queen got all flustered, like her skirt had just fallen around her knees.

"Who is this?"

The whore slammed the volley. "Honey, you

sound tired. You should see a doctor about your nervous condition. I'll take care of Jesse, now, and you just get your rest."

She hung up, lay back on his big bed, and kicked her feet up in laughter.

She heard Brucker clanging pots and pans. Quickly she took a $20 bill from his wallet and went back to her dusty spare room to hide the coke and the pill bottles.

Brucker was distracted as he chopped vegetables and stew meat for the soup he was making. He was going over it all in his mind: Ramsey. Yates. Farron. Masters of their games. Gods. Or . . . maybe devils. Which one of them, Brucker mused, would kill to save his reign.

She heard him make two phone calls, but she didn't understand it all from her end. He told somebody to have a uniform cop bring him right away the evidence box of stuff picked up around the dead bag lady. And he called a guy, must be a photographer, the besotted whore thought as she watched the afternoon sun sparkle on a pond nearby, and he asked the guy for pictures from some banquet.

Caressa sat up straighter. On the edge of that nearby pond she saw a small rowboat and—just beyond it—the main highway. She sighed relief.

Brucker took another call. The whore sat on the floor inside her bedroom door, covering her mouth to keep from laughing like a crazed schoolgirl. The

stoic cop had a plaintiveness in his voice suddenly
as he cooed into the phone.

"No, baby, naw, there ain't no woman here. You
got the wrong number, is all. Patrice, sugar, there's
nobody else, I swear." He was cut off by her bitchy
monologue. Finally he said—and the whore could
hear the tempered elation in him—"Okay, baby,
first thing tomorrow, I'll come over. We'll play
house."

When Brucker came into her room and stood
over her in the dark, the whore pretended to be fast
asleep.

# 41

$\mathcal{A}$rthur Yates's waist-length black hair fanned out in the heated indoor swimming pool water like an oil spill. From beneath the willowy blue water, he saw black cowboy boots on the edge. He popped up, panting from his daily laps.

Victor Farron stared down at him and said grimly, "Brucker called the governor."

"What the fuck for?"

Farron was the color of stale white bread. "He only said police business."

Yates treaded slowly, rippling the water so his oil spill of black hair tentacled around him. "This ain't good, pahd'ner."

"No, it ain't, Yates. I don't give a damn if Brucker hangs Ramsey for killing the bag lady. But you know Brucker, he's got an idea . . . he's a deduction machine. What if he's working angles, and one of them is that maybe we took Ramsey's car and framed him for the murder, and he'll ask himself why we might do that—"

Yates giggled. "Fuck him. Let him ask—"

Farron yelled, and it echoed in the moist air of

the big enclosed pool, "Goddamn it! Harding has to be absolutely sure that he did *not* see Ramsey put down any keys—none of this not-to-my-recollection bullshit! And *you* have to prompt his goddamn memory!"

From the pool's edge Yates picked up a damp cell phone. "Noble, bring martinis to the indoor pool." To Farron he said with that grin that only needed canary feathers to fly from his teeth, "Relax, Vic. What the hell, maybe it's time for curiosity to kill that damned alleycat Ramsey. Or maybe we need us a Jeep with a smashed grill and Ramsey's plates."

Victor said like leaking acid fumes, "We can't do that. And you know we can't."

Yates chuckled, sinister and rude. "Hell, Brucker ain't nothing but a peasant with a pitchfork. I'll take care of it."

Victor frowned profusely, like a man with a noose around his neck atop a nervous horse. He asked Yates dryly, "How?"

Yates said, "Hey, you know those folks who say money can't buy happiness? They're mistaken." He went underwater and slithered around the pool.

Noble came with martinis. Victor brushed past angrily.

Yates slid out of the water when Farron was gone. He stood dripping by the elegant lawn table by the pool, sipped lazily on the icy clear martini and took up yet another cell phone nearby. Into it he said, "Have the garage put my car around front in thirty minutes. The pickup, not the Rolls."

The martini was as delicious to him as the taste of fresh female flesh in his mouth. Out the clear dome over the pool, Yates watched the churning gray clouds. It would rain soon, but not on him. Not so much as a drop would dampen Arthur Yates's privileged world.

# 42

The big fat guy with the face of a blowfish was bundled like an eskimo, even inside the office of the dilapidated motel. Two windows were smashed out, so the frosty breeze whipped through at random, which was good, because the smoke from his four-pack-a-day habit got pretty rancid.

He said to the Asian hooker, "I don't know. He calls the desk here and tells me there's an envelope of money in my drawer when I come back from the shitter. So I look and there it is, so I says to him, okay, I'll get one of you right down here. What do I give a fuck if he's a cop? I'm renting a fucking room. You're the one pressing the flesh."

The afternoon had gone colorless, as if somebody took the bright blues and yellows and washed them in bleach. She found the motel room door and knocked. All she could hear was her chewing gum smack and the cars on the interstate. The door opened. The room was pitch dark. Something was draped over the windows.

She never hesitated. The motto was, She who hesitates don't get no money. But this time she hesitated. When the door fell open inward, nobody stood to greet her, like it was a grave or crypt, she stopped the gum smacking. An arid breeze rustled old fast-food bags in the deserted parking lot. She looked around, for the first time ever wishing a cop car would turn into the lot and she'd have to say, Not now, baby, the heat's on. Meet me later.

No cop cruisers came. Only the gray wind and the chug of people safe in their cars and this sight—this open grave before her.

She stepped inside the room, which smelled like a sewer. The door closed behind her.

Her demise would be more agonizing than the others' because there was truth in her eyes when she said she knew Caressa Dicks, that they shared a locker sometime at the bus station. She said this, of course, with a coat hanger coiled around her neck, which was pulled tighter every single second that she hesitated with her answers.

In return for her pleas of ignorance she got a flaming cigar tip smashed firmly into her hand, and she lost consciousness for a while. When she woke she was facedown and naked and bombarded by maniacal screaming about where did the cop take the nun.

The motel hooker cried, and the wire hanger around her throat got pulled tighter until she could see drops of blood falling onto the filthy sheet under her face.

The nun was Caressa? Well. Without the hanger strangling her, the motel hooker might have laughed, but now she could only shake her head and make gagging sounds.

"Where are they hiding her? It's worse now than ever. If she tells the truth now, it's worse than ever so *tell me* where they took her. You're getting drugs to her. She's not on the street buying them, and she won't quit using, and you know her. I can tell that you know her. Where are you taking the drugs to her? Bitch! Where are you leaving her the drugs to pick up! Goddamn it! *Where is Caressa?*"

She heard the sound of paper being crumbled. But that wasn't it at all. The sound was her larynx being crushed just before she died.

Bloodied black gloves pounded the wall. The dead motel hooker stared hollowly into eyes behind the black ski mask. Her burned tongue protruded.

The bathroom window had been an entrance and now it was an exit that led to the dusty river levee where a car was hidden in the dense brush.

Screams of maniacal agony chewed at the bleak, crisp air, shaking the car windows. Finally, hysterically, cruising the interstate there came a sign for tourists, "St. Patrick Historical Mission and Chapel Next Downtown Exit." Insanity veered, destined for the cover of impending nighttime, hungry for the blood of Father David.

# 43

Mick took the time to walk to the downtown public library, but not for a novel to read on his romantic getaway with Amazon.

He sat at one of the library's public-access computers and called up Governor Harding T. Green's personal profile, along with all financial disclosures. He hit a wall that he knew he would encounter. When Kuwait was invaded, Green may have been CEO of Haslon Oil, but he wasn't a public official. Records from those days were not public information.

But Green's current bank accounts and income sources were. And they listed on the computer screen like jolly little lines of dancing girls. Harding, of course, was living now on his salary as governor; all other income sources had been diverted into trusts, which he couldn't use until he was a private citizen again, avoiding any conflict of interest in state business.

Jesus. Mick sat back and blew air. The guy was rich. Mick ran a hand through his black hair and spun in the chair, nervous, then he looked back at the screen, deciphering, saying aloud, "Okay, all stock transactions on the floor are public information, so let's throw in the year of the invasion, 1990, and let's pick a date, say, two weeks before . . . and Haslon Oil, Inc., and let's rock."

The private holdings totaling 12 million shares of Haslon Oil in a prospect drilling project in Bahrain went public on July 8, 1989, with stock prices at $6 per share. Within twenty-four hours of Haslon's acquiring drilling rights, stocks were $30 a share. The bathroom phantom had it on the nose.

Mick's mind raced. He read on. At that time, Harding Green and Victor Farron through a blind trust held the majority stock—3 million shares each—while the rest was parlayed out among minor players.

And that is where the story ended. Until Mick's pocket phone rang.

"You're there, Mickey, where you said?"

"Yeah. I'll go to a secure phone. Wait."

He rambled blindly to a pay phone in the library's huge marble foyer, twisted the short cord around a corner and huddled. He started with his credit card and then realized how totally stupid that would be, laughed at himself nervously, and started clanking in the pocketful of change he had brought.

The voice picked up. Mick said, "Talk to me."

"It's true."

He looked around the library at all the sedate browsers, and he envied them. His world had just gotten extremely dicey. He said, "I need a source."

"Yeah. I need your rich girlfriend to get her next

movie financed by our investors here in New York. Her production company doesn't take outsiders, and some of our guys want in *bad*. She's the entertainment industry's golden goose, Mick. That's our deal."

His notepad was unsteady, but he was ready to write. "Okay, I told you. I'll swing it."

"Your unnamed source is a high-ranking official on the floor of the New York Stock Exchange—"

"You," Mick stated.

The voice screamed back, "I don't want to see my name in any stories."

Mick dropped his pad, fumbled for it. The glass foyer was being licked suddenly by a misty rainfall. "Oh, you don't want the headline to say 'Robert Davidson tells all.' Come on. I've never burned a source."

The voice calmed. "I traced it. Harding and Victor Farron in the Bahrain deal had three million shares each. Four other guys—Max Newman, Charlie Rutledge, Sammy Borneo, and Frank DeCamp—each bought a million shares. That left 3 million shares to go public, which happened instantly when they opened it up. You know what the prices did after Harding and his boys bought into the drilling fields; they skyrocketed overnight. Now here's where you get the sweaty palms, Clark Kent."

Mick scribbled and said, "Victor Farron doesn't have that kind of investment money. I'll trace his tax returns and prove it . . ."

"Mickey, forty-eight hours before the invasion of Kuwait, two days before Saddam turned the oilfields of Bahrain into infernos, Harding and Farron sold.

Bailed like sinking sailors. They each made out like bandits with $100 million a piece—"

Mick lost a breath. His hands were cold and he had trouble writing. "Tell me the exact dates." He scribbled fast and realized he was holding his breath.

The voice went on. "Boom. Hussein invades Kuwait. The oilfields are black smoke. Haslon Oil stock prices finally bottom out two days later at $4 a share. Everybody holding Haslon stock can eat the paper and hope they choke on it. They're all busted. Except Yates. And Green. And Farron."

Mick swallowed. "Sure, because he didn't put in any investment money; he just got a fee for being go-between. Look, I've got to put it to Yates."

"First, you might want some quick life insurance. Sammy Borneo is the only one surviving. Newman and Rutledge had coronaries, in the pool and on the back nine of the golf course respectively—both alone at the time. Frank DeCamp went cliff diving in his Mercedes. All of this within months of the sour stock deal."

Mick's dread came out sounding like he was collapsing when he said, "And Borneo. He's in the nuthouse. It was you who told him to contact me to do this story."

"Yeah, Ramsey, I owe Borneo. And you may be a prick, but you're a hell of an investigative reporter. Now, I've got to own twenty thousand shares of Jackie's next movie—"

"Okay! Give me Yates!" It got away from him. A few library browsers frowned at him from the main area near the foyer.

"Within two weeks after he cashed in and went home with his hundred-mil from Haslon stock, Yates set up a trust in just that amount."

Mick asked, "Interest bearing?"

"Yeah. In Switzerland. I did the cash draft."

Mick said, "Fine. Then I can cross it with the IRS. And Harding Green?"

He sensed a sinister smile when the voice said, "Ah, well, at the same time, the president's wiley, smiley little brother bought himself $100 million worth of real estate in the Bahamas, Colorado, Miami, and Maine."

"He still owns them?"

The voice said unpleasantly, "That's your job."

Mick thought aloud, "If he does, I can verify purchase dates. He's the governor. Properties he owns and when and how he paid for them will be public info. What about Farron?"

"There won't be any records of any transaction of $100 million to him. He was just the gopher, and that isn't illegal."

Mick said, mostly to himself, "This story will bring federal criminal indictments and investigations into the deaths of those men. Hey, you took this risk. Thank—"

The line went dead. The rain lapped dully at the glass foyer's windows and ceilings. Mick picked up the phone and dialed the number of a cab company so nobody could redial the number he had called. He closed his notepad and started away, trying desperately to look calm in case—and he had no doubt—someone was watching.

# 44

Jacqueline Sofiya opened the gate from a button inside the pink stucco mansion. Bianchi gawked as she drove up the long winding driveway. The windowboxes were European and ornate. White border lights gave the place a Hollywood elegance. In back, the kidney-shaped pool glistened even in the barrenly cold early evening, and steam rose from it. Heated. Bianchi was impressed.

The man who answered the huge French front door was so handsome that Bianchi dropped her jaw and lost her train of thought.

He introduced himself after Bianchi showed her badge, saying to her, "Detective Bianchi. I'm Robert Davidson, a family friend. Would you like coffee or tea or a cocktail?"

Bianchi gushed, sounding goofy and girlish, "Naw, nothing, thanks. I just had a bar of soap."

He was gracious, too, a gentleman—and Bianchi didn't come in contact in her world with many gentlemen. He led her through an entryway where a chandelier bathed the pink marble floors and the winding stairway. They sat in what appeared to be

Jacqueline Sofiya's office, a sunken room of oak and leather and silk.

The place reeked of intellect and serenity. Mr. Gorgeous oozed an urbane sex appeal. She asked about his big ring, and he said yes, it was a Texas Christian University class ring. He went on to say that he'd been a venture capitalist for a while, trading with other people's money, and finally made enough to go into ranching in Montana, his life's dream. He said, too kindly, that it wasn't nearly as heroic as being a police officer, and Bianchi felt a clumsy blush on her face.

When Miss Jacqueline Sofiya swooped in like a beautiful goddess on a magic carpet, Bianchi stood. Mr. Gorgeous excused himself and left.

"Miss Sofiya, I love all your movies. They're so scary and sexy." It came out dopey and wrong, but this major babe, she figured, was used to people going all dopey when she was around. She was so captivating in person, dark and warm and buxomy. She wore simple jeans with a turtleneck and cardigan—nothing showy—and suede loafers. Her suntan was golden. Her eyes were gold and lighted from within.

Bianchi said, "You know why I'm here?"

"Yes." Bela Lugosi lived in that accent. "My secretary said you phoned this morning and would be dropping by." The lighted eyes had a hypnotic quality that was like looking into melted topaz.

"You're Hungarian?"

Her hair was piled up, but little wisps of it fell around her brows and cheeks. She pushed at one of them. "I'm from Bucharest, Detective. Until I was eighteen. My father was American. He had left us, though my mother did not know where he'd gone. So I came here for college, and to find him. When I did have a reunion with him, I wrote a fictionalized screenplay about it, and a studio made it a movie. The rest," she waved a fragile hand, "is cinematic grandiosity. They wanted more scripts from me."

Angie shifted uncomfortably. "Mick Ramsey is a suspect in a hit and run, Miss Sofiya—"

"I know."

Angie stopped, shifted again. "He told you?"

"No. Victor Farron told me. He phoned last night."

This didn't seem to faze Jackie, but Angie was floored at the webs spiraling out from this hit-and-run lair. "You know Victor Farron?"

"Quite well. When I first found my father twenty years ago, Victor was a business associate of my father's. Over the years we have kept in contact."

"And that's how you met Mick? Through Farron?"

"No." The heavy eyelids stayed half shut, so calm, a temptress without trying. "At a social party at Victor's home, Mick saw me. He later asked friends to arrange an intimate dinner and introduce us."

Angie said flatly, "Look, I need to know about Ramsey, and I don't want to insult anybody, but . . . you don't seem like his type. Not deformed or defective. I mean, your father, he approves of Mick Ramsey for you?"

Jackie suddenly needed a drink. She wafted to the small bar, poured, turned to Bianchi and looked so lovely that Bianchi wanted to applaud. "They have never met, Mick and he. Mick has never even asked me my father's name. Mick is not . . . familial."

Bianchi smiled. "Somebody ought to teach that boy a lesson in respect, you know, cut off one finger at a time until he agrees to play fair. That's how we did it when I was in the Mexican Mafia, you see."

Jackie smiled and relaxed. Her hands were lovely and cinnamon colored on the crystal glass, and her nails were unadorned. She said in that Vampira tone, "For three years Mick was like the sun that came up. Linear. Loving beyond belief. I adored him. And then one day six months ago, Detective, the sun didn't come up." Her eyes darkened. "He told me that he intended to have sex with as many women as he could as often as he could. He wanted, as he put it, sex without a relationship. It's the classic American invalidism of mortality, isn't it? The male middle-age crisis. So." She shrugged her thin shoulders, poured more wine over ice.

"I let him go. Of course drifting barstool to barstool disquieted him. He had affairs, frowzy dalliances, but impotence plagued him—"

Bianchi didn't mean to screech in the placid setting but she did. "He told you all this?"

The brown goddess half smiled. "That was the point, no? Because he asked me at Thanksgiving time to marry him, and I declined, though I loved him so. I suffer my unrequited past, Detective, of learning to yearn for the love of my dear daddy, and so I must have an unvanquished future, no encumbrances. It is my . . . id."

"You jilted Ramsey."

A Dracula laugh, somehow frightening and sexual. "Mick is, I believe, in your culture's banal terms, a pathological liar. I begged that he stop lying. Veracity eludes him. And I know, Detective, that when we women ask a man not to lie to us, we are asking the man not to do things he must lie about."

The room was silent. All the many textures of the walls and chairs and the floor absorbed the soft lighting, and Bianchi thought she could see the essence of real grief in the moment.

Bianchi said, "There's a girl. I swear to God she's got altitude sickness. And she actually loves this shark."

Jackie sat again, so enviably thin and agile. "Yes. Loretta. I know about her. We have spoken. I warned her."

Bianchi looked up from writing. Buzz word. "Warned her?"

"She phoned me. Mick was coming here most nights and pleading with me to be with him, even after he met her, and she wanted me to eschew him, to dissuade him. So her method of madness has been to simply tolerate his obsession with me." She smiled sadly and took a long black cigarette from a small porcelain box. "She will abide, she says, not realizing, as I do so clearly, that hurting her is his revenge toward me. Because he can't hurt me anymore. And the girl who hanged herself—"

Bianchi shot up a stern glance again. This broad with her tranquil dispassion and her sharpshooter analysis was just too . . . clement. "Janelle Brucker," Bianchi added.

"Yes. I should have warned her, too. That Mick's integrity has collapsed into ravenous madness."

They were silent again, not poignant this time, but fraught with tension.

"You hate him, don't you, Miss Sofiya?"

"On the contrary. I feel unconscionable pity for him." She blew smoke languidly. "He is a racist, our Mick. And so he picked the Brucker girl because he feels minorities are inferior. This girl, now, what is her prostration?"

Bianchi said, "It's not like I can really talk myself, but a guy would be real lucky if she likes getting it from behind. She ain't Helen of Troy exactly."

Jackie grinned kindly. "And the next one will be impoverished. The following one, perhaps an abuse victim, and then one who feels she is overweight. Ones after that, they will be flawed in Mick's eyes. Because he tells me that lying to them is not his fault. He says that they are blighted, and he must lie to them out of kindness. So he is . . . a missionary of lust."

"Miss Sofiya, do you have keys to Mick's Jeep?"

The question floated like poisonous gas bubbles. "No."

The phone rang. She answered, **and** she signaled that it was Mick Ramsey. Bianchi listened intently. "Yes, darling, all right. No, please don't come here before you leave. No, don't. Please. Mick. Don't call anymore. This is six calls now, today. Stop. No, I can't go along with you on your trip. No. I can't! Yes, yes, I'll see you tomorrow. Calm down. All right. When you return you can tell me everything, the whole story."

She hung up, turned to Angie. "He is going to Red River City, to the hospital there for a story." Her eyes pleaded with Bianchi to understand the pathos. "He said he'll call me the minute he arrives, and he will, Detective. No matter who he is with tonight, he will leave the bed and call me repeatedly."

Bianchi could only whisper, "Why?"

Jackie suddenly had a chill. She wrapped her arms around herself. "Because, he sees himself as a rhapsodist, when quite frankly he is nothing but a sex addict. And because, Detective, he is quite insane."

Bianchi joined her at the window. The glistening pool made sharp reflections across the deck in the evening rain.

Bianchi asked, "The girl, what does she say to you?"

"That he will change for her." She pierced Bianchi with those brilliant, illuminated eyes. "And I say yes. Like Jekyll and Hyde." She turned to Bianchi, and Bianchi felt a chill along her arms like she did when the evil killer lurked in the darkness in a Jacqueline Sofiya suspense thriller on the screen. Something just as sinister lurked in those topaz eyes. "When Mick sees a woman, Detective, anywhere, anytime, one question burns in his mind. 'Can I have sex with her?' He doesn't care anymore who she is, or what she is, or what she feels. He cares only for the answer to the question. And he doesn't stop until he knows."

"Miss Sofiya, would he kill a pedestrian and drive away? Would he kill anybody? Like maybe a hooker or an old security guard?"

The answer was disjoined from the question; Jackie was lost in somber thought. "In the beginning, I was going to use him. I needed something. Along the way, I fell in love. And then? He began to hate me. Because I succeeded. And now, now that I love him, he punishes my success by being with other women."

"But would he kill someone?"

Jackie's sigh was profoundly gloomy. "I don't know. Because I don't know him anymore. He is a stranger to me, and I am sad about that."

"Would Victor Farron?"

Jackie gave a strangely perverse smile. "In my world of thespians, I find the homosexuals to be particularly kind and conscienscious."

Bianchi said flatly, "Farron is gay."

"But he doesn't want to be, Detective. And so over and over he tries with women. The night after the banquet he was out with a woman I know, and she could not satisfy him, no matter her expensive perfume and lust." She penetrated Bianchi's gaze. "But he can perform with men. Ah. You look incredulous. Well then. Ask his lover, Brian Connelly. Good evening, Detective. Come back if I can help more."

# 45

They watched her car pull away. Mr. Gorgeous said with a smack of sarcasm, "The state mental hospital. Right where Ramsey belongs."

Jackie asked sullenly, "You have everything ready at the mental hospital?"

The hunk moved closer to her. "I built them an entire new kitchen cooking area this month. They'll give him your father's file without hesitation."

"Oh God, Robert, Mick has to write this story. He has to help my father be set free. I could never tell him my father's ordeal because I had no proof. It would only have been my conspiratorial rantings, and they'd have hidden my father farther away. Then you came, and you brought their motive, the insider trading my father knows about."

Mr. Gorgeous looked sadly into his drink. "I knew I had to find you. The letter to me in my uncle's safe deposit box laid it all out. He wrote it in case something happened to him, something like his car going off a cliff with him in it. He must've seen his murder coming. Are you sorry we're using Mick?"

"My Mick of earlier days? Yes. This Mick. This psychotic walking erection. No."

"Jackie, I told Ramsey everything on the telephone today. He has no idea that I know you. And you told the cop the truth, enough to keep her off Mick until the story is published and Yates and Farron are exposed."

Mr. Gorgeous uncorked champagne and brought two crystal glasses for a toast. "Red River City," he groaned, "I spent two weeks there one day. I bet ol' Amazon is going along for the ride."

"Surely to god not. Surely nobody in their right mind would go to that godforsaken town. Even for the sick pleasure of being Mick's flavor of the month sex queen."

And at that very moment Loretta was packing those Victoria's Secret panties, eating diet pills, and swilling booze. He was two hours late already and hadn't bothered to call. She took a boozy breath and said to herself, "That's okay. So he's late. I'll just prove how undemanding a good woman can really be."

Mick stopped off for a blow job from Lola, which she was delighted to give him after he stepped inside and told her she was the most beautiful woman in the world. He didn't take off his shirt or his socks, but she overlooked it because he said he was on deadline for a big important investigative story and had to go. And she overlooked it because before he left he brought her to orgasm twice. It all seemed okay, but there was that one disquieting remark he made as he kissed her at the front door.

She said, "Mick, sometime I want you to meet my little boy, Kyle. He's with his daddy tonight, but you should see him. He's real cute."

His handsome brown eyes made her feel undressed and wet. He said without blinking or thinking, "Meet your kid? Why? I'm not fucking your kid. I'm fucking you. Man, you must've been spectacular when you were thin. I'll call tonight, babe. Stay out of the cookie jar."

# 46

Brucker bent deeply over the sleeping whore and snapped back at the smell of her liquor breath. He checked her pulse. She didn't wake when he slid the handcuff around her small wrist. He lifted her arm and locked the connecting cuff around the knob of the bed's headboard. To leave, she would have to drag the bed.

He fought gusty wind to get to his car, had to hold on to his Stetson and duck down. An afternoon storm was driving in. He pulled away, his stomach heavy with a sense of how wrong he was to protect this girl, a murder witness, and how completely erroneous it had been to involve Angie Bianchi.

The priest stood at the front windows of the rectory, nursing a cup of coffee. The sun was sinking behind tall skyscrapers, outlining them with purple and gold. Behind the sun a bank of clouds journeyed toward downtown from the countryside. The priest sipped. And he remembered.

The first time he had gone to Ireland, just after he was ordained. He could taste the ale, bitterly beautiful on his tongue. He could feel the backslaps of the crusty old fishermen when he sat in the pubs and they saw his clerical collar. He never bought an ale. Everything was on the house for the "Gewd Fay-thur Kee-noon." He smiled lazily. Wind whipped the rectory windows.

Everywhere he went in Ireland he thought of her. As well he could taste her sugary lips and feel her hand on his back, up and down, adoring.

As flashbacks go, it was a good one, and he went to this delicious one often. Back to her. Mary Catherine Frances O'Sullivan. Skin like an abalone, pearly, pure. Eyes of the sea foam. They were at St. Mary's University together back then, and he couldn't draw air when she was around, nor now when he thought of her. Red wavy hair that skipped against her back when she ran; ever the coquette, she was. She was having nothing but him, she said in her brogue, and damn the heartless saint that tried to take him away. Ah. Those legs of hers. Gams, they were, and she showed them to him when they studied on the grassy slopes, just to make sure he knew what was in store.

The whipping wind against the rectory died a moment, almost in reverence to his thoughts. She got sick, Mary Catherine Frances O'Sullivan did. She all tethered to weird lines, and he, young David Keenan, handsome as a soldier saluting, mourning until he began to weep without shame. He walked a long way the last day, to a cathedral near the hospital, and he sat a while. Then he stood.

"I know that you know, Lord, what's on my

mind, what's always been on my mind. I know that you know my heart, because you put it there, this calling."

He remembered himself that day alone in that chapel as Mary Catherine lay dying. He remembered saying, "So I'll do it. If you make her well. If you save my Mary Catherine, holy father, I'll give you my life in service. I will come to you and take the vows." He had kneeled then. "Oh, God, you don't make deals, I know that, so it's my deal then, you see. Jesus. Mary. Please let her live. Father, take my life. It's what you want. And for her, it's what I'll give."

In just days she began to come around, to beat the mysterious, paralyzing virus. They took away the breathing machines and the tethers, and Mary Catherine ate broth. And David Keenan went away, to seminary. Mary Catherine came to his ordination years later, pregnant and vibrant. She named her baby boy David and sent pictures that made the priest weep alone on Christmas nights.

Yes, as flashbacks go, it was a sweet one. Others were less so. The night he cut his wrists twenty-five years later. The first time he ever spoke the girl's name aloud, just hours after hearing first reconciliations from a group of second-grade girls from the school.

Standing there now at the window, he had to clutch his chest at the memory of that moonless night. There on the altar. He had slashed and screamed. *Diddia!* And he didn't remember much of it, except that for one evening he had been an evil skeleton and life became Hell. The ballerina. Jesus.

He thought of her and of the angel voices and eyes of the tiny girls, one by one, approaching him. Their fancy white little gloves, their rippled pastel dresses, their ice-cream smooth skin. Their eyes, as clean of slate as blue satin. She had been them. Diddia had trusted him and obeyed him and played rock-scissors-paper in his lap to win candy. Oh, Blaspheme! he had wailed at himself. Defiler!

And on that night twenty-five years later, the pastor was ill. Would Father David hear the girls' first confessions? He had chosen his ministry so it kept him from young girls, because he couldn't face their guileless love for him. Their puffy hands on his cheeks. Their quicksilver giggles. He couldn't face them without seeing her. Diddia. And the skeleton.

After that evening, he knew that what he had done would never end, that in those guileless eyes he had seen God saying, "End it." So he went to the altar and to his knees and slashed his skin, over and over, until blood soaked his black robes and the altar of the church. And the other wrist, too, with a nearly severed hand holding a straight razor.

The ballerina's face swirled at him that night like floating masks that he tried to swat away. He didn't remember taking the straight razor to the altar and cursing God, but he had glimpses. Himself, blood covered and screaming, "I'm dying to see you, Lord! What the hell difference does it make how I get there? *Jesus!*" He had collapsed, woke in a psychiatric ward where he stayed for a long time.

From behind him a voice spoke. The priest turned from the storm brewing at the windows.

"You should have every door locked," Brucker said. "I came for her stuff. She wants some books you gave her, and a rosary."

"Yes, Jesse. Come in. It's just knickknacks to you and me, but the whole world to her. How is she?"

Brucker was iron. "She's a holy terror, that's how she is."

The priest smiled. Brucker did not.

"Remind me again, Father, why we're doing this. Why I'm risking my career and possible charges of impeding justice."

The priest faced him solemnly, and Brucker remembered his one and only ride in a police car, handcuffed—another black kid going bad. He could see Janelle screaming and weeping on the city sidewalk, telling the burly cops that their mama and daddy were long gone and Jesse was her only family and couldn't they please believe that he stole the food for them and he didn't even hurt nobody and how he was only fifteen years old.

He said, "Never mind, Father. I know why we're doing it. I'm doing it for you, because you saved my life at that Jesuit home. And you're doing it for her. But that night, you were out of body. You didn't mean it."

"And she doesn't mean it either, Jesse. She didn't ask to be haunted the way she is. She was a beautiful, precious little girl, a little soul so fresh from God, until that night."

His face splintered. Brucker abided. The priest said to him, so poignantly, "The bag ladies and the bad boys, the poor, the lost, Jesse, they don't mean to be that way. It's just life, son. I will not let you be in trouble for this. But I promise you, I'll stop at nothing—not a damned or holy thing—to save her life."

Brucker stepped in. They embraced. The wind howled through the cold, old house where the priest lived alone.

Brucker said, "And that must be, Father, how you felt about me when they brought me, and you loved me, and without that love I'd have been a statistic. Thank you."

They held each other a while. Brucker had to go. The whore would wake soon. He stopped at the door and had a sickening fear that he wouldn't see his savior on earth again.

"Father, please, lock up at night. There's a cruiser out front, but don't take chances, okay?"

The priest's kind eyes squinted in a sad smile. "You'll bring her to me in a few days, when the danger is over?"

Brucker nodded. He bowed his head, and the priest's willowy hand put a blessing on the cop's forehead.

# 47

The roads leading out of the city toward the mental hospital quickly became flatlands dotted only by tumbleweeds. Loretta drove—her car, her gas, even though it was Mick's trip—and the harder she chirped, grasping for ersatz intimacy, the more sullen he became.

Finally she succumbed to the lonely grind of the windshield wipers. When she asked if she could play the radio, he grumbled "No," and went back to ignoring her.

The Victoria's Secret special hot-stuff perfume didn't seem to be working on him.

Mick was so deep in thought, he couldn't swallow—forget about smelling or seeing her. The story that would fry the governor and Yates and probably Farron was half written on a disc from his home computer. The disc was in his suitcase.

He turned every two minutes to see if they were being followed. The rain obscured what he could see behind them, but Mick didn't imagine that they would let him leave town and not come along to watch what he was doing.

In the little hick town that was spawned solely by the weird, hunkered people who kept care of the mental patients at the hospital, Mick dumped Loretta at a gruesome motel. He did not go with her inside or offer to carry her bag or kiss her good-bye or say when he'd be back. She stood in the rain and felt her first tear of unabashed shame.

The complex of a hospital loomed on the outskirts of the hick town like a giant flesh wound. Windowless. Doors with bars. An assortment of mentally crippled people wandering a large covered, fenced area where they were locked in. They were stooped in their robes, shuffling, medicated beyond oblivion. Some talked to themselves, or yelled bizarre things to Mick as he clipped along the sidewalk past their outside area. Some danced, or sat slumped and drooling. They were in a mind palsy—nothing left but a body still working even though the brain inside it was mush.

The hospital secretary smiled when he asked to see the administrator. Mick frowned . . . nobody ever smiled when he showed his press credentials. And the hospital administrator smiled when he asked for the files of Mr. Sam Borneo, said she had a copy of them right in her credenza.

Mick's frown turned to hardened anger. He said, "No argument that they're confidential. No bureaucratic jockeying to keep me from seeing them."

She was perky. "Mr. Ramsey, we're a state institution. Our books are public information."

He narrowed his sandy eyes at her. "Uh-huh. Except I didn't tell you my name when I flashed my card for a half second. And I know that patient files are confidential unless court ordered."

She sat slowly. She was a heavy woman in a heavy winter suit and a scarf tied too big under her large face. Her hair was a crisp white helmet. Her face faded to match the color.

"Mrs. Jordan, did you know I was coming for Mr. Borneo's patient records?"

She did what people do when they lie and want you to know it. She looked squarely at him. "No."

"Then why are the files so handy?"

Her neck tightened. "Because he's committed for life. The lifers' files are with me. There aren't that many."

"And why's he here for life? Doesn't everyone get a psychological review along the way? Isn't that part of the judicial process in declaring someone insane?"

She raised an eyebrow at him. "Mr. Ramsey, Sam Borneo was deemed by the Texas courts to be non-rehabilitative—"

"The whole court?"

"Yes. Based on a report from Governor Harding's office and the FBI."

Mick sat somberly, thumbing the pages, his stomach tight and his hands shaky. "Why?"

"The reports show that Mr. Borneo had for years been stalking and threatening Governor Harding in his private life, and it escalated when he became governor. Death threats. Attempts at public physical assault. Seems there were many incidences—"

Mick looked up. "So why are there no police reports?"

She sighed. The money she took from Mr. Gorgeous suddenly didn't seem like enough to tell all these immutable truths that had been hidden so long. "Harding said he didn't ever call the police when it happened. They had been business partners, friends, I guess, and he didn't want a scene. He wanted Sam put away quietly. There was a hearing. By then Harding was governor, so he brought in the FBI and told them he feared for his life and his family, but it needed to be surreptitious to spare his friend any shame or embarrassment—"

Mick shot up. "Wait, wait! He was committed here in secret—for the rest of his life—with no continuing psychiatric analysis because the governor *said* the guy was stalking him? Do you know what that sounds like, Mrs. Jordan? It sounds like Communist Russia. So who okayed it for the FBI to scoop up Borneo without process and bring him here?"

A crazy man in a far off hallway screamed, and it echoed with the sounds of his leg chains rattling, "I am the Devil to slaughter the sheep! I am the Devil to massacre the meek!"

Mrs. Jordan stood and came around the desk, six inches from Mick. "The process was suspended for Borneo's committment hearings by Harding—that is Lamar Harding, then president of the United States."

Mick backed away. He had to see her, all of her. "And you're on the record for my story?"

She came to him again. "The committment papers are in that file you've just pirated here from an unknown source. Do you understand, Mr. Ramsey? I don't know how you got it. And I trust, because I was told, that your integrity as a member of the Fourth Estate is stellar."

He glared at her. Rain bled on the glass behind her. The crazy man echoed again, his screams almost bloody, "The Devil is lovely, the Devil is nice! The Devil will woo you with your own favorite vice!"

Mick didn't back away from her sober expression this time. He said, over the sound of the man's desperate screams, "Someone knew I was coming for these records, Mrs. Jordan. Who? Who paid you to give them to me? Who wants Sam Borneo out of here badly enough to expose the governor and the former president?"

She told him flatly, "An influential family friend."

Mick squinted at her. "Just now? He just now decided he wants him out?" Then he sighed. "Oh. Okay. He just got grown enough, or he just got rich enough to do something about it. But . . . but how would he know to get me involved? Why would he pick me? Who is he?"

"I can't tell you that, Mr. Ramsey. I've done what I was asked. I released a copied file to you on his word that you'll protect me from exposure."

Mick was thinking aloud, racing. "Davidson. Davidson has some connection with Borneo's family, and that's why he leaked me the SEC confidences."

Mrs. Jordan waddled back to her cluttered desk and sat heavily, with a sigh so great it almost fogged the room with shades of human despair.

Mick felt himself laugh stupidly, at the thought of it all, and he said, "Mrs. Jordan, I need to see Sam Borneo."

She didn't look up, just shoved at him a stack of papers as thick as a big-city phonebook, saying, "Then fill these out. It takes approval from his doctors, all eight of them." She eyed him meanly. "Even for the Fourth Estate."

The hallway smelled like pain, and it seemed to wobble before him as he walked, so he looked like a patient, holding the wall and mumbling to himself.

"Davidson, you bastard. How are you connected with Borneo? And why does that connection make you want to burn Harding and Yates?"

The crazy man screamed, "He isn't ugly! He isn't ugly. The Devil don't scare you. He comes in beauty, like a goddess, and he feels good and you take him and love him! And then . . ." The scream intensified. Mick hurried for the door, where a security guard waited to buzz him out. "And then he murders your soul with the evil you loved so . . . goddamned much! Hear me! Help me, oh god, pleeeeeeeeeeze!"

She was waiting there on the bed in those Victoria's Secret black panties, burning some candles that made him feel putrid. Mick made ravenous love to Loretta, assaulted her with his prowess to give her ecstasy and feel absolutely nothing himself except revenge and rage.

She said afterward, "Kiss me, Mick."

He turned to her, those evil eyes laughing at her, and he said, "Kiss you? And ruin a perfectly good fuck?"

He laughed. She went to the shower, turned on the water and stood sobbing.

# 48

In the morning Bianchi came into Brucker's farmhouse kitchen bundled up, saying like gunfire, "Farron's gay. His boyfriend was the bartender Brian."

Brucker poured coffee. He was crisp again in jeans, boots, a wool sports coat. "So we'll find traces of Farron in Brian's apartment, very likely, and that connects him to another murder victim—if we get the forensics to prove Brian didn't hang himself. Good work, Ace."

Bianchi flopped and opened a bag of croissants laden with cheese or cherry filling. She talked while she chewed. The sun wasn't up yet, and the house was prairie dark and quiet except for the flicker of a fireplace at their feet in the den. Caressa was a snoring clump in the bedroom, cuffed at the wrist to the bedpost.

Bianchi said as she smacked, "You show me yours, I'll show you mine."

He plopped a file and an envelope onto the coffee table. "I went through the evidence box, stuff from the hit and run. The hooker said there was a blindfold and she ripped it off and tossed it. I didn't figure the driver hung around looking for it." He dug in the big envelope. "So look here."

She peered, gulped. "A red bow tie? It's the blindfold?"

"Yeah. So it was somebody all dressed up for a big party. And now lookee here." He opened the file of photographs from the awards banquet.

In the warm lamplight Bianchi sucked a wad of croissant when she gasped. "Holy shit. Ramsey and Yates, both in red bow ties?"

Brucker's frown intensified. "Yeah. I got all the photos." He leaned at her. His face was deadly serious. "The thing is, when we picked up Ramsey's tux, he also sent a bow tie, a red one."

"Creased? Like this one?"

"Wadded into a pocket."

"So maybe Ramsey realized it was missing and stuck this one in the pocket."

Brucker countered, "Or else Yates is our man. He was at the table with the keys, too."

Bianchi whispered, "But wait, the hooker said somebody from the backseat blindfolded her. So who was driving?"

Brucker stood by the fire. In the outline of it, he looked like a massive prizefighter. He said sullenly, "Yates didn't have a tie in the laundry bag that you got. So I send the uniforms to his mansion today to find it, and the butler, Mr. French, he shows them a damned walk-in closet of bow ties, six red ones among the blacks and plaids and on and on. Mr. French tells the guys that Yates keeps only fresh ones in there. He keeps so many of them because he goes to so many after-five things. So after he wears one, the crazy fucker throws them away!"

Bianchi said excitedly, "Cross this bow tie for Ramsey's hair and fibers. But you got a problem. We didn't get Yates's shoes from that night. Without those fibers and the Jeep, I can't put him in the Jeep ever, with anybody."

Brucker shrugged, sipped from his steaming mug. "I don't know. This bow tie here laid in the rain for a couple of hours while the crime-scene boys worked the perimeters. There's the Rolex. Nobody's wearing one in the photos—none of our players anyway."

Bianchi toddled beside him at the fireplace.

She whispered furtively, "But guess what? Mick's girl Loretta is the dying congresswoman's frigging niece! She's taking calls on the cell that night, because she's the family spokesman, for Hooter Brown's sake! Like the little whore said, she's banging on someone talking about the resignation the next day! And Loretta wears a gold and diamond Rolex. I saw it. And our hooker didn't suck a penis, she gave a chin slam, like you might do to a woman—"

He cut her off, "Or like you might do to a guy who's impotent with women but keeps trying, like Farron." He moved to close the hallway door in case the cagey little hooker was listening. "And the big gal told you Mick's got noodle dick sometime, too. Man, this is driving me crazy! You got the lab yet on Yates's pants?"

Brucker answered, chewing, "Yeah. No blood, just like none on Farron. There is blood on Mick's tux, remember, but he told that yarn about the beat-up bum, which is an alibi for him and an explanation of the blood. I've got all my street urchins looking for a bum with corrective shoes, but nothing yet."

"How about the Sofiya chick? You said she's spooky."

Bianchi huffed, "She's as weird as riding sidesaddle. She says Mick only picks losers so he can victimize them, that he likes hurting women emotionally because he doesn't think much of himself, so when they fall apart on him he can enjoy it. Then she tells me that she 'warned' this Loretta broad and she says she 'should've warned' Janelle—"

He was cologne and coffee breath right in her face, with the yellow fireplace flames dancing in the shadows. He asked her, "Warned them of what?"

Bianchi said, "That he's a sexual pervert, that he considers women prey and he has no conscience."

Brucker posed it. "So she keeps him why? And how is a sexual pervert and a pathological liar so good at a job that demands veracity?"

Bianchi came closer. "Because he likes his job. He hates women. Brucker, maybe it isn't that he keeps Sofiya; maybe for some odd reason, she keeps him, huh?"

He stared at her, concentrating past her. "Who else but Yates could dispose of a Jeep so completely? Mick isn't that shady. If he hit the bag lady, he'd take the car the next day and get it fixed, for cash, no insurance, and probably in another city. We've checked the garages here."

"The tall girl is a candidate, Brucker. If Mick

wanted kinky, to watch her with another girl, this fruitcake broad would do it. Ramsey could easily have slipped you a substitute tie."

He leaned on the brick mantel and swept a hand across his tired eyes. "What about bullet chips in the buildings from the shots fired at the hooker?"

Bianchi went back into the bag for another croissant. She plunked into Brucker's comfortable couch and mumbled with her cheeks bulging, "No bullets or fragments. We combed her route." Her eyes flared at him from above her fat cheeks. "And remember, the bartender and the newspaper security guard can't talk. But I did find out today that Arthur Yates's mansion on the hill does have guard dogs at night. Dobermans. In an hour the judge will issue me a probable cause to impound the dogs and get their teeth prints to see if he set them loose on Archie Dane."

"Which he would do why, Bianchi?"

She grinned, cocky. "This is a test, right? Yates would off Archie Dane because there never were any keys at the security desk, which would make him and Farron and Ramsey real strong suspects."

Brucker grinned, too, more cocky. "Wrong. Yates would put his dogs on Dane because somebody did drive that Jeep out of there, and Archie Dane saw him . . . or them. And Brian the bartender was killed by Mick because Mick was never there that night."

Bianchi chimed in, "Or by Farron because Mick was there, and Farron wants Mick to have no alibi. Man, this sleuthing stuff is fun!"

Brucker smiled, "Hey, you do damn good work."

Bianchi smiled, too. "Keep the praise. Give me a raise."

Brucker laughed. "God almighty, Yates will go apeshit when they haul off those dogs and match them to Archie Dane's leg bites. We'll have him, Angie."

She said, her smile fading, "Until then, the priest and the hooker are both in grave danger. You know that. Maybe it's not Yates. We'll know in twenty-four hours if the dog bites match and if any of the hooker's fibers are on his pants. Meanwhile, our bad boy is still on the loose. He knows the priest is helping her, but he doesn't know if she's talked. So he figures she hasn't told us who he is yet because we, after all, are the pigs and she's a hooker. So he figures he's still got time, if only he can find her."

Brucker pulled on his black bomber jacket and stuck the Stetson on so it shadowed his comely black face. He said, "Anything else on Ramsey?"

Bianchi dusted her fingers and mouth with a napkin and settled in to wait for the hooker to come awake. "Yeah. Jackie Sofiya says he's a racist."

Brucker said thoughtfully, "Hmmm. And what've we got dead here? Four dead hookers. A black, a Hispanic, an Asian, and a white male. How does the white male fit in?"

Bianchi picked her teeth. "Hey, every killer makes mistakes."

Brucker chuckled dryly. "Let's hope so. And let's hope he makes it real, real soon. Before Father Keenan lets him in and doesn't live to tell about it. Take the girl to your house. Lock your doors and keep your weapon on you."

# 49

Bianchi rumbled in and uncuffed the whore, pounding her butt and hollering, "Hey, Rip Van Twinkle, daylight's wasting!"

The whore made gagging sounds and struggled to sit, covering her face against the dastardly sunlight and the cop's bellowing cheerfulness. She managed to say, "What the hell—"

"You're going with me for today. In the morning you have a meeting with the priest, and then you're on bus number nine to paradise." She tossed a wad. "I brought you some old warm-ups of mine that I haven't worn since somebody spray-painted Goodyear on my ass. You shower and put 'em on, kid. I'll scramble you some eggs."

The whore said, "I need a drink."

Bianchi said stoutly, "Me, too, Sheeba. But you start without me. I'll make you a screwdriver."

The whore squinted. "You're going to let me drink? Really?"

Bianchi went about unlocking the handcuffs. "Baby, if we stopped you cold now, you'd be dead in twelve hours. Go. Wash up."

An hour later the whore and the cop pulled away from Brucker's cabin. The whore toted her bag and a manhandler size glass of orange juice and vodka. She had smoked a joint in the bathroom after her shower, so the day looked better now.

The cop played country music and sang along— really loud. And Caressa felt herself put out the smallest smile at her, at this fat broad who was like life's loudest love song.

She asked Bianchi, "How come Brucker didn't try to fuck me?"

Bianchi laughed. Her Moe haircut jostled, just like her belly. "Brucker? Oh, baby, he's in love with another woman."

The whore smirked. "I never knew that to stop one of them."

Bianchi was like the percussion section. Loud. Cool. Paced. "Well, our boy Brucker, seems he doesn't have sex with just his penis, honey girl. Seems he needs his heart in it. Hey, we're going to the grocery store. You pick out some junk you like to eat, then we'll go to my house, watch some movies."

"What kind of crazy cop are you?" The whore meant it as an insult.

Bianchi laughed like a wild woman and shouted, "You think I look crazy from out there? Baby, you ought to be inside here where I live!" She laughed crazylike again.

The whore smiled dimly and took a deep swig of booze.

An hour later at Bianchi's boxy track house, they unpacked groceries. Mostly they unpacked things the whore only dreamed of eating. Chocolate cup-cakes. Chips and dips. Twinkies. Bologna and sala-mi and ice cream. They unpacked their run from the liquor store—scotch and beer and limes.

Bianchi played music. Bonnie Raitt. She's No-body's Girl. She showered and sang loudly. The whore did two lines of cocaine in a back bedroom and poured scotch and sat down with Bianchi.

When Bianchi came in toweling her hair, the whore asked pointedly, "How come Brucker loves a girl who doesn't love him?"

Bianchi poured scotch over ice. Her hair dripped on her bulldog face. Her paunch came through the warm-ups like she was hiding a balloon. "That's the deal, little one. Life is all about what you have the courage to give up—because it all goes, baby, your looks, your kids, the guy you love, your money, whatever you got, it goes one day. And there you are, having to prove how resilient you are. He'll have to give her up someday. It'll take courage, and he'll think it was a wasted five years. But it's like college, you know, those years seem so wasted, but hell, you learned something."

They were coiled cross-legged at Bianchi's low coffee table in the living room while Bonnie's torch songs floated.

The whore said, growing woozy again and loving the feeling, "Well, what I think is—he wants her, and she only needs him."

Bianchi dug into the chips and dips. "Very percep-tive. Now explain."

The whore lit a joint and sucked deep. Bianchi

flinched, but stayed still and waved away the sweet smoke.

The whore said reflectively if drunkenly, "My customers, they need their wives for—whatever. The kids or the money. So I figure what's wrong is, you ought to not be with somebody you need. You ought to be with somebody you *want*. But most of all, they've got to want you, too. Like, if you want him and he only needs you, phooey, it won't work."

Bianchi poured another stout shot from the bottle, and the whore said, "I can't believe I'm sitting here drinking with a cop. Why are you helping me?"

Bianchi changed the music. Indigo Girls. She said to the whore when she sat again, "I'm not helping you, exactly. I'm helping Brucker, because Brucker is a comer. He'll be a captain soon, and eventually deputy chief, probably chief someday. He's a swell guy to have owe you a big favor."

The whore smiled, not like a schoolgirl but like a disbeliever at a tent revival. She said, "You're weird."

"Yep. That's what my ex-husband says. Of course, he rivals Quasimodo himself, in my view."

The whore opened a beer to go with her scotch rocks and lime. "You were married? I don't know. You don't seem like the marrying type. You seem more like a girls' team wrestling coach."

Bianchi cackled. "Oh, yeah, I got an ex. I bet you've seen him in some of those motels where you sat and watched TV. He's on TV, for real, he is. He has that fishing show on Saturdays on local cable. Fishing with Buck Bassman. I swear to God! You've seen it, haven't you? You've seen him?"

"My god! That fat guy with the ear flaps on his

cap? We used to sit around, all us girls, and look at him on that channel and just scream about how awful it would be to fuck him. That's not your ex-husband. You're lying!"

Bianchi pounded the table. "Swear. Sex with him? The whole time he's about to come, he yells over and over, 'Reel me in, baby, no slack, I'm coming, reel her in!' He taught me the definition of eternity—the time between when I come and he goes."

The whore felt her first real laugh in—well, ever—that she could remember. Then the fat cop said, "So if that's not enough, he's my ex-husband *and* my boyfriend, because I'm so desperate that I still date the dumb bastard—"

The whore yelled, "Oh god! Why? You got rid of him once. Oh, he's so gross! Why do you date him?"

They were screaming drunk. "Because. He pays my bills!"

The whore yelled. *"Ahhh!* So you're a hooker, too!" She said suddenly, "You shouldn't eat all that stuff in there. You should get skinny and get a different guy—who *wants* you and doesn't just need you because he smells like bait and nobody else will have him." She poked Bianchi. "Go on a diet!"

Bianchi slurred. "Oh, pooh. I'm on that see-food diet, honey. I see food—I eat it!"

The whore pulled her up. "Come on. I've got makeup in my bag, fake eyelashes and stuff. I'll phoof up your hair. Instead of a dowdy old wrestling coach, I'll make you look hot enough to burn their retinas. I always wanted to be a cosmetologist, you know, but hooking paid better."

Bianchi giggled. "Me, I wanted to be a weather reporter."

The whore was gathering stuff from her bag, including a brunette wig that looked like it came straight off of Joan Collins's head. She asked, "A weatherman? Why?"

They tramped down the hallway, toward the bathroom, the whore with a joint flaming in her mouth and Bianchi carrying the scotch bottle.

Bianchi hollered, "Well, think about it. What other job could you have and be so wrong so many times and still get paid? I mean, they say it'll be sunny tomorrow and it rains and the next day the same lyin' puke is right back at work. Like, what if your doctor said there's a tumor, and then he did all this surgery and then came out and said, oh, well, it wasn't a tumor at all, it was that Tootsie Roll you ate. Would he be at work the next day?"

The whore smirked at Bianchi's rant and said, "Sit in front of this mirror while I transform you into a Latina Love Goddess. First, we'll use these. Lee Press-on Nails. Look at your stubby fingers."

Bianchi mused, "Why don't they make Lee Press-on Tits? And why doesn't anybody say 'Mexican'? I'm not Spanish or Hispanic or Latina—I'm a Mexican. But nobody will say the damn word! Viva Mexico!"

The whore went to work, saying, "When we're done here, you go in there and get me a cucumber and I'll teach you to give cheater head to a man. For when you've got strep or chapped lips."

Bianchi started, thought better of it. She stared as the whore stuck Joan Collins's hair onto her head,

and suddenly Joan Collins had the face of Walter
Matthau. Then Bianchi said, "Cheater head. What
is—no, never mind."

At night, when the whore had drunk enough and
done enough drugs to pass out and escape the
nightmare, Bianchi got up quietly. In the living
room she found the cigarette butts the whore had
smoked. In the bathroom she found the hair brush
the whore had used before bed. She bagged them.

Now, she had herself a whopping big load of Caressa Dicks's DNA to compare with whatever—and
God willing there would be something—the killer
had inadvertently left of himself on a harmless red
bow tie.

Sometime before dawn the whore blinked awake,
not from the usual nightmare, but from the need
for more of the goodies from her bag. She fished
through it, found a bottle of street-grade potent
Xanax and took three. Before she slid her bag under
the bed, she opened it again. She had stolen something from Brucker. She had stolen an old, worn
photo album. It was the size of a record album and
full of old black and whites now fading to brown.
She didn't know why she took it, or why she wanted it, but when he was sleeping she had found it
and put it into her bag.

She couldn't look through it now, too doped, but
in a few hours she wanted to wake and look at it, at
the images of Jesse Brucker as a boy. She drifted
away on the downers, thinking of how it would feel
to wake and put her fingers on Brucker's face in
those photos, without him knowing she was touching him at all.

# 50

The priest prepared for the 5 P.M. Mass. He moved stealthily, his black clothes covered by white robes. His soft shoes made no sounds on the altar, and he stopped only once, long enough to tousle the golden hair of a young, yawning altar boy.

From across the street in the familiar alley, danger lurked, and danger watched. Parishioners filed inside.

There were nuns. It was tricky, trying to glimpse under their umbrellas to see which one was the whore in disguise. Most were recognizable instantly as elderly women. Some were too fat, others too short or tall. But the notion was planted. Of course, the priest would hide the whore among the nuns, in the convent just down the street, hidden behind ancient oaks and a brick retaining wall. It would be necessary—no matter how unsavory the thought—to enter the convent later and look for the whore. That would mean, of course, taking a weapon in case one of the doddering women saw a ski-masked intruder sneaking from room to room. Surely the whore had told by now. And they hadn't come to make the arrest because they were building evidence for the arrest warrant. The matter now was to see that she did not live to testify about the hit and run, because the hit and run would connect to the murders of the hookers.

The priest came to the chapel door. A cop in a marked cruiser got out, went to the door, and they spoke. The priest and the uniformed cop shook hands, and the priest used his thumb to make a cross on the grateful cop's forehead. The cop car pulled away. So they were only guarding him certain times, not around the clock. Okay. Okay. Fine. But they weren't guarding the convent at all, even at night. The nuns who were hiding the whore were like shrouded crows on a wire. Easy pickings. Done deal.

Mick and Loretta left the seedy motel by noon. He drove, and he drove too fast, but she didn't remark. He was already so far gone from her, a cross word from her and he might vaporize. He got in his car at her house two hours later and started to get in without a word. She took his face to kiss him, and he let her.

She said, pouting again, "Mickey, why did you sleep on top of the covers all night?"

He sighed like she had asked for money. "I don't know. Just get over it, okay? And don't give me shit."

He patted her butt then and added that she could blow him at lunch that day, he'd come back if she wanted—because in an hour his big story would be written. He went on about how it would be copyrighted and picked up by every major news service, and that as soon as he shipped it on the wire he would be ready for a good, wild romp.

She, of course, salivated. He, of course, hit the pedal too fast and fishtailed away.

At 4 P.M., Mick stepped into Victor Farron's office where Governor Harding Green lay napping on an oversize sofa, obviously waiting for Farron to arrive late for the editorial board meeting. Mick cleared his throat. Harding opened one eye and then closed it again. He was a thin, well-groomed man, handsome in an effeminate way, slight and with a full head of silver hair.

Mick announced, "I'm running a story about the stocks you sold on Haslon oilfields in Bahrain two days before Hussein invaded Kuwait. I have the particulars. Any comment?"

The governor said smartly, if softly, not bothering to open his eyes, "Sure. Quote me: I know where the Jeep is."

Mick sat slowly. His heartbeats drowned away the sinister thunder rumbling the windows.

Mick said dryly, "My prints are supposed to be in that Jeep, remember. So you bring it on. I have a legitimate alibi. The fact that you know where it is will implicate you."

The governor sat up finally. His expensive gray suit and thick silver hair were impeccable. His eyes were like volcanoes. He stood, and, in his gray cowboy boots he had the look of a well-dressed undertaker who liked his work.

He said with the effect of cement shoes hitting a river, "Boy, if we're going to have us a pissing match

here, you remember three things. I'm a decorated
Viet Nam conflict hero and I'm the former president's brother." He took a step. The storm in the
windows made a twisted fury at his back. Mick
smelled booze and death threats.

The governor smiled slowly, as if someone had
just put a greasy campaign donation into his palms.
"Last but not least, boy, you remember this. I'm
trustworthy and honest, I mean, how could all
those shithead voters be wrong?"

Mick said dully, "If my story runs, it'll be proof
that you and Yates and Farron had reason to frame
me for a hit and run, a reason to get rid of me in
jail. Nobody will doubt it. Nobody will think a reporter who exposed your insider trading scheme
would hit a bag lady and keep going."

The governor plunked on his cowboy hat and
said with a growl that could blister skin, "Did you
know, boy, that a car runs its very best, the
smoothest, just right before it runs out of gas? Pure
vapors are the purest power. You're on fumes, and
you can run, but you cannot hide."

Arthur Yates was not at his palatial mansion
when the police came with Animal Control people
to take away his guard dogs. He was at his private
airstrip, just boarding his Lear, when a police cruiser came flying up the runway, dangerously fast in
the rainstorm. Arthur stopped, dipped the brim of
his cowboy hat so he could see them, but they
couldn't see his eyes.

The bigger cop, whose chest was a concrete
block, said, "Mr. Yates, we have orders to confiscate

all animals from your homes and to detain you. We
need to take you to your residence, and you must
stay there until further notice from the District Attorney's office. Here's the papers."

Yates looked behind him, into the plush jet, at the
lavish upholstery and the stemmed crystal, at his
world. He said to the officer, "Fair enough, boys.
Y'all drop me at my place downtown, and I'll call
my lawyers."

# 51

Bianchi was in her attic, hauling things around and grunting. She wore a baseball cap over her Joan Collins wig, which doused the glamour a bit. Country music blared in her headphones, and she sang like a saloon gal on stage.

The whore, dressed in the loaned warm-ups, sat lazily by a big window, smoking marijuana and thumbing through the photo album she had stolen from Brucker. There was a huge gap in the chronology. In the first pictures he was in grade school, and then junior high school, and then it dropped off. With a turn of the page he was a teenager. And, funny, she thought, she had seen the place he was standing. Or a place like it. She walked to find Bianchi's reading glasses and brought back with her the scotch bottle to swig from. She bent closer and peered at the photo. Brucker was surly, on the steps to a stone building. There were big kids lined up behind a bunch of little kids sitting on their feet in the first rows. It was a school picture.

She stood too fast, and the photo album fell. A slight scream left her. She doubled over as if a fist had hit her, and she held herself against the window where rain glanced the glass.

She picked up the photo album again. Brucker wasn't smiling; he was a tough kid back then, the trouble and insolence showed on his face. But a girl in the front row was grinning. A beautiful girl with shiny, long black hair and eyes like tiny stars. The whore said breathlessly, "It's me. It's that place. And Brucker. My god, my god. He was there with me."

She sat, shaky and nauseous, though she didn't know why. The nightmare was coming. She looked back at the photo. She saw a priest in the back row, his white collar and his smile both gleaming in the sunlight that had gone dim in the photo. She pulled the album closer, feeling the nightmare come at her in clawing tidal waves. It was the priest. It was Father David Keenan.

She cried out, threw the album, and she felt the nightmare breathing on her, hot, sucking away her sanity. She had a feeling of momentary blindness, and then chest pains, and finally such weakness that she went to the floor.

The nightmare. She remembered now. He looked so different, the priest in the picture and the priest she had just come to know in the chapel. She saw it on the wall. A skeleton rankling toward her, and she scooted backward, crying and whimpering.

"No. No. Don't. Oh god. No."

The whore stood. She walked in a circle. Thunder rolled.

She remembered the hand clamped over her little mouth, and how her eyes widened like bloody

moons when he began taking down her ballet leo-
tard.

She covered her mouth, sure that she was going
to faint on Bianchi's wood floor. The blood pounded
in her throat and her ears, and she couldn't get air.
She could feel the physical pain of the penetration,
and she remembered not being able to breathe
through his big hand. And she remembered his hollow eyes boring into hers, and he grunted with each
excruciating thrust, and the tears, her tears, like
pearly pieces of a broken little spirit dripping from
her soul and her heart.

She held the wall and fought hyperventilating,
mute with a crushing grief, a will to die, a shame
and pain so big it shadowed Bianchi's whole room
like a filthy, godless hand over her life. She climbed
to her feet. She was ashen. Her voice was bone dry.

"You *did it!*"

She found her bag. Brucker had taken her bullets
when she shot at him along the highway. But
Bianchi would have a gun somewhere, in her purse.

The whore found it. And she found Bianchi's car
keys. She darted in the goopy rain, sobbing, sick to
her stomach with hatred and rage.

She drove away, screaming to the thunder and
lightning, "You son of a bitch! Father David. Yeah.
You were Brother Dave back then. I remember now.
You son of a bitch rapist! I'm going to *kill you.* You're
the dream. You're the nightmare! You're *dead!*"

She clutched at the big gun, grasped it with all
her might. She would find out soon—and too late—
that Bianchi had wisely taken out all the bullets.

# 52

The governor said to Mick, "You kill the story. Or I produce the Jeep. There's a detective coming to see me at six this evening. I can tell him that I never saw you set down any keys . . . or Mick, I can say that you did put down some keys, but I am not aware what became of them. I can corroborate your story, or not. If the Bahrain story runs, your Jeep turns up faster than a born-again Christian can buy white shoes, boy."

The evening was falling. Streetlamps along the downtown street clicked on. Mick saw them. He asked carefully, "What was supposed to happen in my Jeep?"

The governor chuckled meanly. "Well, you know, she wasn't going to see anybody's face. But she saw the Jeep. Your license plate and a hooker getting in, that's all we wanted. But the plan went all haywire with that hit and run."

Mick said dryly, "The story's in. All I needed was your quotes and the push of one send button."

"Well, son, the Jeep's in, too, in a safe place, and

it's had what those talk shows call a makeover. Made over so nobody's been in it but you."

Mick had to think, to clear his throat. He walked, poured a shot of whiskey into a glass on Victor's small office bar. He asked, "Who was going to tell about the hooker getting into my car?"

"So," the governor chuckled again, "you're not as dumb as you look. Why, the hooker, of course. She was gonna get some money the next day with instructions to come on down here and tell Victor all about how you beat her up and fucked her and then paid her."

Mick said, "So the hooker was in on it."

The governor spat it out. "Oh, hell no. You can't tell a damn woman a damn secret. She was gonna get called on the next day and persuaded, with the money. But hey, don't take it personally. What's a little butt-fucking among friends?"

Mick jolted, almost lost the glass in his hand. He said, "Loretta. She told you I got a call from someone at the SEC." He slapped his forehead. "I talked right in front of her, asking questions on my phone." He turned chalk white.

Weakness got him. He sat, gulped the scotch.

The governor said mildly, "Don't get your bowels in an uproar. Loretta liked you, she really did. So here's where we are now. The plan to have the hooker come down here and blackmail you got cockeyed by the hit and run. Now, it's murder because your Jeep ran off. Your Jeep, Mick, and maybe I never saw you put down the keys on the table, huh?"

Mick said, in a painful rasp, "I've been your

friend for twenty years. I have a right and a duty to write this story. You cheated people who put their hard-earned money into the stock market, and they don't cheat, they take the risk. Sometimes they lose. Goddamn it, Harding, you can't do this to me!"

The governor grinned, twirled his hat. "Aw now, Mick, see, we've got the Jeep, and there aren't any signs of anybody in it but you and a dead gal's hair and blood on the grill! Yes! We can do it, and we will."

Mick looked up. "All you have to do is say you saw me put down those keys."

The governor's wicked eyes glowered. "All you have to do is kill the story."

On his way past, the governor patted Mick's shoulder saying happily, "It's the good ol' boy game, Mick. You stab my back, and I stab yours."

# 53

At his desk, Mick sat quietly. The newsroom was busy with reporters on phones and the three television sets muted on three network news shows.

On his computer screen he called up the story, and the letters of the heading blinked at him like fireworks. With one finger, Mick Ramsey pushed a button.

Z, for zap. The story of insider trading was gone.

He picked up his phone and dialed.

"Jackie, listen to me. Don't hang up. In the lobby at the hotel down the street, by the water gardens, I'm leaving you an envelope. You must go now and pick it up." He swallowed, looked around, nobody was paying attention. "If something happens to me, Jackie, you'll know what to do with it."

He hung up and stared listlessly at the rainy, grimy windows.

A print-out of the whole story was in his briefcase. He walked briskly to the hotel and left the envelope with the concierge. In the rain, walking, feeling every stranger's eyes were a gun pointed at him, he muttered to himself, "It's like they say, Governor, never fuck up on a slow news day. Too bad for you."

# 54

Into the phone—and into Victor Farron's ear—the governor screamed rabidly, "I'm a dollar down here waitin' on a damned dime! Where are you?"

Victor mumbled an apology, hung up the phone, and quickly and quietly made himself a stiff drink. The leaves on his patio percolated in the falling rain. He heard the glass doors open and close, and he stepped into the dark living room.

Loretta was dripping wet and pointing a .357 at his chest. He didn't move. She was simmering and seething and crying, but the gun was steady.

Victor said calmly, "Loretta, don't point that at me."

She cried out, "He knows! He left me a message from a bar and said, 'Fuck you, you goddamned spying whore. I'll deal with you later.' He knows, Victor!"

Victor stood motionless, but he was concentrating on things in the room, something he could throw or somewhere he could run before she could pull the trigger.

She went on, sobbing. "I told you weeks ago that I was in love with him, that I didn't want the money anymore." Her expression was pure pain.

Victor said sedately, "The hit and run complicated things, Loretta. And you weren't paid to fall in love with him. You were paid to find out who he was talking to at the SEC. That's why Art got you the job doing their cubicles."

She screamed. "Goddamn it, Victor! I arrange fucking office cubicles! I'm not Mata Hari. I didn't mean to fall in love with him, but I did. And I stopped the money. But he won't believe that." She wiped her nose on her raincoat sleeve. "And you killed Brian. My friend. Your lover! You and Art went in there and made it look like he hanged himself while he was masturbating."

It hit him that she could be wired for sound. He said, "Nonsense. I don't know what you're talking about."

She came a step closer. The gun's barrel looked cavernous to him. "Yes, you do." The tears stopped, and rage came, and Victor felt his belly tighten. "You killed Brian, because I told you that he served us drinks, that he saw Mick just before the hit and run, and you were afraid it might be an alibi for Mick." She was haggard, out of her brain with booze and drugs and fatigue.

She called out to nobody, wailing, "Oh god! You lying, whoring, heartless, selfish men!"

He tried, "I'm sorry, Loretta—"

"And you think that saying you're sorry means it never happened? I hate you, Victor Farron, for showing me what a victim I can be. I could've lived all my life with a nice guy and not known myself at my worst."

He reached to set down his drink on the hearth. Loretta fired twice. The second shot went straight into the middle of his forehead. He stared for a moment, shocked, and listed lazily before he lumbered facedown on the floor, dead long before the ice melted in the glass by the fire.

# 55

Jacqueline Sofiya sat in her Jaguar outside the bustling hotel, rain spewing her windshield, and she read the damning story aloud to Mr. Gorgeous, who was smiling like a jack-o'-lantern.

She said, "It is done. Our friend at the Associated Press is waiting."

Mr. Gorgeous said, "Let's go drink to our loved ones. You'll be able to bring your daddy home tomorrow, after it runs." His handsome face fell into sadness. "And I'll be able to go to my uncle's grave and finally tell him it's all okay now."

She touched his arm, saying, "Thank you for helping me. I know you have risked your job at the SEC."

He said, "They won't find out. The girl, Loretta, she might put it together. She was put there by Yates, is my guess, to find out who Mick was getting tips from. But she has no reason to suspect me. We never even had a conversation." He looked at Jacqueline gravely and said, "They'll kill Mick."

She closed the envelope, started the car and said, "Good."

* * *

Loretta flew straight to Mick's house and banged relentlessly, pleading. "Mickey, please, please, oh Mickey, please open the door and talk to me."

He did, dressed in black slacks and a black turtleneck sweater. She fell straight to her knees on his entryway bricks. She was sopping wet and smelled as if she were drenched in whiskey. Mick stared down.

"Mickey, please, I'm sorry. I'll take any test, a lie detector test, and I'll pay for it. I don't care how much it costs. I'm not here pleading for you to keep seeing me, baby, but please don't leave me thinking I'm a traitor or a spy or a whore. Please." She had her hands folded in prayer, and her black eye makeup was running down her face.

She cried out, "Oh! I don't want it to be over! Please!"

He said tartly, "Well, it is over, Loretta. Now get up and go home. And leave me alone. You're pathetic."

Her stained face and pained expression made him want to bend and spit on her. She said, "Can we still . . . can't we still have sex, Mickey? Like when you want it, you call me. Can we?"

He bent to her face. "Let me see here. I believe that you told me you wanted to be with me because you liked feeling smaller than someone, finally. Well, honey, I think I made you feel plenty small, didn't I?"

He turned to leave her kneeling, the sound of the rain deafening behind her. She called his name. He didn't turn back.

# 56

After reporting her car and gun stolen and Caressa missing, Bianchi found Brucker playing basketball on his dinner hour at the YMCA with a bunch of sweaty guys. The loud thumping of the game behind them didn't detract from her urgency. In tow, like she was hauling a sad-faced clown, she had a bum by the scruff of the neck.

Brucker padded to them, blowing sweat off his top lip.

Bianchi said, "This here is Mr. Horatio Duckworth, better known on our fair streets as Ducky."

The bum gave Brucker a toothless grin. Brucker put out a hand. Ducky winced backward like he was going to get slapped.

Bianchi announced, "Duckey is skittish, a bit, so go easy on him. What he lacks in looks, he makes up for in heart and brains. Ducky, let's do it the way we just did it downtown at my desk."

Brucker asked, as the bum chewed, coughed, hawked, gurgled, and spit, "Where'd you get him?"

"From the railyard. I got word on the street that Ducky had recently pawned a . . . shall we say unlikely item for him to have. So I followed my nose. Ducky, ready?" The toothless bum grinned like a caricature of himself.

Bianchi asked, "On Saturday night did a tall, good-looking hunk take you and pay for your breakfast at a twenty-four-hour diner on Rosedale?"

"I told you he did. What are you, slow or something?"

She humored him. "I am. Slow as sorghum in a meat locker. What'd he look like?"

Ducky rolled his bloodshot eyes. "You ain't just slow, you deaf. I told you. He looked like Bill Holden."

Bucker squeaked, "What?"

Bianchi answered, "Ducky's older than dirt. He's referencing *Sunset Boulevard,* the last moving picture show he actually saw. So, Ducky, you'd been all beat up by some gang mem—" She checked her frame of reference with his. "Some hoodlums, and Bill Holden took you into the diner and paid for your food after he washed you up in the lavatory, uh, check that, the latrine. What time was it that he took you into the diner?"

Ducky struck a pose of dignity, never mind that his overcoat was a black plastic trashcan liner. "One fifteen in the A.M., and if I'm lying I'm dying."

Bianchi's eyes sparked at Brucker. She asked Ducky, "And that's when he left you. So what time did Bill Holden find you, first off?"

Ducky didn't hesitate, even through his lisp and his own stench, he was a man of his certainties. "He picked me up from the gutter at 1 A.M. I had just heard the bells of St. Pat's. My gutter, you see, is a stone's throw from there. And it was fifteen minutes later that he give me the money and left the diner."

Bianchi was about to pop like a bottle rocket. "And how do you know the time so good, Ducky, my main man?"

He beamed. Most cops arrested him. These two were just damned near in love with him. He said, " 'Cause he give me his watch, and I got pert' near $70 for it at the hock shop."

From her pocket Bianchi handed Brucker a gold and diamond Rolex.

"This watch, Ducky? With the letters M.R. inscribed on it."

"A Rolodex. Bill Holden give me his Rolodex watch. Miss Angela, am I in trouble, 'cause I didn't steal it. He give it to me as sure as I'm standin' here."

Brucker breathed out, "Holy shit."

Bianchi threw back her head and hollered, "If he's lying, he's dying, did you hear that, Brucker? Mick Ramsey wore a gold and diamond Rolex. Ramsey lied about the time he found the bum—no offense, Ducky, I love ya, I really do. Brucker, Ramsey is our . . . what would Bill Holden say? Ramsey is our *perp!*"

Brucker paced in a circle. "Okay. Shit. Get search warrants. His place. The tall gal's. Yates. Farron. We'll bring them all in, separate them. Did you hear anything about the girl?"

Ducky broke loose and went to join the basketball game, though his body odor caused some of the guys to shrink back and yell obscenities.

Bianchi switched her heavy bag to the other

shoulder, away from the weight of her big gun.
"No," she answered, "but she took my personal car,
you know, and my revolver. She's probably just
going to hock the gun. And there's a bulletin on the
car. The cruisers are on it. She's probably working
the streets again by now."

Brucker was shiny with sweat, his breath slowing
after the basketball game. He pumped Bianchi's
hand.

"Aces. You're aces on finding this bum. Look, I
have a feeling the girl will go back to the rectory.
She likes the priest and feels safe there—"

Bianchi interrupted before she forgot her
thought. "She had your old photo album, from that
orphanage. She took it from your house, I guess. I
found it on the floor when she bolted my place—"

Red alert. Brucker hollered. "What? Did she look
through it? Aw, shit." He grabbed his towel and
walked backward from her. "Angie, pick up Ramsey right now. Jesus, if that girl remembers the
priest—"

He left Angie standing, Ducky dunking. He took
an instant shower, dressed in lightning speed, and
he said it to himself, if the girl remembers, if the
trauma comes back . . .

She'll kill Father David.

Into his car radio he started to give the command,
but he stopped himself. Sending a marked cruiser
with sirens to the rectory would make the whore
run. And he needed to know where she was. He
needed to catch her, to hold her down and make
her listen.

# 57

The priest poured coffee and stood in the kitchen, listening to the rain and the jumbled ramblings of his thoughts. The whore had run off from Detective Bianchi's house. Brucker called in the early afternoon.

The phone rang and rang. Finally it switched over to the convent line. Brucker cursed at getting no answer so he could warn the priest. He had just hung up when his cell phone rang in the seat beside him. The guy identified himself as so-and-so blah-blah, Brucker didn't care, with the Associated Press. The guy talked. Brucker listened, driving frantically toward the rectory.

At first he listened halfway, but soon he was listening with rapt attention, and suddenly Brucker cared very, very much about what blah-blah was saying. Brucker's reporter friend was telling him all about Mick Ramsey's story of insider trading, which was minutes from hitting the international wire.

The main hallway of the convent was soothingly dark. All the nuns were huddled in a small chapel,

chanting some kind of spooky blather. Through a
slit in the doorway to the chapel, they looked like
peaceable crows lining their pews.

In the bedrooms and bathrooms of the convent
there was no sign of anything a fugitive hooker
might bring. No cigarettes, and she smoked, the
smell came back to memory now, after seeing the
nun in the window. In the nuns' bedrooms and
bathrooms there was no nail polish or jewelry, no
sign of the big bag that she carried.

A nun started up the stairway, her soft steps
creaking on the old boards. A small bathroom was
the only place to hide and stay still. She passed so
closely that her humming sounded almost loud.
Her long robes flowed after her in murky shadows
like a giant soft cave bat. She fluttered past, into an
unlit bedroom, and suddenly lamplight flooded the
hallway. The ten-inch butcher knife was ever ready
if she came too near. The nun hummed placidly as
she searched for something in various drawers that
she slid open and shut.

She turned off the light and started down the
hallway again. At the bathroom door she stopped.
She was demure, even in the wash of her thick
black shroud.

"Oh, my, I've dropped the bookmark."

The nun scampered back to the bedroom, fished
around in the dark, and found her Bible bookmark
on the floor. She floated down the steps, creaking
away, humming.

The back door of the convent closed quietly. The
shadowed stranger went out and headed for the rectory down the deserted, rainy street.

# 58

The priest sipped. The church bells pealed softly. A clock chimed. He sighed, worrying that Brucker wouldn't find the girl and his chance again would be lost . . . to apologize to her, to set her life right, and restore her soul.

The lights flickered out. He furrowed a brow, but didn't worry. The wiring in the old place was bad; every thunderstorm daunted the ancient lights. He went to his office to find candles and carried them into the kitchen.

The whore, watching through the kitchen window, took the opportunity to use the key she had stolen, open the kitchen door quietly, and slip into her covey that led to the musty attic. She nuzzled Bianchi's gun at her side and stepped lightly.

It was dark, but the priest knew his way by now. He felt along the walls, found three candles and brought them back to the kitchen table, then he found the kerosene lamp under the sink and lit it with matches.

He sat very still, pondering, thinking of an early

evening gin and tonic, asking God to let it be that the girl had run away to come and find him again. He had tried to be a refuge in her life the days she was with him.

A voice behind him said, "I want the whore."

Father David turned and squinted, but it was too dark in the corner where the voice came from. He began to speak, and then a strong, violent arm took him by the throat and smashed him face first into the wall. He felt his nose crack and begin to bleed.

"I want the goddamned whore."

"She's not here."

There was a knife suddenly in his face, candlelight glinting off it.

"You see this? I'll cut your fucking throat, you pompous bastard, if you don't tell me right now where Brucker took her."

An essence of amazing calm came over the priest. He said—and his voice became hypnotic—"I have lived my life preparing to meet Christ. I do not fear death."

Something happened, a sort of release on the pressure of the grip.

"You don't want her. You don't even have sex. What good is a dumbass whore to you? You'll die for her? Fine. I'll kill you."

The knife went into the priest's shoulder, and the priest went to his knees. The strong arms that gripped him turned the priest over, face up, and then pulled the ski mask off.

The priest recognized Mick Ramsey immediately.

The priest was in horrible pain, pain like fire

leaking into his left shoulderblade and taking his breath. He said, "Finish me, Mr. Ramsey."

Mick sat. The kerosene lamp made his face disfigured.

Ramsey yelled, "Goddamn it! I got to have that bitch. She's here, isn't she? She's hiding. I'll find her. You crawl one inch and I'll come back down and gut you like a mountain trout. Stay still."

The whore heard the commotion downstairs, watched through a crack in the ceiling. She could see the priest down below, in the dull flickers of candlelight.

Mick stalked to the little cove he had found behind the door in the wall. He found the doorway to the small attic where the whore was hiding.

She heard him mutter, "Damn, there's a doorway behind here," and she heard the door open. The driver of the Jeep, giant knife in hand, was on his way up.

Caressa cried as she scampered. She took up the position she had seen cops do on TV, feet spread, back straight, and she pointed the gun and cocked it. Footsteps trudged upward toward the door to the attic.

Something told her, not a voice or an apparition, but a sensation like a dream: The gun is too light. In a small stream of streetlight through the pigeons' circle, she checked the cylinder. Empty. She clucked a moment, spinning in the dark attic, and then she went behind the wooden Christ, shivering. It was time to die, she thought. Mick Ramsey was going to slaughter her.

Light sliced in when he opened the attic door. He

stepped inside, his footsteps like tribal death drums. He called to her. "Little whore, oh little whore, daddy's home."

The priest lay very still, seeing his own blood pool and smear as each breath felt like another stab. He thanked God aloud that Caressa was not anywhere in the rectory.

The whore could barely breathe. She scooted into a tight ball behind the wooden Christ, panting, scared of death more than of the pain of him chopping her flesh and stabbing her to death.

Mick looked around. The knife dripped with the priest's blood. He took a step into the attic, called to her again, and then he froze, as if he'd been zapped by a ray gun.

He narrowed his hard eyes and felt his pulse quicken. He felt the blood drain from his head and heart so that his knees went rickety.

The eyes of the wooden Christ were glistening, illuminated. They did not blink at him, nothing so human, because he would've known then that it was a prank, a trick crucifix designed to look alive and vital. No blinking. He wanted to step forward, but he was afraid the horrible thing would speak to him or reach out and grab him.

Under the crown of thorns on the wooden crucifix's head, red paint streaks webbed out onto Christ's forehead and cheeks. Mick backed up. One solemn streak of red paint began to flow, to drip, and he could tell that if he touched it, the blood would be warm. The living eyes became brighter, moist, focused.

They focused on him, and he felt not love—but wrath.

He managed to squeak out, "Jesus Christ—" before he backed out and flattened himself against the wall. He had the thought that the wooden monster Christ would chase him, so he ran.

# 59

Brucker found the priest bleeding on the kitchen floor, and heard heavy footsteps rambling quickly down the stairs.

At the bottom of those stairs, Jesse Brucker was waiting.

He held out the gold and diamond Rolex that Bianchi had recovered from the pawn shop.

"I know what happened, Ramsey. I know about the story that will in an hour be all over CNN. You had the story about stock fraud, so one of your buddies, Farron or Yates, asked you to go joy riding with him the night of the banquet and pick up a whore. You were just supposed to get caught with a whore so Farron could fire you, but somebody hit the bag lady, and everything went awry."

Mick rasped, "Brucker, I didn't know that Farron knew about my SEC leak that night. And I didn't mean to hit the bag lady. She was a nobody. I didn't want anything to complicate my chance for the story of the century."

The priest moaned from where he was coiled on the bloody floor.

Brucker said, "Drop that knife, so I can call 911 for this man. I mean it, Ramsey—"

Mick said, "They killed those hookers, looking for the hooker we picked up. Because they thought she might ID the guy who was in the backseat. Yates was killing them. The first and only work he ever did that got his hands dirty. Murder. And he did Archie and Brian—"

From the kitchen doorway Bianchi said, "No, he didn't. There's blood on your tuxedo, but it isn't from some bum, Ramsey. It matches the blood of Yolanda Garcia, the first hooker who was murdered. And nobody did Brian. Brian was an autoerotica freak. He hanged himself by accident. Yates only did Archie, because Archie saw you drive out with somebody. Who was in the car with you?"

She kept Ramsey covered with her gun, but she knelt to the moaning priest. "It's bad, Brucker. He's in shock already. Goddamn it, Ramsey, drop that knife or I'm shooting your lily-livered ass."

Mick said, in what was almost a sob, "Did my story hit the networks?"

Brucker said, "Yeah, you evil lowlife. Now come on in with us. But first, we need to make another arrest. Who blindfolded the whore? Who hid the Jeep for you?"

Mick had a crazy look, puzzled, bewildered, catatonic. He said, mummified, "The governor."

Brucker lost a breath. "Why? Why would the governor go joyriding with you to pick up a hooker?"

Mick answered, "To frame me. To stop my story. I'd been in so much trouble before with women. The sexual harrassment suits. They thought if the whore came forward, I'd cry uncle and just quit my job and leave the story alone before I got started. And the whores. Shit, Brucker, they're just dumb whores. Women. They're like fucking fire ants, man. So many of them, and they all hurt you if you don't burn them first."

Brucker persisted. "But why would the governor go in the Jeep with you? Why would he take that risk?"

Mick half smiled, a man gone mad. "Ah, Harding Green. The governor. He's a Republican, you know. A regular autocratic, tyrannical, imperialistic, elitist . . . frat boy. We were gonna get this whore, take her back to my place, bang her, all of us, me, Farron, Yates, Harding. I figured out tonight that there were going to be photos of me with her, not them with her, of course. So you know why the governor went along with me? Because he's a Republican. And before the banging at my place, he wanted to do her first. So. His kingdom for first dibs. The vain prick. Then I got the dumb bitch in the car and he takes off running, like the school principal is coming toward us. Leave it to a Republican to queer a good gangbang."

Brucker said, "And then you hit the bag lady."

"No, man, then the bag lady got in my way. Women! They're so much trouble!"

Bianchi pointed her pistol square at Mick. "I'm going for my radio, to call for help for Father David. Drop that knife."

The bloody knife clamored to the floor.

Brucker started forward with the handcuffs. Bianchi radioed frantically for an ambulance.

Just then the glass of the kitchen window shattered in an explosion, as did Mick Ramsey's head, and Brucker and Bianchi hit the floor, Bianchi covering the priest's limp body.

Brucker screamed, "What the hell?" and took out running.

But Loretta ran faster, down the back alleys where she had followed Mick when he left home. She stopped only seconds long enough to throw her handgun into a smelly Dumpster. And then she darted through the dark like a happy hyena.

Mick Ramsey convulsed and died.

The eyes of the Christ went dark again. Struggling despite her tiny size, the whore crawled out of the attic through the pigeonhole and disappeared into the stormy night.

# 60

Arthur Yates knew he was tasting his last breath of cool night air. He inhaled the freshness of freedom deeply, pushed himself lightly in the porch swing.

The inside of his sprawling rancher, which occupied the most prime property around the lake, was full of lawyers. They milled just as dumbly as the cattle that Yates could hear rumbling in the pens across the pasture. The lake beyond was an expanse of black glass, barely rippling in the frigid night air.

One of the pinhead lawyers swaggered onto the porch. Yates didn't look up. He'd seen enough lawyers' faces to know that most of them looked just like his own hairy ass.

The pinhead snarled, "Artie, all Hell's broke loose in there. It's bigger on the TV than Diana's damn car wreck, I tell you. Harding's been arrested at his hotel. Farron's been found dead at his house, shot and killed. Ramsey just got his head blown apart through the window of some damn church or something, and they think it might of been you who did it. The cops are on their way here to haul you in for popping Archie Dane. All 200,000 of your telephones are ringing from reporters calling."

The lawyer sighed. Yates puffed a cigar.

The lawyer griped, "I mean, I'm in there like a one-legged man in an ass-kicking contest trying to field it all and if you want my opinion—"

Yates stood. The lawyer felt himself back away.

In a soft growl, Yates said, "Let's start with the easy questions, Counselor. Did I ask for your opinion?"

"You pay me for it—"

"I pay you," Yates snarled, cold as dry ice, "to ask how high when I say jump. Now, I have some instructions for you. Let's see if with your law degree you can figure out how to follow these instructions: Go away."

The well-paid automaton took his hurt feelings inside. Yates slumped into the porch swing again, letting the darkness swallow him. The thick leaves of the magnolia trees swayed all around him. Yates heard the crack of a twig behind him. Footsteps. He stood when Loretta stepped into a small pool of moonlight. She looked like a zombie.

"Yates, you said it was the perfect plan. Find Mick's leak at SEC. Frame Mick with a whore. Fire him. Pay off my gambling debts. You said it was smooth as a baby's butt."

He asked, "Where's your car?"

Loretta smiled like a witch. "See how dumb you are. I'm in Victor's car. The guards waved me in like I was your first-born son."

He said, "Nobody was supposed to get hurt. I didn't know Ramsey would run down some old woman and then start killing whores. I didn't know the governor would be dumb enough to sit straight up like a fucking prom queen as they pulled out of the garage under Archie Dane's nose." He blew smoke, thought a moment. "It ain't true, you see, that what you don't know can't hurt you. How much you want, Loretta, to get out of the country and not talk to anybody about any of it?"

She came forward a bit. Her black raincoat was drenched and seemed shiny with something like glass shards all over it. Her hair was a total wreck.

"People like that word: whore. It's so easy to say, and it's so hard to really define. There's all different kinds, you see, Artie. There's the girl who takes money for sex—just a working girl, really, a prostitute. Then there's the girl who only does it with whom she pleases, for her own pleasure. And then there's me, girls like me, who do it with anybody and everybody because for a few lousy minutes we can pretend we mean something to somebody. I give out sex in return for nothing at all. I'm the whore."

"I could call out, Loretta, and in five seconds there'd be twenty gun-toting bodyguards around you."

She laughed. The tree limbs dipped in the wind like talons pointing at Yates. The last sliver of moonlight vanished behind a cloud.

"Yeah, Yates, you could call out and in five seconds I'd be dead. But see, that would be four seconds longer than you have to live."

She shot three times in rapid succession. She was

flying low across the muddy paddock toward the road before the legion of pinhead lawyers had time to find the porch light and find that Yates had no pulse. He was splayed on the steps like an octopus—a slimy, smelly, flat-dead octopus, good for nothing anymore but fresh-cut bait.

# 61

$\mathscr{C}$ stooped woman, young but bent with constant grief, heard the letter fall onto her unkempt carpet from the mail slot in the door. She shuffled to it, picked it up, studied it intently.

No return address. She never got mail, not since Annetta died, not since the color went out of her life. Or maybe she did get mail, but since she buried her precious daughter, maybe she just didn't remember hearing anything, much less the light touch of a letter falling to dirty carpet.

She opened the envelope. Inside was thin, pink paper with delicate handwriting. "Dear Cora May, you might remember me. A long time ago we were neighbors on the Air Force base when our husbands were just youngsters. You had your baby just before I had mine, and we made the funniest jokes about how awful that base hospital was. My girl DeeAnn finished high school last year, and now she is in college and going to be a schoolteacher. I hope your daughter is doing well. She was the prettiest little thing, I recall, and how she giggled, like fairy dust!

"I don't know why I'm writing. I don't even know

if this is still your address or not. But I wanted to say I'm thinking of you, of when we were young wives, and for some reason, I can't say exactly, I wanted to send you this . . ."

From the bottom fold of the letter fell a tiny blue flower. It fluttered, and it landed soft as a saint's kiss in the woman's fragile hand.

The gay man sat alone on the park bench. The air was good for him when it was springlike in the afternoon. The tree limbs over the bench were barren, but he knew soon there would be buds, white and pink nuggets.

He heard church bells in the distance, and he thought of the quirky nun on the telephone prayer line, the night of the day he found out he was HIV positive. They preached to him, the doctors did, about how it wasn't an instant death sentence anymore, about how the drugs were so effective now. It had buzzed in his ears like cannonfire. It was from that moment on that he contemplated not just death, but also his life as a homosexual. Had it meant anything? Had it separated him from God's love forever like the fundamentalists screamed from every corner?

He cried a lot at first. He did what the nun said, he prayed to God and to Saint Therese of the Little Flower—for a sign that he was and would be always God's child and welcome to God's love. The doubts drove him to his knees in agony sometime, the fear of burning in the Hell that the gay haters spewed so constantly and convincingly.

He put his face in his hands, and he felt himself

grow weak again with that sorrowful dread of being lost forever, even in Eternity.

A breeze blew. It was too harsh. He looked up because it was alien on this sedate afternoon to feel such a sudden rush. For a moment he saw the snow, but then it wasn't snow. He stood, put out his hands and let the flower petals fall all over him, and he sang out into the sunshine, "Oh! God! Thank you!"

Madison Renee Fitzgerald blubbered like she hadn't since she was just born. Her mama was being so cruel! Madison tugged at her mama's legs and kicked her feet and wanted to pull her own fluffy curls until all this torment stopped.

"Mama, please, no, don't put Cinnamon's bed away in the attic! Mommy, listen to me—"

"He's not coming back, Maddie, honey, please calm down. We'll get another puppy when Uncle Mack's new litter is in. Maddie, let go of me, honey. Let me climb the attic stairs now. This big dog bed has got to be put away."

Madison Renee ran, just as mad and hurt as when she fell all stupid-looking off the beam in gymnastics, and she sat right on the curb in her overalls, and she'd have cursed if she thought for sure nobody back there in the house would hear her say it. She just couldn't think of one other thing to do, so she lay down in the grass and turned her face to the wetness, and she sobbed like her heart was broken, which it was.

A car stopped by the curb, and cars stopping by the curb scared Madison Renee because of stranger-danger, so she scooted back toward the bushes by the house. The car only stopped for a half-second, and the driver sped away so that the tires screeched, and Madison could see that the people in the car had dumped a baby wrapped in a blanket right there where it was about to tumble into the gutter. The baby was crying.

Only it wasn't a baby. Madison inched up to the bundle, and her pink tennis shoe touched it, and the head of the tiniest puppy she had ever seen poked out. Its eyes were open, but just hardly, and Madison gasped. In about two seconds she had that puppy scooped right into her tiny hands and went running, telling the puppy, "You'll be Spice. That's your name. Imagine such a thing, someone treating a puppy like nothing but trash. Well, you're just a little treasure, is all, and just to heck with people who don't know treasure from trash."

Inside his dirty blanket, which was really just a bloody towel, Madison Renee and her mama would find the funniest thing, one petal stuck on the muddy puppy, a rose petal, heart-shaped and soft and very pretty.

## 62

Detective Bianchi sighed as she looked at the swamp of gory homicide reports she had yet to write. In defiance, she put her head down on her desk and let out a big sigh. Her Joan Collins wig went kind of sideways when she put her head down, but she didn't care.

A voice said, "Detective Bianchi?"

She looked up, and there was Mr. Gorgeous, a walking talking orgasm in a corduroy sports coat, with those perfect teeth and that smile that could make a woman eat her own young just to impress him.

"Oh. Yeah. Uh, here, sit down. If this is about the Ramsey murder case, you'll have to see Detective Brucker. He's in charge."

A slant of sun hit Mr. Gorgeous, and Bianchi could hear the seashore lapping her feet and feel his lips on hers. She snapped back when he said, "No. This is about . . ." he went sheepish. "Uh, it's about eating—"

She frowned, joked, "Oh, you're from the diner, and you came to warn me to stay away from the all-you-can-eat buffet."

He laughed. Bianchi was sure a bead of sweat slipped off her top lip.

"No. It's about lunch. I mean, with me. You and me. You know."

She squinted at him. "Are you vision impaired?"

Mr. Gorgeous twirled his hat. "You seemed so funny. And nice. Smart. And I love how you do your eyes, so smoky and erotic." It was odd, watching a playboy grovel. "I've had so many beautiful and fatuous dimwits. I just, uh, saw you and knew that this is something I really . . . want."

She stood and clucked weirdly and spilled her purse. He said winsomely, "I'll hold your hand if you're nervous."

Bianchi cackled, "Honey, don't hold this hand yet. I'm not too good with these damn fake nails. Did you know if you pick your nose with these things you can give yourself a lobotomy?"

Mr. Gorgeous chuckled. Bianchi prissed him right through the whole division while all the detectives watched speechless. She hollered as they gawked, "The Fleet's in! I got a date!"

Brucker snapped up the phone on his desk. He was in no mood for bullshit. He softened instantly. Patrice's voice brought a warmth all through him. Until she said, "I can't come over tonight, Jesse. I'm so tired, and tomorrow I go in at 6 A.M. Let's just do it another time, okay?"

He leaned back in his creaky chair and let the sunshine bathe him. He said gently, "Sure. Another time is okay because, you know . . ." He felt himself smile wickedly, "you are my sweet Patrice."

She went silent, a thoughtful pause. He had spoken magic words during her orgasms lately, and if Caressa was right, Patrice would never know why it was magic. In all her pleasure she couldn't hear the words, but she obviously could feel them.

"Oh, Jesse, never mind, baby. I'll bring dinner. See you tonight."

He hung up, shook his head and said, "Thank you, Sister Mystic."

# 63

The priest heard the glass break. He had hardly time to sit up in the dark and get a clear thought before she was on him.

She pinned him not with her strength but with the deadly sharp switchblade she pressed to his throat. He could see her in the glow of streetlight through his sheer curtains, and he lost a breath at the sight of her.

"My god, child. You are dying."

She was sunken, terrible black caverns under her eyes, and her black hair was tangled with debris and her own blood. She had bled from the nose and mouth so it dried there and stained her as if she had been beaten.

She pressed the knife. He could have thrown her off, except his left shoulderblade was fresh from surgery and still stitched and bandaged. He lay very still.

She hissed at him, "You raped me."

The priest heard his own swallow, and he said, "Do what you have to do to be whole."

* * *

The uniformed cop parked outside the rectory had his car windows down in the brisk night air. The car radio crackled dimly, police calls and terse chatter. He put his head back, checked his watch and decided he would walk the perimeter of the rectory again in five minutes.

Caressa could not cry. She wasn't alive enough. But she knew about his shoulder, so she mashed there, to be cruel, and she put her face against his. "It wasn't just once, either, you sick fuck. It was over and over, because I was so tiny and so help-less. And you told me each time that if I'd come to the shed, you'd have my mama for me. You promised a little orphan girl her *mama*, you bas-tard!"

Brucker's car pulled in slowly behind the uni-form. He got out. His shoes clicked on the wet ce-ment. He leaned his head in the open window.

"Eddie, everything okay?"

"Tight as a drum, Lieutenant."

"You done the midnight perimeter?"

"Just about to."

Brucker said, "I'll walk it. You call the division and get the hockey game score for me."

Inside, the priest did not plead. "Caressa, it was not what you think, little girl. Listen to me—"

She slapped him so hard in the face that he saw stars. "What I think, you godless child rapist, is that you put the pain in me, the one I've had night-mares about, the pain I've died trying to medicate

out of my soul with drugs and booze and all the
self-destructive things I do—" she slapped him
again; the first tears came from her. "So that I don't
have to stop and feel anything because it all hurts
so fucking bad!"

She pounded his chest. He couldn't help but cry
out in pain.

She wailed at him, "Do you know what happens
inside a little kid when you pull down her panties
and take away every safe place or thing she has
ever had? When you destroy all the innocence and
you ruin all the fantasies about how good life is? Do
you know, you son of a bitch, what happens?"

He could see her bloodied face twisted in gritty
hatred. "From that moment, the moment a grown
fucking man *violated* all the goodness that ever ex-
isted, I was never the same! Never the same as
anybody else. Never the same as I was before. Different. Shamed. Guilty." With her fist she hit his
stomach. "And I was *seven years old!*"

She lost sanity and began to shake him. "God
damn you." She could at last sob. "God please damn
you, you sick, cruel, terrible . . . oh, Jesus. I hurt. I
didn't want it. I didn't like it. I didn't cause it. I
wanted my mama. Oh, god."

The whore fell onto him. The priest lay still. He
saw Brucker in the bedroom doorway, solemn and
scared. He knew Brucker had seen the broken glass
and quietly come inside. Brucker saw the knife in
her hand, and he spoke gingerly.

"Your name is Diddia LeBlanc. Your mother was a
French girl at an American university. She got pregnant. She gave you up in adoption, and the people

she left you with abused you, they hit you and didn't feed you. Diddia. Look at me."

She turned to him, and Brucker jerked in horror. The whore rasped, "Go away, you. I'm going to cut his throat. He took me in that shed, and he put his grimy, filthy hand over my mouth and he took down my panties and he—"

Brucker took one step inward. "Diddia, why would the priest's hands be grimy and filthy? Talk to me."

The priest moaned, "Don't, Jesse. Let it end here."

Diddia lost a moment. She said, "I . . . don't know. But his hands were so dirty . . ."

Father Keenan whispered, "Go slowly, Jesse. I beg you, please. Easy."

Diddia was in the shed. She had scampered, moonbeams dusting her ballet slippers. My mama. My mama. Oh, joy! The bad things he did, he did them because she didn't have money to pay for her mama to come home, so he said if he could touch her privates a few times, that would be payment enough.

She had learned by now to close her eyes and clamp shut her mouth and let him touch. He said if she told anybody, then her mama would never, ever come home, so Diddia didn't tell.

Jesse was talking to her. "Who's in the shed with you?"

Diddia was a broken pile on the cold floor at Brucker's feet.

Father Keenan was dressing slowly in the shadows so he could move to her when it was time.

"The skeleton. The skeleton is in the doorway, and he's cursing me, and I'm so scared."

Brucker bent to her. "Then how can he be on top of you?"

She looked hollowly at the priest, a little ballerina soul wanting to scream out in pain. "He's not? Oh god. No. He's not. But he's coming in, and he's screaming at me—"

Father Keenan said, "No. Not at you."

"No. You're screaming at him. *Him.* Another man." She scooted backward. The men stayed away, so she would feel safe. "And the skeleton, he comes at us, I'm lost, wait, I'm bleeding, where are my slippers, he'll never bring my mama now because the skeleton is my teacher the priest, and now we're caught and my mama will never come."

They let her swim in digression for a few moments. Brucker asked flatly, "Do you remember it? Not what happened next—but anything at all."

Diddia put her eyes totally on Father Keenan, into him. Her voice was almost gone. "You—"

Father Keenan knelt to her. He took her face in his hands. "I killed him."

Diddia put her hands on his. "For me."

Brucker was in the darkness. "Father Keenan threw him, too hard. It was the caretaker, just a drifter who did work at the school. He had no family. I told Father Keenan to get you and take you back to clean you up, that I would take care of the body. It's never been found. He died because David was in a blackout rage, and when he threw the guy, a pitchfork in the shed went right through his heart. It truly was an accident."

She saw Father Keenan's mangled wrists again. "Then why—"

His voice broke when she put her arms around him. "Because, Diddia, I murdered him in front of you. I did nothing to help you. No counseling. No intervention. To save my worthless self, I did nothing for you. And you lived with the pain. And you are what you are because of it, because I am a coward."

He was holding her. He turned to Jesse and cried out, "Jesse. Dear Jesus. She's not breathing."

She was gone. Brucker put her down straight, threw off his coat, and said, "Call the ambulance. I'll start CPR."

He bent to her and began compressions. "Come on, baby, breathe for me. We love you, you hear?"

Father Keenan was stricken. "Jesse, tell me what I can do."

"What you do best, David. Pray to God she comes back to us."

# 64

All was white and soft. Diddia floated in the wave of numbness, blinded by a soft light. She felt no pain anymore, just like a big splinter had been picked out of her heart. Ah. Maybe Heaven. She could hear singing. And . . . wait, from the sound of it, maybe this was Hell.

Foot tapping? Not angels. One voice was precise and clear as it sang, and the other voice was a wrench in an engine.

Detective Bianchi? Here in Diddia's afterlife? No harps. No tweaks of angel's cheeks. No. This was Detective Bianchi singing as loud as a bullhorn with a Ray Price cassette, Bianchi flapping along like she was chopping wood. The steel guitar slathered and twanged.

"You've got me under your spell again, sayin' those things again, makin' me believe that you're just mine . . . you've got me dreamin' those dreams again, thinkin' those things again, I've gotta take you back just one more time . . ."

Diddia LeBlanc opened her eyes. The light wasn't divine at all, it was a bruising stream of sunshine from the hospital room windows that Bianchi had thrown open so she could smell the magnolias and the honeysuckle on the lawns.

Diddia stared. Bianchi was eating from a box of candies, singing with her mouth full, wearing a denim skirt and a TCU jersey and cowboy boots. Her Moe haircut was dyed blond. Her contact lenses were in. She finally glanced at Diddia.

"Oh, hey, babycakes, you're awake again! Well, praise the Lord and pass the plate!"

Diddia groaned. "Oh. I feel horrible."

Bianchi smacked chocolate. "You'll be okay. They've got you all hooked up there, so don't move too fast. You've detoxed. Now you get to stay a while and learn your twelve steps, the first of which should be to eat one of these here chocolates Brucker brought you. While you were unconscious. Jeez. Men."

She laughed too loud. Diddia felt her own weak smile.

"Where am I?"

Bianchi stopped singing to say, "Hospital. You've been out cold for two weeks—ever since you ran off from my house. Died twice. Somebody beat the bejesus out of you. You did some heroin, it seems, good grade of stuff, and you got all dehydrated and started bleeding inside. Could be worse though."

"Good god, Bianchi, how could it be worse?"

"Could be me."

Diddia could not bear to laugh. Bianchi said, "You've been waking up, saying weird stuff to us. They told us to talk to you and make noise. You're firing on about two cylinders, but you'll rally. By the way, they recovered my car. From the floor-board alone I could harvest a kilo. You sure had a yabba-dabba-do time. Want some water?"

Diddia sipped, asked, "Where's Father Keenan?"

Bianchi took the glass away. "Jail."

A well of grief gushed. Diddia felt slayed. "No."

"Yep. Turned himself in for the guy in the shed. So it has to go to the DA or the grand jury, because there's no statute of limitations on murder. Man, you've missed all the excitement. The guy who blindfolded you and walked away was the governor. He's resigned, facing charges of insider trading. I wouldn't give you a bent dime for his life right now."

Diddia could only stare into the sunshine blank-ly. She said softly, "I want to see Father Keenan."

Bianchi pulled a blanket over her and said kindly, "Take care of yourself, little girl. Father Keenan is in God's hands."

Ray Price sang.

"Don't look so sad. I know it's over. But life goes on and this old world will keep on turning . . . let's just be glad we had some time to spend together, there's no need to watch the bridges that we're burning. Lay your head upon my pillow . . ."

# 65

The Jeep was dredged from the lake on the governor's massive, sprawling ranch.

Loretta had not been found, but Victor's sedan did turn up at the airport. Brucker and Bianchi figured she was by now lounging somewhere in Europe—with more than a million of Yates's dollars that they discovered she had drafted into a foreign account back when she'd been his girlfriend. On his desk, it seems, she had her way with him in two ways, one in the missionary position and the other by finding some magic buttons on his computer when he passed out drunk.

Bianchi grinned at this development. Brucker laughed loud enough to bust a gut. Loretta remained at large.

Brucker handed in his badge, gun, all the goodies that made him a cop. He sat one cool morning by a granite waterfall called the water gardens and told the chief of police about seeing a murder and burying a body twenty-five years ago. The chief declined at that point to arrest Brucker. Brucker took a long walk.

*   *   *

The body of the caretaker was unearthed from a huge septic tank near the Jesuit Home for Neglected Children. The concrete cap was mud- and grass-covered and had not been lifted since the night a teenage boy pried it with all his might and a crow-bar.

The medical examiner went over every inch of the skeletal remains. Two rib pieces appeared to have been nicked by a sharp metal object—that most likely being the pitchfork that was found rotting at the bottom of the septic tank. He found no other fractures or lacerations on the bones, so nobody had tortured the guy or beaten him with deadly force. Father Keenan's story could be corroborated. Death had most likely come with one fatal injury to the chest area.

Brucker sat in the chief's office, where he had been summoned and advised not to bring an attorney.

Father Keenan sat in a six-by-six jail cell, wearing jail-issue cottons, his reading glasses, and his silver crucifix.

# 66

Katie Chan, the young prosecutor, indicated right off that she was speaking in behalf of her boss, the district attorney.

This was no sexist, racist profile of a cartoon geisha girl, Brucker thought to himself, this was a savvy sex bomb with brains and power. She sat in the chief's chair, her blue-black hair sliced just at her chin, her eyes so clear he could see the amazing brain power glistening. They were alone, she and Brucker.

She said, "Let me tell it to you this way, Detective Brucker. We are not sentimentalists. Your friend the priest will be treated no differently because he is clergy. You will be extended no special consideration because you are a police officer."

She glared. "In fact, you have been scrutinized most carefully, more so perhaps than most, because you know the law and you know you broke it. However," she lowered her voice. Brucker bent in. "We will apply the law to its fullest extent toward both of you."

Brucker asked dully, "Why was I told to come alone?"

Chan snapped, "Mr. Brucker, in this state deadly force is legally justified in defense of a third party who cannot protect themselves. Do you understand?" He nodded. She continued like a gorgeous machine gun. "Then you understand that it is possible that you are the only one in this situation who is guilty of commiting a crime. At this point, only the chief, you, and I know that."

Brucker raised a brow. "Come again?"

"Father Keenan, by law, did not confess to a murder. He confessed to a killing, which he committed against someone who was in the act of aggravated assault of a defenseless child—"

"That's one major fucking loophole—"

"Detective, I am the one with the power here. Nearly 100 percent of the time a grand jury follows our recommendations for indictment or not. They will rely heavily on what I say for both of you. I am prepared to have these charges administratively dismissed against the priest. It is not a loophole. You committed the crime—after the fact of a justified homicide."

Brucker hung his head, took it like a man. "Okay, Miss Chan."

She snapped, "You violated penal statutes. Failure to report. Denigration of a corpse. Suppression of evidence. And the priest, he did, too, but I am not calling for his indictment."

He stood military erect, calm, resolute. "I got it, Miss Chan. I beat the ride. Now I'm going to take the rap. So let's do it. Let's go the the booking room and—"

Katie Chan did not like him, and it showed in her frown. She was doing him no favors, except to be in charge here and to be a scholar. "Mr. Brucker, sit down."

She cleared her throat and rose, no bigger than a butterfly but not nearly as pleasant. She wore a man's suit, tie included, and high heels, red lipstick, and her black, severe hair glimmered.

"You were a juvenile. Juvenile records are sealed. I deem that at the time, as a juvenile, you did not have the mental capacity to commit a crime under the law. We cannot legally hold a juvenile accountable."

"But my career—"

She cut him off. "I said, sir, that juvenile records are sealed."

"You're saying that nobody will ever know." He felt the first shivers of a certain joy, even in the face of this stern professional who had just manhandled him.

"Your chief is very excited to have you back on the force. You may go."

He walked backward to the door, trying not to smile because his elation might piss her off and she'd change her mind. She stopped him just before he hit the hallway running.

"Detective, remember, absolute power corrupts. But in the hands of a woman of integrity, power also provides the privilege to do what is right."

He just wanted to pick up that little ol' gal and hug and spin her. He managed a calm smile, saying, "Ancient Chinese proverb?"

She cracked the dimmest grin on her serious face. "No. Don Imus, I think. Good luck, Detective."

# 67

Diddia's morning therapy included another successful walk without the wheelchair that she had used for several weeks now because of her frailty. It felt good to feel her feet on the ground.

She had been to her morning psychological counseling session. She had eaten breakfast and lunch, real food. She bathed, dried her long hair, and noticed that without the drugs and booze it was just beginning to shine again, not quite, but sort of. It had been more than three weeks since she regained consciousness, and she was not yet allowed visitors in the rehab hospital. Bianchi and Brucker phoned often. But not today.

Father Keenan, the whole time, had been in jail, his future in the balance of whether there would be an indictment. Brucker had quit his job.

She sat on a bench in the sterile hallways, watching nurses and doctors fiddle with charts and medicines. They smiled at her nicely when they looked up. She was a cooperative, willing patient so far. And she was dressed, looking groomed if somewhat unhealthy. She was tired, though, and the newspapers grinded her each day when she read . . .

"Father David Keenan, accused in the murder twenty-five years ago of an itinerant caretaker at a Catholic orphanage, remained jailed yesterday pending action from the district attorney . . ."

She wanted her bed first for a few minutes, and then the chair by the window that looked down on the verdant, sloping lawns and the circular drive lined with flowers and fountains.

She looked listlessly out the locked window. She couldn't feel the billowy, cool winds gracing the lawn, but she could see them touching the trees and the flowers.

She went to her bed, laid down, and drifted to sleep.

Detective Brucker came to Father David Keenan's jail cell, and he brought with him the jailer with the keys, and Father David was set free. Brucker embraced him, and told him their troubles were ended, and Father Keenan thanked his old friend with a blessing waved over his forehead. Brucker smiled brightly. When they drove up in front of the rectory, and before Father Keenan got out of the car, Brucker took hold of him.

"Father, I'll come back this evening. We'll go to the rehab hospital. Diddia is asking for you every day. Okay?"

Father Keenan smiled kindly. "If Diddia wants me, I'll go."

Brucker stopped him again, tugging at the sleeve of his black shirt, his white collar back on now, the way it should be.

Brucker said to him, "Most of us, you know, we never do anything significant. Sure, we do junk that turns out to be important, but we don't get to do stuff that's really significant. You, Father Keenan, your life is significant."

Father Keenan laughed upward and said, "God bless you, Jesse Brucker. You collect me in time to go see Diddia, let's say seven-thirty tonight."

He went into the rectory alone. The Church had sent in cleaning people, but the priest imagined he could still see all that blood, his and Mick Ramsey's. He got a bucket of water and a sponge, and began to swab the floor, down on his knees.

# 68

Diddia woke from her nap just after sunset. The breeze woke her, and she noticed right away that there shouldn't be a breeze. But the window was open, and the air was flowing through the room, and the priest was sitting there by her.

She rasped, "Father Keenan," and put out a hand to him, which he took in his hands.

"Diddia."

"How did you get the window open, Father?"

He smiled like an angel. "Magic fingers. You're okay now. You're getting well."

She sat up, pushed back her long hair. "I did that thing you said. I hit bottom one night in here, and I told God, Hey you've got to heal me. I'm a wreck. I'm a hooker and an addict and a nobody to nothing. And I said to him, So, it's all yours."

Father Keenan smiled, sadly this time, and said, "I'm sorry I failed you for so long."

"Well, you didn't fail me. You're no more perfect than anybody else. You just try harder to be perfect."

The whipping breeze through the open window

was delightful. They sat that way for what seemed a long time.

She asked, "What time is it?"

He answered, "Ten after eight in the evening."

And then he said, "God comes to us each through other people. The world can be so lonely. And so it is other people who bring us the love of God."

She said, "I can't give what I never had. I can't give people God or love or . . . any good things. I never got good things. I'm just learning all that." She sat up and faced the window. "Oh, I do love that breeze. Thanks for opening the window."

Father Keenan said, "I have to go now."

"Come back soon. Will you?"

He kissed her forehead. "Anytime. Always. I'll be close if you need me. Just say my name."

Father Keenan left her hospital room, and Diddia breathed deep a fresh breath of wind through the window and smelled a wonderful wash of flowers in the rushing air.

69

Diddia fell asleep again quickly. She woke when Detective Brucker came into her room. The window was closed now. It was pitch dark outside. She had slept a long time—without a nightmare.

Detective Brucker was hat in hand as he closed the door behind him and stood quite still.

She sat up. "Hi."

He said, "Hi, Diddia. How you doing?"

"I'd like some water there, from that pitcher."

He poured, handed it to her, sat down on her bedside. She drank deeply and laid back.

Brucker said to her, "You're all set up now to be released tomorrow. Bianchi's looking forward to having you as a roommate for a while."

There was something odd about him, something missing, like his tough-guy glare. He was having trouble looking right at her.

Diddia said nicely, "It's amazing that Angela would have me live with her."

Brucker sat on her bed, still hat in hand, and tried a smile. "Yeah, she said you promised to show her some trick with a cucumber. She said now that she's got a boyfriend, she needs to know about it."

Diddia laughed upward.

Brucker grinned, and then he got serious and told her, "I was going to bring Father Keenan earlier tonight, but, Diddia, I gotta tell you something about that . . ."

She said quickly, "It's okay. He came earlier tonight, on his own. We talked. He said I can see him often, whenever I want."

Brucker made a face. "He came here? When?"

"Oh, what time is it now, Detective?"

Brucker checked his watch. "Nine-thirty."

Diddia said peacefully. "He came at ten after eight. I asked him the time and he told me. We talked. He promised he'll always be there for me. I believe him."

Brucker got up, stood by the window, looked at her, away from her, back at her.

"Diddia, Father Keenan died tonight. I went to get him at seven-thirty, at the rectory, and he was dead in the kitchen. He apparently had a heart attack while he was scrubbing the floors. You couldn't have seen him at ten after eight. Maybe you dreamed it."

Brucker didn't say anything for a while. Neither did Diddia.

Finally Brucker put on his hat and said to her, "Who're we kidding? You didn't dream it."

He went out. The door closed slowly behind him. Diddia went to the locked window and sat in the moonlight.

# 70

The day came, and Bianchi pulled up front of the hospital, and there stood Diddia LeBlanc at the big glass front doors with all her earthly belongings in a shoebox.

The sun shone, maybe too brightly. And Bianchi's car radio played, definitely too loudly. Bianchi got out and made a show of giving Diddia a big hug, and then she stepped back to take a look.

She hooted, "Girl, look at you. You're almost as pretty as my new boyfriend." She took the shoebox and threw it in the car, still hollering, "Damn, that's sad there. You need some stuff! Some dresses and some cowboy boots and, of course, a pickup truck with mud flaps. Let's go shopping."

Diddia looked at her funny. "Bianchi, I don't have any money."

Bianchi winked. "Aw-contrary, my little chick-adee. You're rolling in it."

Diddia shaded her eyes with her hands to see clearer if Bianchi was joshing. "Yeah? And where'd I get it to roll in?"

Bianchi slapped the car. "There's this chick, you

see, Jacqueline Sofiya, and she makes movies, and she read in the paper about the priest hiding you, and Mick Ramsey stalking you. She wants to buy the rights to the story and make a movie of your life."

Diddia was just beginning to smile. "Bianchi, don't you pull my leg."

They got into the car. Bianchi cranked the music up even louder, and hollered over it like she was calling hogs, "I am not pulling your leg, child. Hey, you okay? I'm sorry your friend the priest died. You gonna make it?"

The bright sunshine was blessedly warm. Diddia felt it penetrate her skin, and she answered softly, "Yeah. I'm okay. And I'll make it, one day at a time, you know?"

Bianchi wanted a high-five. Diddia gave her one.

As they pulled away from the hospital, Bianchi yelled over at Diddia, "So, in this movie, who you got in mind to play my role, huh? 'Cause, I'm thinking that to be me, well, you'd probably want to cast that sophisticated English gal. The perfume chick."

Diddia said, amazed, "That magazine model? The skinny one with the big—"

Bianchi laughed, all wild and happy. "Yeah! Elizabeth Hurley is her name. Yessir, in the movie, she's me! Huh? Why're you laughing like that! We do resemble each other, me and her, don't you think?"

"Oh, Bianchi, this is a crazy world, and you are its mothership, I'll tell ya."

"Crazy world?" Bianchi sang out. "Hell, this is a great world. Look there. The sun is shining. God is in his Heaven. The Dixie Chicks are on the radio.

This day couldn't get better. Hey, look right up there, would you? Damn, it's a rainbow."

There it was ahead of them, an arc of all of God's colors waiting for them, just the way Jacqueline Sofiya would end it in one of her splashy Hollywood movies.